DOUBLE vISION

DOUBLE VISION

Annie Ross

HEADLINE

First published in 1997
by HEADLINE BOOK PUBLISHING

10 9 8 7 6 5 4 3 2 1

British Library Cataloguing in Publication Data

Ross, Annie
Double vision
1.English fiction - 20th century
I.Title
823.9'14[F]

ISBN 0 7472 1455 7

Typeset by
Letterpart Limited, Reigate, Surrey

Printed and bound in Great Britain by
Mackays of Chatham PLC, Chatham, Kent

HEADLINE BOOK PUBLISHING
A division of Hodder Headline PLC
338 Euston Road
London NW1 3BH

For my American friends,
Barb, Cori, Don, Jim and Mary

ACKNOWLEDGEMENTS

I could not have carried out the research for this book without the generous help of my friends Dr Mary Mira and Dr Jim Risco and his wife Kathy. I also owe heartfelt thanks to Ellen Hanson, Chief of Police of Lenexa, Kansas for answering all my questions and introducing me to invaluable contacts. Sheriff Michael Dailey allowed me to tour Wyandotte County Jail accompanied by Captain Ricardo Alvarado – and let me out again – while Sheriff Mike O'Brien arranged for Deputy Dale Swiderski to show me round Johnson County Detention Center. I am very grateful for their courtesy and patience but wish to stress that none of these law officers is responsible if I've got my facts wrong!

I am also very appreciative of the time taken by Dr Don Steeples, McGee Professor of Geophysics at the University of Kansas, to explain the geology of the western part of the state. Jennifer Green and Jama Akers were delightful guides to the Kansas City Art Institute while Randy Attwood was kind enough to show me round the University of Kansas Medical Center. Last but not least, I would like to thank Kenneth Baum for spending almost an entire day driving me across his land to view various old quarries and derelict houses. Without the help of all these people, this book would not have been possible. Thank you.

Chapter One

'I'll do what I damn well like!' the woman was shouting. She was American, in her late thirties perhaps, slim, dark-haired and very attractive, her lips painted scarlet, black eyes flashing with anger.

'You're my wife, for God's sake! If you think I'll let you get away with this . . .' His face suffused with anger, he caught hold of her arm as she tried to struggle.

For a moment, they stood there as if paralysed by the force of their rage, he towering above her, a heavily built man who looked at least twenty years older than his wife, with fine sandy-coloured hair smoothed back from his face, revealing strong chiselled features. Then the spell was broken.

'You can't stop me!' she spat at him, raising her chin in defiance. 'And anyway, you're getting a little *old* for me, Malcolm.'

His fury erupted. Suddenly he had picked up some object, it looked like a stone, and was swinging it over his head. The first blow elicited a scream of terror and agony and she began to sink slowly to the floor.

Now he could not stop.

The second blow caved in the side of her skull. Still he could not stop. Again and again the powerful muscles flexed as he struck at her until her face was almost obliterated and blood spilled and seeped and flowed everywhere.

The screen went blank. Martin dropped the VCR controller on to his desk with a loud clack and swivelled his chair to face me, eyebrows raised. My shoulders were hunched up, still flinching away from the images I had just seen.

'Can they get away with that?' I asked with a mixture of incredulity and horror in my voice.

He shrugged. 'Different laws. US telly companies do a lot of these reconstructions before the case comes to court. If the reporters can find the witnesses and persuade them to talk, they're free to piece together their version of events and broadcast it, whereas we'd be clapped in jail if we did something like that before the trial.'

He swung his feet up on top of his desk, dislodging the gleaming nameplate which read Martin Kember, Head of Factual Programmes. Leaning back with arms behind his head he added, 'What d'you think? Wealthy local farmer visiting his in-laws in America accused of murdering beautiful wife who just happens to have inherited millions of dollars. Exotic location . . .' He paused. 'Where is Kansas City?'

'No idea. The United States.'

'Oh well.' He shrugged dismissively. 'Anyway. Friends here say he couldn't have done it – he's being framed because he's foreign and the American police are corrupt anyway. It'd make a nice little doco.' There was a wheedling note in his voice now. 'The network will take it for that series they're doing on true crime.'

I leaned back in my chair and gazed outside. It was four o'clock on a Friday afternoon. From the window of Martin's office high up in the Regional Television building where I worked as a director, I could look out over the spires and skyscrapers of the city, crisply outlined in the clear blue light of late spring, a few fluffy clouds blowing across the sky.

'I've only just finished that film on faith healing,' I said.

'Julian's doing the EDL as we speak, I'm off to check on the music, I've got the on-line Monday and the narration and dub next week.' I paused, then unable to resist, I asked, 'When would this other one start?'

Martin shifted his feet off the desk and gave me a breezy smile. 'Monday.'

'Monday!' I was outraged. 'I can't start anything on Monday! I'm owed holidays from last year and I really need a week off to get myself—'

'Oh no!' Martin wailed, doubling over as if in pain. I scowled at him. 'Not the one about how you just need a week to get your life straightened out once and for all, catch up on ironing your knickers, get the Inland Revenue off your back, bury the cat – brings tears to my eyes –' he pounded the desk with his fist in accompaniment to the next three words – 'every single time.'

I found myself laughing. 'Well, what about my dub and narration?' I countered, but even I could hear from my tone of voice that I was weakening.

'Leave it till later. That show's not going out till the autumn anyway. This one has to be done asap because the trial's starting in a couple of weeks and we want to try and film some of that.' Martin suddenly glanced at the Rolex watch on his wrist, clicked his tongue in irritation and leapt to his feet. He adjusted his silk tie, dusted down the smart hand-stitched grey suit and ran a hand nervously over his close-cropped dark hair streaked with silver.

'I must go. I've got to be at a board meeting in fifteen minutes to give my end-of-the-financial-year report,' he muttered hurriedly, tossing an electronic organiser into his briefcase, followed by a couple of manila files. I watched him, amused that someone I'd known as a pal for so long, whom I'd sobered up after drunken binges, had now joined what he once considered to be the enemy. The hard-drinking newsman was an up-and-coming exec. Martin was raking around in one of the desk drawers.

'Anyway,' he said, returning to his earlier theme, 'you are genetically incapable of getting yourself organised. Your car's falling to bits, the cleaners refuse to go in your office because there's so much stuff piled on the floor . . . Damn!' He straightened up. 'Where is that thing?' His eye lit on a small package sitting in the middle of his blotter. He snatched it up and threw it into his briefcase.

'How many filming days?' I rose to my feet.

'Oh.' He snapped his briefcase shut and came round his desk. 'I thought a couple of weeks prep, another two filming over there and probably a few days back here and then maybe a month in post. But it's a movable feast. Just get cracking.' He had me by the elbow and was propelling me out of the door and down the hall. 'You should get over there really as soon as you can – by the end of next week if poss, because I doubt if you can do much of the research from this end.'

We had reached the lift and he let go of my arm and leant forward to press the button. From somewhere in the depths of the shaft we could hear machinery groaning.

'What about a crew? I'll never get anyone decent at this short notice.' I wasn't going to let him off the hook.

'Oh, I should have mentioned that,' returned Martin distractedly, tapping his foot and staring at the list of floor numbers on the lighted display above us, as if willing the lift to move faster. 'You're in luck. Joe Bolton already called me to ask if we were doing anything on this. He's just done a job in the States and it was all over the papers there. As he put it, "sex, money and murder, an unbeatable combination". He's really keen and he'll shift stuff around to do it, he said.' Martin turned to look at me. 'You've always said you'd love to work with him.'

I had been prepared to raise objections, but this silenced

me. Joe Bolton was still relatively young but already he had won awards for creating images that changed the way you saw the world for ever. The lift had finally arrived and Martin stepped into it smartly. I stayed put, intending to walk down the stairs to the music library on the floor below.

'Mags will be your on-screen reporter,' he was saying as he scanned the panel of buttons before selecting one. 'We're meeting for a drink across the road after the news tonight, by the way. Come and join us.' The door was starting to close.

'What about a researcher?' I yelled into the narrowing gap.

'I've thought about that.' The door clanged shut and his last words echoed back to me. 'I've got someone coming in to see you . . .' I couldn't make out the rest.

Halfway down the stairs to the music library it suddenly hit me. I was going on a three or four week paid trip to the United States, with one of my best friends as reporter and a brilliant cameraman. Never mind that Kansas City could be on the moon for all I knew and I was going to have to fit in some work while I was there. I let out a whoop of excitement that reverberated alarmingly round the stairwell and brought Jeanette, the secretary in Religious Programmes, out of her office to peer over the banisters to see what was going on.

I was still in a euphoric mood an hour later when I waltzed into the editing room clutching a little stack of CDs. I came to an abrupt halt. Julian, the editor, was pressed flat against the wall next to the window peering through the Venetian blinds in a thoroughly suspect manner.

'What the hell are you up to?' I asked.

'Ssh!' he hissed, putting one hand to his lips. He craned to see better. I almost burst out laughing. Julian is an extremely tall, gawky individual, with soft hair cut short so that it stands up in a little coxcomb at his temple. With his long neck, round eyes and beaky nose, he always reminds me of an ostrich who's just had a bad fright. Now, spread-eagled against the

5

wall playing Sherlock Holmes, he looked ridiculous.

He beckoned to me. 'Come and take a decco at this.'

Dropping the CDs on to the table, I strolled over to the window. I knew that the Venetian blinds made it virtually impossible for anyone outside to see in, so I made no attempt to hide myself.

'Don't let her see you!' squealed Julian, yanking me in behind him. He pointed to the wing of the building which was immediately opposite. 'There.'

I strained to see what he was looking at. To begin with, I couldn't make out anything unusual, but then, as I bent my knees a little and craned to look up between the slats of the blinds, I realised he was watching a young woman leaning out of a window on the floor above.

Even from this awkward angle, I could see that she was extremely beautiful. She had a mane of glorious Titian red hair which shimmered with each movement of her head so that it was a living kaleidoscope of golds and auburns and reds. Her complexion was flawless, pale and creamy with a subtle flush of pink over her cheekbones, and her features were even and delicate. I couldn't see her eyes. They were closed tight. One elegantly tapered hand was clutching a packet of cigarettes and what looked like a silver lighter. The other held a lit cigarette.

None of that would have seemed particularly extraordinary. RTV had adopted a no-smoking policy a couple of years ago and the building was fitted with alarms to detect those criminal enough to break the rules. Normally I would just have assumed that this woman had become desperate and this was the best solution she could find. But what had obviously attracted Julian's attention was her evident state of mind. She was shaking violently in long convulsive spasms, eyes tightly closed, teeth chattering. There was an anguished expression on her face and she was clearly in great distress. Suddenly she gave a lurch forward so that she was leaning perilously far out over the sill.

'D'you think she's going to jump?' Julian looked at me, his eyes, full of concern, gleaming myopically from behind thick pebble glasses.

I was reaching for the phone. 'I don't know. She might be having some kind of seizure.' I began punching in numbers. 'Do you recognise her?' Julian shook his head emphatically.

One of the security men on the front desk answered. 'Dave, it's Bel.' I spoke urgently. 'There's a woman on the fourth floor outside Graphics who needs help fast.' I glanced up. Julian was watching me anxiously. 'She's hanging out of the window and she seems to be ill or having some sort of breakdown or something.'

'I'll be right there.' The line went dead.

I turned back to Julian. 'They're on their way. Can we get that window open and talk to her, d'you think?'

'Brilliant idea!' Julian reacted with alacrity. The Venetian blinds rattled and shook as he hauled them up and reached for the latch on the window. Then he stopped, his hand poised in mid-air. 'She's gone.' He looked at me blankly.

I leaned past him to see. The woman had disappeared and the window opposite was firmly shut. If I hadn't had a witness standing next to me, I would have thought I'd imagined it.

'Oh well.' I shrugged. 'She must be all right. If she'd jumped, she'd hardly have paused to close the window behind her, would she?'

Julian looked worried. 'But she can't be all right. She looked dreadful. I really thought she seemed suicidal. She couldn't have recovered that fast.'

'I'll let them know downstairs,' I said, dialling the number for security again. Tersely, I informed them that the woman had now disappeared, but that I thought it would still be worth finding her and checking that she was all right.

7

'Don't worry. Dave's on his way. He'll make sure every-thing's OK,' Eric assured me.

Julian was persuaded to tear himself reluctantly away from the window to listen to some of the tracks I had brought from the music library. No one called from the front desk to report on the red-haired woman and I assumed the situation had been dealt with. When we finished almost an hour later, I glanced at my watch. It was just after six, which meant that Mags and Martin wouldn't be congregating in the pub across the road for another half-hour. That would give me time to check on my telephone messages at least.

My office is in a corner of the building, and opens off a big open-plan area where the secretaries and production assist-ants have their desks. Since it was a Friday evening, most of them had already left and the room was deserted when I entered. Even from the far side I could see a flurry of small pieces of yellow paper stuck to my door. I groaned inwardly because that meant that a lot of people had been trying to get hold of me this afternoon.

But when I inspected them, it turned out that three were from whoever was on reception asking me to ring as soon as possible. The first had been at four thirty, the second at five and the third at five thirty. I could detect the increasing irritation underlying the messages from the way the words 'Please call back asap' were underlined in the second one and capitalised in the last.

Sighing, I ripped the other pieces of paper off the door, noting that there was a message from Mags repeating Martin's invitation to join them for a drink and another from the finance department about the US trip. Doubtless the latter were already girding their loins for a battle royal on the budget.

I walked into my office, reaching out behind me with one leg to close the door. But something was blocking it. I glanced round to see what the problem was. Standing in the doorway was the red-headed woman I had seen earlier. Only now it was as if a different person was inhabiting her body. She stood there smiling at me, exuding a relaxed confidence.

'Hello.' She held out her hand. 'I'm Amanda Greer.' Startled, I shook the hand she offered me. 'Martin Kember told me to come in and see you this afternoon but the people in reception couldn't track you down,' she rattled on. 'They said you were still in the building, though, so I decided to wait.'

My brain was doing somersaults. Was this the person Martin had mentioned as a possible researcher? I stepped back so that she could enter. 'Come in,' I said. 'Have a seat.'

My office was pretty much as Martin had described it. Open shelves round the walls buckled under the weight of books and videotapes. Piles of scripts and papers were festooned over every available space. I never seemed to have time to clear up.

Lifting my briefcase off a chair near the window, I offered it to my guest. Then I squeezed behind my desk and attempted to clear a space between us by moving a stack of books.

'What can I do for you?' I inquired politely.

She smiled warmly. 'I've come to talk to you about the US project.'

I couldn't help staring at her as she spoke. She was exceptionally lovely, but that wasn't what held my attention. I was finding it hard to adjust to the fact that this woman sitting so calmly before me was the same one I had seen earlier. It was odd and unnerving, as if I were talking to a puppet masking the real person.

'What have you worked on before?' I asked, automatically going through the routine of a job interview.

For a split second, her composure faltered. 'Well, I didn't have any formal education after eighteen,' she began in a high voice, 'but I worked as a nanny for five years and I think that's very good training for dealing with all kinds of situations.'

My heart sank. The researcher's job is one of the most demanding in television. A programme can stand or fall according to how good they are. They must have the gift of establishing a rapport with strangers over the phone, of sensing the right questions to ask to tease out the intricacies of a story or unleash pent-up emotions. If they don't get the facts straight, checking and re-checking them, we could end up being sued, and if the arrangements the researcher makes aren't watertight, thousands of pounds of crew time can be wasted.

A strictly academic education might not be necessary to do the job, but I was pretty sure that being a nanny, however good you were, definitely didn't qualify as adequate training. Then, of course, there was the question of her state of mind. Researchers come under a lot of pressure and it was only a couple of hours since I had seen Amanda apparently on the brink of a nervous breakdown. That image still hung in the air between us like some ghostly presence and it made me uneasy. Mentally I decided I'd be much better off hiring someone from our regular pool of freelance researchers.

I asked politely, 'Whereabouts was that?'

'A small town near Kansas City.'

I jolted upright. 'Kansas City? That's where we're going to be filming.'

Amanda looked confused. 'Didn't Martin tell you? That was why I applied for the job. I lived there for six years. I've been back here for four or five months. But I still have good contacts,' she added eagerly.

I passed my hands across my face, trying to gather my thoughts. 'Do you know anything about this story already? It's been in the papers quite a bit.'

Amanda nodded eagerly. 'Yes. I've read all the reports. It happened after I left Kansas City, but I may know some of the people who knew the murder victim. It said in one newspaper that she'd inherited the family farm in a place called Rapid Falls in western Kansas. Some of my friends come from there and it's such a small community that I'm sure they'll be able to supply some background information.'

I glanced at my watch surreptitiously. Six thirty. 'Well, that could be extremely useful, but I need to think about this.' I smiled and rose to my feet. 'Thanks for coming in, Amanda. There are several people I'll be interviewing about this job, but I'll be in touch sometime early next week.'

Amanda also stood up and for the first time I registered how tall she was – at least five foot ten or eleven. She had a perplexed expression on her face.

'Martin told me I could start on Monday.'

It was my turn to look nonplussed. 'Start what on Monday?'

'This job. That's what he said. That's why I hung around this afternoon because I thought it would be nice to meet before I actually began work.' She was smiling at me calmly, but there was something in her eye, an edge of something – panic perhaps, or fear.

My mind was riffling through all sorts of possible ways of handling this and discarding most of them. 'OK,' I murmured weakly. 'Then do whatever Martin said. I'd better have a word with him and find out what he's arranged.' I managed a feeble smile.

Amanda held out her hand and said with the assurance I was lacking, 'I'm so excited about this and I'm sure I'm going to enjoy working with you.'

I shook her hand in a daze and gave her directions for finding her way out of the building. Then I grabbed my shoulder bag and headed down the back stairs en route for the pub. Martin was going to have a lot of explaining to do.

'What do you mean I *have* to hire her?' I was shouting to be heard above the hubbub. All around me was a jostling crowd of my colleagues from the evening news programme which had just gone off air. Under the circumstances, the corner booth where I was sitting opposite Mags and Martin was a relative haven of peace and serenity.

I lifted my glass and took a sip of vinegary white wine, glaring at Martin. I had just told him and Mags of my first sighting of Amanda Greer and the outcome of our interview. I hadn't minced my words concerning my worries about her mental state. But he refused to meet my eye, and was absorbed in flicking a beer mat off the edge of the table and catching it in one move.

'Come on, Martin. You may as well tell us the worst,' Mags admonished him in a resigned tone of voice. She pushed a silky strand of dark hair off her face. It always amazed me how, even at the end of a frantic day covering the news, Mags invariably managed to look immaculate. She is a single parent with three smallish children and her home is a deathtrap of discarded schoolbags and toys which shoot out from under the feet of the unsuspecting – like me – but she herself always seems to be perfectly under control. Her dark hair swung smoothly round her fine features, the large green eyes were cleverly emphasised with make-up, and the grey suit she wore on her neat frame looked fresh and uncreased.

Martin sighed and then looked up at me with a placating smile. 'She seems like a nice woman.' This was met by a howl of protest from Mags and me so he took a deep breath and began again. 'The thing is, I thought we should give her a try. After all, she's familiar with the location and she may know some of the people involved in the case and could get us inside info.' He paused and cast a sideways glance at us to see how well that had gone down.

'A map would have done just as well,' said Mags tersely.

12

'Tell me, Martin.' I looked him straight in the eye. 'This woman is extraordinarily beautiful. Is she the girlfriend of someone important – someone's bit on the side? Is that why she's got the job?

Martin's gaze travelled round the room searching for escape then, finding none, came back to us.

He gave a sigh of resignation. 'I didn't have any choice. Benny Upperton phoned me and asked me to give her the job. He's my boss. I could hardly refuse, could I? Anyway,' he continued in an aggrieved tone of voice, 'she seems quite bright to me.'

Mags groaned and threw herself back into her seat.

'But what about her mental problems? What if she cracks up?' I objected.

Martin shifted uncomfortably. 'I'm sure that was just nerves. The prospect of a job interview affects some people more than others.' I rolled my eyes and he carried on hurriedly, 'You said yourself she seemed perfectly fine when you spoke to her. She was probably just a bit anxious and now she's got over it.' He reached for his beer.

I was shaking my head in despair. 'But even if you're right – and I'm not sure you are – it still doesn't alter the fact that she has no experience, not even any background in journalism as far as I can make out.' I leaned forward. 'Look, this is serious, Martin. We're going to be thousands of miles away, totally dependent on this woman to come up with the goods. We don't have time to spare and it's going to be a bit late if we get there and find after two days she's no use.'

Martin shrugged. 'Sorry. Nothing I could do. It's just one of those things, Bel. You'll just have to live with it.' Mags made a face. 'You'll have me,' she said consolingly. 'We'll just have to do the whole thing between us if we can't count on this – what's her name, Amanda?'

I nodded, unconvinced. 'Sounds like it. Hey ho.' I rose to my feet. 'I may as well get us another round.' I went up to the

13

bar and ordered drinks, still trying to come to terms with what Martin had just said. I was unhappy about being forced to accept Amanda as my researcher; the only thing that made her appointment acceptable was the fact that I'd have Mags to help me. Although officially the ultimate responsibility for making the documentary rested with me, while Mags's job was to appear on camera, do the narration and ask the questions, in practice we always work closely together. This is partly because we are such good friends, but also because Mags is an ace journalist and I trust her judgement as well as her research.

I glanced back to the table I had just left. At that moment, Mags lifted one hand and softly touched Martin's cheek. I had known and been delighted about their budding relationship for several months, but they had kept it secret from the rest of our colleagues. This was the first public display of their affection I had seen.

I looked round the room. The crowd had thinned out suddenly. Most people had one quick drink after the programme then headed for home. Apart from a raucous group of darts players in one corner, there were only a few couples lingering. Loneliness washed over me, sudden and piercing. I glanced towards the entrance where grey light leaked into the cosy lamplit room. There was still time. I had been putting this off for weeks. Abruptly, I scooped my change into my pocket, picked up the two beers I had ordered and walked over to join my friends, leaving my own glass of wine on the bar.

'I have to go,' I announced, carefully lowering the glasses on to the table. They looked mildly surprised, but did not argue. Within minutes, I was outside and heading for my ancient TR6.

There was still light enough to see when I arrived at the cemetery. It was an old one with gravestones dating back to the middle of the last century, not far from the farmhouse which my husband Jamie and I had bought together and where I now lived alone.

Spring had come late this year, pushed back by punishingly cold winds blowing in from Siberia. The daffodils hadn't come out until a few weeks ago, only to be battered by the heavy rains we'd had since. They swayed in bedraggled clumps around the burial plots.

I stood by Jamie's grave. Small, gnarled trees had let loose white blossom which drifted like snow around it and was strewn across the grass. It had been the fourth anniversary of his death just over a month before, and it was three years since my foster sister, Rosa, had died. They had been the only family I had left. I had always come here to find comfort in the past. But I had been avoiding it for weeks.

I shivered as I looked around. A chill wind had got up and the sun had set, draining everything of colour as twilight encroached. The place felt empty. There were only rows of tombstones, standing impassive. I picked up a handful of petals and let them fall through my fingers until the last one was gone. Then I turned and went home.

Emmet, the retired fisherman who looks after my garden, was lying in wait for me. I parked my car, which Martin had accurately described as falling to bits, in the lane leading to the garage alongside the house. Squeezing through the hedge, I could hear Emmet clanking tools in the shed, clearly loitering with intent. He straightened up when I called out to him.

'Ah, there you are. I was hoping you wouldn't be much longer. There's something important I have to talk to you about.'

My heart sank. The domestic details of my life always threaten to overwhelm me.

'What this garden needs,' he continued heavily, 'is some good muck.'

I looked round blindly in the gathering darkness. 'But

there's plenty of muck, Emmet. The place is full of it.'

'No. *Muck*,' Emmet intoned with even greater emphasis. 'Manure. What you need here is some good matured muck. Now –' he was obviously settling in for a long lecture – 'I noticed the other day when I was out with my daughter and her family that the farm just past the Barnsley roundabout keeps horses. They'd have good stuff. You could go out there and see if they'll let you have some.'

I felt a band tighten round my head. 'Emmet,' I said weakly, 'you do it, please. I'm leaving for America next week and I've got so much to do before I go. I just couldn't cope with anything else at the moment.'

Emmet sighed. 'It's about time you got your life straightened out and your priorities sorted,' he told me sternly. He stretched his neck muscles. 'All right. I'll order the muck and I'll give this place a good clear-out. There's that much rubbish and dead wood I'll have my work cut out for me, I can tell.'

With relief I escaped indoors and found bread and cheese for supper. Then, plate in hand, I roamed restlessly from room to room. Until recently, I had shared the house with Lucinda, one of my oldest friends. But a few weeks ago she had moved in with her boyfriend. I wasn't used to being alone again. The rooms seemed emptier than I remembered. I climbed the stairs to the attic which Jamie had used as a studio. But there was nothing of him there except a few half-finished canvases, his paints, an easel and a small stool.

I walked across to one of the dormer windows where Jamie had liked to sit while he painted. The light was good there, he said. Pinned to the wall, just at eye level if you sat on the stool, was a small snapshot. It was his favourite picture of the two of us, showing our younger selves – twenty-eight years old we were, I think. It was taken on a boat somewhere. We were laughing and windblown, my eyes screwed up against the sun.

I stood gazing at it for several minutes. For the first time, I had a sense that I was looking at someone distant from me. Jamie had been only thirty-two when he died of cancer and since then I had carried his memory close within me and felt him still a part of my life. But he would always be young. I had moved on. Recently I had found during my internal conversations with him that there were things I could not explain to him. He was fading into the past, and I was terrified.

I turned and went back downstairs and got ready for bed. Just before I drifted off to sleep, it occurred to me that perhaps a trip to the States would do me good. The last thing to run through my mind before I sank into oblivion was the realisation that I hadn't given a second thought to the murder I was going to make a film about.

Chapter Two

'The weather in Kansas City could be anything at this time of year,' RTV's tame man at the Met. Office informed me over the phone. 'It could be rainy, cold, stormy, very hot—'

'Fine, fine,' I interrupted him. 'I get the picture. Take everything.' So I spent a large part of the weekend disinterring my summer clothes from the back of the wardrobe, dumping piles of garments into the washing machine and dragging most of the rest to the cleaners.

On Sunday morning, sitting up in bed with my second cup of coffee, feeling inordinately smug about this display of domesticity, I telephoned Lucinda. After a general gossip, I told her about my forthcoming trip to the States. She readily agreed to check on things while I was away and water my dying pot plants.

'One other thing,' I said as our conversation was drawing to a close. 'I don't suppose you could nose around at police headquarters, could you, and see if you can turn up anything interesting on this guy Malcolm Laurie who's supposed to have killed his wife?'

Lucinda used to be a police detective until she decided to go back to university to study law. She sounded doubtful. 'I'll try, but don't hold your breath. A lot of my contacts have moved on and anyway they wouldn't be doing any of the investigation here unless it was a favour to the US cops.'

'Well, give it a go,' I pleaded before hanging up.

One way or another I was feeling pretty pleased with myself as I drove in to work on Monday morning. My clothes were all clean and ready to be packed, the house would be taken care of while I was gone, and doubtless there was a load of manure on its way even as I sang along off key to some opera on the radio.

When I arrived in my office, I found Amanda pacing around, nervously smoking a cigarette which she guiltily dropped into a dirty coffee cup on my desk as I entered. Evidently she had already figured out she wouldn't set off any smoke alarms in private offices.

'I wasn't sure what time to start,' she began with a bright smile. 'So I got here sharp.'

'We need to find you somewhere to work,' I returned, finding all this enthusiasm a bit much so early on a Monday morning.

'Oh, I've got somewhere,' Amanda rejoined hurriedly. 'It's just there was something I thought I should tell you.' I braced myself. 'I was at my aerobics class on Saturday and there's an American woman who works at the health club and we've sort of got to know each other.' She was talking very fast, so that all the words seemed to be strung together. 'Anyway,' she took a deep breath and spoke more slowly, 'it turns out she was the murdered woman's best friend.'

I blinked. On her very first morning on the job, Amanda had landed a scoop. None of the local newspaper reporters had tracked down anyone who knew Marlene Laurie well. This was exactly the sort of background we needed to build up a picture of the murdered woman and the events leading to her death.

'How the hell did you manage that?' I asked bluntly. 'It seems an amazing coincidence.'

Amanda looked anxious, as if perhaps she feared my words

implied some criticism. 'Well, you see,' she said quickly, 'I became friends with this woman in the first place because I had just come back from the States and I missed my pals in Kansas City. And it suddenly occurred to me that there aren't that many Americans in town and they do tend to gravitate towards each other if they get homesick. So there was a reasonable chance that this woman and Marlene would have been acquainted. It turned out they met at some health club years ago and have stayed in touch ever since.' Amanda paused, watching me closely.

'Brilliant,' I said. 'Will she talk to us?'

Amanda nodded eagerly. 'Yes. She's not sure if she'll do a proper interview for the cameras, but she claims she knows why Mrs Laurie was killed.'

'Well, that's more than anyone else does,' I said drily. 'Give her a call and set up a meeting as soon as possible.' Amanda beamed with delight. 'And,' I continued, 'as soon as you get a chance, can you do a trawl through our cuttings library and see what you can find about Malcolm Laurie and his wife, please?'

She nodded and rushed off. Ten minutes later, she called to say she had arranged an appointment with Marlene Laurie's friend first thing the next morning at the health club.

I spent the following hour with the hitmen in the finance department, arguing over the budget. Amongst other outrageous demands, they tried to insist that I hire an American crew whom I knew nothing about in order to save money. This was merely a tactical manoeuvre, however, because they knew I would never agree. I came out of my meeting bloodied but unbowed. I'd conceded that I would hire the sound recordist and camera assistant in Kansas City, but I had it in writing that Joe Bolton could fly out to do the filming.

Mags was finishing off her latest project and wouldn't be able to help with this one for several days, so I spent the rest of the morning sorting out a rough schedule. If possible, I decided, the three of us would leave at the end of the week and then Joe would follow us out later in time for the shoot. I also had to decide about technicalities such as whether we would take our own recording equipment and tapes, or ship gear in from somewhere like Los Angeles or possibly Chicago where there might be companies using cameras and recorders for the British PAL system.

So my mind was on other things when there was a knock on my door, and a tall, muscular man with a blond crewcut walked in. This, it turned out, was Joe Bolton. He'd decided to stop by, he explained with a smile, because he was working on night shoots Monday and Tuesday of this week, which meant he had the mornings off.

I guessed he was in his early thirties, wearing the standard cameraman's uniform of black T-shirt and jeans. He had a lean, intelligent face, with luminous grey eyes, and wore one gold earring which gave him a slightly piratical air. As we chatted about the shoot and discussed equipment and schedules, his manner was bright and friendly, but his eyes were watchful. I had a distinct sense of someone permanently on his guard. That didn't disturb me unduly. Freelance crew members were used to working in close proximity with new people all the time, having to adjust and accommodate themselves to all sorts of idiosyncrasies. So they learned to hold back, hiding behind an easygoing courtesy until they had the measure of the people they were working with and knew what topics to avoid, and how they should handle prickly personalities.

An hour later, we had most of the practical details taken care of and had agreed that we would hire Joe's camera gear and take it with us.

'I was thinking,' Joe said, looking idly out of the window.

'What?' I asked absently, still scribbling notes on what we'd decided.

'I was thinking I might fly out with you and the others and have a bit of a holiday before we start filming.' I looked up at him. He was gazing at the building across the road as if it was of extreme interest to him.

'Fine,' I said. 'OK by me. We can probably get some deal on the hotel room for you if you like and of course all your travel will be paid for.'

I was rewarded by a dazzling smile. Evidently Joe Bolton could be quite a charmer when he pleased. 'Well, exactly,' he said. 'It seemed a pity to waste the opportunity since RTV are picking up the fare.'

'Of course,' I said and returned his smile. I could be charming too when I felt like it.

When I returned from lunch, there was a huge pile of photocopied newspaper cuttings lying on top of the assorted rubbish on my desk. Amanda had been busy. I was beginning to think it might not have been such a mistake to hire her after all. The acute anxiety attack I had witnessed seemed to have been a one-off event, as Martin had said. She was proving to be an enthusiastic and resourceful member of the team.

I began to look through the assorted photographs and articles about the man now standing trial for murder in Kansas. Some of them dated back forty years or more. Malcolm Laurie came from a family which had farmed in the region for generations. Their beef herds had regularly won prizes both locally and in national cattle shows.

There were photographs of Malcolm as a young man, standing beside his father, fair hair smoothed back, big and handsome, dressed in expensively tailored tweed jackets or occasionally in suits, sometimes with a grey trilby and a heavy dark overcoat carried casually over one arm. He was the image of the wealthy, confident landowner's son. Only now he was on trial for murder.

Looking at these images of privilege, I wondered why he

would kill his wife. Was he a habitually violent man, perhaps, whose secret vice had burst into the open with this killing? Could it have been a drunken accident? Or perhaps a crime of passion? It would be interesting to hear what Marlene's friend had to say.

I turned over a sheet of paper and came upon a picture of his wedding, dated fifteen years earlier. The photograph was grainy but I could still see that they made a handsome couple. The tall, muscular man, head held high, stood proudly beside his very slender wife, her hair dark and curling over her shoulders. She was looking straight into the lens, with an expression at once open and vulnerable.

It was an elaborate scene, with arum lilies arranged on either side on white columns and candles glowing in the background. The caption simply announced that Malcolm Laurie (38), one of the area's most eligible bachelors, had married rancher's daughter Marlene McKinley (19) in Rapid Falls, Kansas. Then there followed a description of the bride's dress, which had been made from silk and lace ordered from Paris.

After their marriage, the newlyweds had settled at the Laurie family farm in the UK. Over the following years, they made numerous public appearances. There were shots of Mrs Laurie, looking svelte and glamorous, presenting rosettes at the county show, and pictures of her and her husband posing beside prize cattle. Only now, when she faced the cameras, there was something more guarded in her expression, a brittleness in the smile, a watchful look in her eyes. Apparently they had no children.

I pondered what could have gone wrong with their marriage, begun like all others with such hope and joy.

I got one answer to that question later that evening when Lucinda called me back.

'I talked to Alan,' she announced, referring to her former

husband, who was still a detective, 'and he says they did get a request to do some checking on Malcolm Laurie. It turns out he's about to go bankrupt. A combination of bad investments and some disease that nearly wiped out his herd a few years back. The only way he held off his creditors was by telling them his wife had inherited a fortune and he'd have the money by the end of the month. So it looks like they've got their motive.'

Her words were still reverberating in my mind as I set off with Amanda the next morning to meet Marlene Laurie's friend. I found it hard to accept that the prospect of financial ruin would have been enough to drive someone to kill his wife. Many couples were actually drawn closer together by adversity. Either Malcolm Laurie had fooled his family and friends for years and was a very cold, calculating killer, or the police had got it completely wrong.

'What is Kansas City like?' I asked Amanda, in an attempt to get my mind off the same repetitive train of thought. I pulled out into the traffic, following her directions.

'Oh, it's an odd mixture of country and big city,' she said, 'straddling two states. There's a road through the middle of town called State Line and one side's in Kansas and the other side is in Missouri. Until not so very long ago you could walk into a bar and get a drink on one side of the road but not on the other.' She shrugged to indicate it made no sense to her.

'Otherwise, it's like any other big city. There's an orchestra and a ballet company and a couple of big art museums and theatre and concerts and cinema – all that stuff. I suppose the thing that is different, however, is the countryside around it. You don't have to go very far before you're out on the plains, hundreds of miles of flatlands with nothing in sight but a small town or two or the occasional farmhouse and outbuildings or perhaps one of the pumps that keeps the oil pipes flowing. You'll see lots of those if we go out to western Kansas.'

'That's where Marlene Laurie grew up, isn't it, in Rapid Falls?'

'Yeh,' Amanda nodded. 'I've been out there a few times. To visit those friends I mentioned.'

'It's an amazing coincidence that you know people from the same town as her,' I remarked.

Amanda shook her head. 'Not really. Western Kansas isn't that well populated and quite a lot of young people move into KC because they have to get work or go to school. Everyone in Rapid Falls knew each other pretty well and they all tended to hang out together. So if you met one, you sort of got to know the rest pretty quickly.' She turned to me. 'I only know a couple of people who knew her personally, though.'

We had reached the health club. Parking the TR at the side of the building, I asked, 'What's her name, by the way?'

'Maryam Cheever.'

If I'd had to choose one word to describe the woman waiting for us in the foyer, it would have been 'glossy'. Although she was probably in her mid-thirties, she could have passed for much younger. She was very slim, with the lithe, toned body of someone who spent a lot of time in the gym. The streaked blonde hair was fluffed out around the carefully made-up face with its tiny sculpted nose.

'Isn't it just awful!' she exclaimed as soon as we were seated. She gestured widely with her hands so that the long orange nails flashed back and forth before my eyes in a dazzle of colour. 'Poor, poor Lenie. I mean, I knew they were having problems but I never imagined –' she fanned her hands out before her – 'that this would happen!' She closed her eyes momentarily to indicate how overwhelmed she was.

'When you say they were having problems,' I began care-fully, anxious not to add to the melodrama, 'what exactly do you mean?'

Maryam assumed an expression of deep concern. 'Well, things weren't going too well. I mean, Lenie was, what, nine-teen when she met Malcolm. He was fortyish, a real hunk she said, big, strong, good-looking and rich, or so she thought. And he was British, so to a young woman who'd spent most of her life in a small town in Kansas, he must have seemed pretty exotic.'

'So what went wrong?' I prompted.

'Well. Just that she grew up, I guess. She turned thirty-four just before she left for the States. Malcolm's in his fifties.' And –' Maryam grimaced and leaned forward, lowering her voice, as if this was the most shocking thing of all – 'I guess there were money problems – in fact I know there were. Lenie wanted out because she'd just inherited all that money from her mom and she certainly didn't want to have it eaten up by a bunch of cows.'

She paused a moment, her face a picture of indignation, before continuing, 'And the other thing, too, was that one of the characteristics that Lenie and I have, I mean had, in common is that we are, were, both real creative and artistic. That's what drew us together in the first place. We were just so different from most of the women we met. I'm an astrologer and really, really intuitive. You have to be a very spiritual person, very sensitive to do that. Lenie was studying to be an artist when she met Malcolm but she gave it up to get married. She really had a lot of talent and she wanted to give it a whirl but she felt that being married to Malcolm was holding her back. She wanted a divorce, basically.'

'Had she told her husband that?' I was watching her closely.

Maryam shook her head, so that the curls shivered and rippled. 'She was too scared. You know –' Maryam gestured

27

with one hand outstretched – 'I really like Malcolm. He's basically an OK meat-and-potatoes kind of guy. But he does have a temper!' She jerked her head back in mock terror. 'So Lenie decided to wait till they were in the States. She thought it would be safer under her sister's roof. My oh my. How wrong can you be!'

'So you believe Malcolm could have killed his wife?'

She shrugged. 'Who knows? He could have. He had a real bad temper, like I said, and he was under a lot of pressure. You know, I often think about that. One moment your life can be OK and then something happens, something triggers that little thing inside you – maybe you could have gone through your whole life without ever knowing it was there – but you explode, you're caught up in this, like, madness.' Maryam paused, her eyes wide, her hands splayed. Then she relaxed and her voice became lower, softer. 'And then when the dust clears, your life is changed for ever. It will never be the same again. And that's what it could have been for Malcolm, you know. Just one little thing she said that set it all off.'

We sat in silence for a moment, savouring that particular profundity. I rose to my feet, holding out my hand.

'We must go, but thank you so much for your help.'

'My pleasure.' Maryam began to move towards the exit. 'Of course, there was one other little thing that probably tipped the balance.'

I stood still and looked at her sharply. 'What?'

Maryam shrugged. 'She wanted her freedom. There was someone else, someone in the States. She hinted at it before she left but she was real coy, she wouldn't give me any details.'

I eyed her carefully. None of the newspapers had mentioned a lover. 'You have absolutely no idea, no guess at who it could be?' I pressed her.

She smiled regretfully as she held the door open for us. 'Sorry. That's all I know.'

'Thanks.' But I couldn't keep the frustration out of my voice. 'We'll be back in touch in a few weeks' time.'

'No problem.' My last impression of her was the neon orange nails twinkling as she waved goodbye.

'What do you think?' asked Amanda as we got back on to the motorway and headed towards town.

'What do I think?' I repeated. 'I hope it does turn out she had a lover. A crime of passion sounds much more interesting than Laurie bumping off his wife just to keep the bank manager happy.'

Chapter Three

The next few days passed in a haze. I spent my time finalising budgets, sorting out crew and equipment, making arrangements to have tapes shipped back safely and, in between times, packing my own clothes and gear and clearing out my refrigerator.

'I've found out where Kansas City is,' I yelled across the car park to Martin one day as I was leaving the building. He looked preoccupied.

'Where's that, then?'

'If you close your eyes and stick your finger bang in the middle of the United States, you'll hit it.'

'That's nice,' he mumbled distractedly as he got into his car. His apparent lack of interest did not surprise me. I'd heard that there was some big political fight going on amongst the board and rumour had it that Martin's job might be on the line.

On Saturday morning, Amanda, Joe, Mags and I flew out to the States. There was a palpable air of excitement, even though this was not going to be a holiday. We landed at Kansas City International Airport about seven thirty in the evening local time, but it was after one in the morning back home and the weariness was showing in all our faces. Laboriously, we reclaimed our baggage and loaded it into two taxis. As we did so, I was struck by the balminess of the air, even at this time of night.

We set off for our hotel in the city centre. Tired though I was, I craned my neck to see what the landscape looked like. But I could tell very little from what was visible from the highway. During the transatlantic flight, an American sitting next to me had told me a convoluted joke about an alien from outer space arriving on earth and being asked to describe Mars. 'Like Kansas with craters!' The punchline made my neighbour double up with laughter while I stared at him baffled. It wasn't until several days later, when I had experienced the monotony of mile upon mile of flatlands for myself, that I was able to understand the joke.

We were driven into town on a wide six-lane highway, which seemed miraculously empty of traffic by British standards. On either side of the road I could see grassy sweeps of land, interrupted by occasional commercial buildings. These ranged from prefabricated warehouses that somehow suited the Spartan landscape to more ostentatious edifices adorned with pillars or grand entryways. The latter stood out stiffly against the fields, with no backdrop of hills or trees to make them look less awkward and out of place.

Finally we reached the outskirts of the city. I could see a cluster of skyscrapers on the horizon to our left and the taxi driver told us tersely that that was downtown Kansas City, Missouri. The area we were headed for, however, was surprisingly suburban and green – residential neighbourhoods of wooden houses set back from the road under the protective shade of leafy trees.

'You guys are lucky,' our cab driver volunteered. 'We've had a lot of rain and it's been kinda chilly, but today it got up to the nineties which is real hot this early in the season. The forecast is for a heatwave.'

He slowed down and turned right into the forecourt of a towering hotel where he deposited us with our luggage. We entered a long, low foyer, designed to resemble the great hall of some English manor house. Waist-high mahogany panels were topped by heavy, cream brocade wallpaper which provided the background to several oil portraits of eighteenth-century aristocrats. Advancing towards the reception desk, I noted the antique tables and the breakfront cabinets containing elegant china. The hotel had obviously gone to some lengths to create a make-believe world of gentility and privilege.

After checking in, we ate a light supper then mumbled goodnight to each other and disappeared to our rooms – Amanda, Mags and me on the fifth floor, Joe on the one above.

I awoke far too early the next morning, unable to adjust to this new time zone. I propped myself up on one elbow, feeling disorientated. I had been too tired to pay attention to my immediate surroundings the evening before, but now I could see that I was in a fairly plush hotel room. The walls were covered with an inoffensive pinkish-beige paper and there were prints of English hunting scenes hanging above the large bed. I pulled back the heavy curtains to reveal a sliding glass door leading to a small balcony. Stepping outside, I was struck by how warm it felt. I looked down on a narrow creek which flowed between the hotel and an area of shops and restaurants opposite.

It was only five o'clock, but the hotel receptionist assured me the pool was open for use, so I pulled on my bathing costume and a tracksuit and took the lift to the basement. The pool was outdoors, but heated to a warm temperature so that it was usable year round, I was told, in spite of temperatures that dipped to minus thirty degrees with wind chill in winter.

I dived into the water indoors, swam through a small tunnel into the open air and began to knock out some lengths, slowly at first but gathering speed all the time. The water felt cool and

33

soothing. By the time I hauled myself out on to the deck half an hour later, I felt ready for anything.

I got into the lift, emerging seconds later at the fifth floor. There was no one else in sight as I padded along the thickly carpeted corridor, moving from one pool of downlight to another. As I passed the doors of other rooms, I caught the muted sounds of activity from within – snoring from one, a fridge door opening in another, then a toilet flushing. Turning a corner, I approached my bedroom. That was when I suddenly became aware of a tearful voice which floated fitfully down the hallway towards me.

As I drew level with Amanda's room, the sounds became clearer. It was impossible not to register the low, anguished tone, although I couldn't catch the exact words.

I unlocked my door and entered. The one-sided conversation in the next room was dulled to a low murmur, but I could still hear the undercurrent of acute distress. I hesitated, debating whether I should do something, then resolutely turned on the shower. It was none of my business. The only reason I was aware that Amanda was in any kind of trouble was because we happened to be staying in adjacent hotel rooms. She was entitled to her privacy, I told myself, rubbing shampoo vigorously into my scalp.

But I found it disturbing. That first impression I had had of her, shaking convulsively, as if she were falling apart, had been swept aside by the Amanda who was enthusiastic, confident and overflowing with positive energy. Now it seemed as if that other self might still be there, buried only just beneath the surface and likely to emerge at any time.

Half an hour later, when I had finished drying my hair and had pulled on a cotton T-shirt and jeans, I went down to the dining room for breakfast. I had expected a coffee shop with plastic-topped tables in booths, but the illusion of grandeur was maintained even here. I was escorted to a table by the window, set with snowy linen and silver cutlery. Joe was already there, sprawled in a chair, half hidden behind a newspaper. All I could see of him were battered canvas shoes and a pair of jeans with a large tear in one knee. Seconds later, we were joined by Amanda.

I gave her a covert glance as she examined the extensive menu but there was no outward sign of the anguish I had overheard earlier. Miraculously, she appeared calm and clear-eyed, although she was pale and her manner seemed a little tense.

Ten minutes later, Mags arrived in an exuberant mood, looking bright and fresh in khaki slacks and a cream silk shirt. Over scrambled eggs and hash browns, we discussed our plans. Since it was a Sunday, we had been given a day off to recover from jet lag – an unusual luxury. Mags had also carried out a reconnaissance from her hotel balcony and insisted that we should explore the nearby Plaza, with its outdoor cafés and speciality stores.

Our hire cars were due to be delivered to the hotel that morning, but we decided to walk there – something we came to regret because by the time we emerged from the hotel, the heat was becoming intense, and the quarter mile or so to the other side of Brush Creek began to seem like a marathon. Once there, we mingled with the crowds of casually attired people strolling around in the sunshine.

I still felt slightly woolly from jet lag and, after a couple of hours, took up residency in the courtyard of one small restaurant, sipping mineral water and later wine and watching the crowds go by. Mags had been given a shopping list by her children and, accompanied by Amanda, had dashed off, full of energy as usual, to see what she could find. After a while I was joined by Joe. He had acquired a selection of magazines so we sat in companionable silence, reading and drinking wine.

When the others came back, they seemed in good spirits. With relief, I noted that Amanda was more relaxed than I had ever seen her before, laughing spontaneously as she approached our table and sank into a chair opposite me. I ordered more drinks while Mags showed off her purchases.

'Right, it's your turn,' she finally said to Amanda when she had displayed the last box of trainers, the last pair of jeans and a collection of electronic games.

Amanda blushed and looked sheepish. But Mags cajoled her into producing her only package from under the table. It contained a beautiful pair of navy kid pumps.

'I really shouldn't have.' She grimaced. 'I can't afford to buy anything just now, but I fell in love with them and I've only got a pair of Nikes and these.' She leant sideways and extended her foot to show us the plain tan loafers she was wearing. They were of sturdy leather and were clearly expensive, but well-worn. 'When I left Kansas City, I walked out with just the clothes I was wearing and I haven't had any money to buy very much since.'

There was a moment's silence while Mags and I digested this odd statement. 'Couldn't you have asked someone to send your things over?' queried Mags, ever the practical mother-of-three.

Amanda hesitated, then smiled breezily. 'Oh, there was nothing I really wanted.' Turning her head away to discourage further questions she added, 'I must go to the rest room.' With a fleeting smile, she hurried indoors.

Mags raised her eyebrows to me, but said nothing. Joe seemed unaware of anything strange in Amanda's conversation and was watching the crowds strolling by. I had noted with some curiosity that in spite of their evident good looks and sexual attractiveness, Joe and Amanda seemed to ignore each other much of the time. While Joe flirted with anything and everything, he appeared oblivious to Amanda's charms.

I was beginning to feel very sleepy. Joe and I had finished a bottle of wine between us during the afternoon which was more than I was used to during daylight hours.

'I think I'll go back to the hotel for a nap before dinner,' I muttered.

Mags had slumped in her seat as if she too had just realised how tired she was. 'Good idea. I'll come with you.'

'Me too.' Joe began to gather together his magazines. 'This jet lag is a funny business. You think you've cracked it then it catches up with you at odd moments.'

I rose to my feet and stretched. 'I'll go and pay the bill.'

I headed for the cool interior. Stepping inside, I paused, momentarily confused by the sudden dark after the glaring sunlight. As my eyes adjusted, I became aware that Amanda was standing only a few feet away. Her back was towards me, and she was peering round a pillar which stood between her and the dining area.

There was something about the intensity of her pose and the way she was hiding herself that stopped me calling out. But just as I had decided to walk past as if I hadn't noticed her, she suddenly dodged backwards, flattening her body against the pillar. A few seconds later, a youngish couple passed by on the far side, heading for the exit.

They were a striking pair, even from the back. He was tall and powerfully built, dressed in shorts and a casual white shirt, above which I could see thick dark hair. When he half turned to wave goodbye to the waiter, I had a fleeting impression of film-star good looks, of a dark brooding face with deep-set brown eyes. All I could tell about the woman was that she was tall and slim, with long, elegant, tanned legs and short auburn hair that swung round her head as she walked.

Amanda watched them intently until they had disappeared through the exit on the far side of the room. Then she whipped round suddenly and crashed into me. For a moment I caught a glimpse of pure fear in her eyes. Then a shutter came down and she pulled back a little, smiling disarmingly.

'Oh, Bel! I'm so sorry. I didn't see you standing there.'

I waved her apologies aside. 'No problem. I think we've decided to go back to the hotel. I'm just going to pay the bill.'

'Good idea,' Amanda agreed. She walked outside to join the others, leaving me full of curiosity about what I had just seen.

We all seemed to go downhill very fast that evening, perhaps because of the wine we had drunk during the day and also because of the unaccustomed heat. So at my suggestion we ate an early dinner and then retired to bed.

I fell into a dreamless sleep immediately, but to my chagrin I woke in the middle of the night again. Switching on the lamp by my bedside, I noted with irritation that it was only 3.30 a.m.

After tossing about restlessly for some time, I finally got up and went out on to the balcony. The city was silent. I might have been the only person left in the universe, except for a car which was approaching from across the creek. I watched it with interest as it pulled into the hotel parking lot and a solitary figure emerged. It was Joe. He walked towards the foyer and disappeared from view. Evidently he had decided to make the most of his holiday.

A clock somewhere struck four. Resolutely I returned to bed, determined to make myself sleep.

Under the circumstances, I felt surprisingly well-rested next morning. As soon as I woke up, I rolled over in bed and phoned Martin. It was a perfunctory call. He seemed glad that we had arrived safely and wished us well, but I got the distinct impression that we were the least of his worries and he would be quite happy if we just got on with the job and didn't bother him except in an emergency.

I had planned that Mags, Amanda and I would spend this first week carrying out research – talking to possible interviewees, looking at locations, piecing together the background to the crime and those involved in it and trying to find an angle on the story that no one else had come up with.

'Of course, the ideal thing would be if we could find a witness or something to prove Laurie's innocence,' I commented as the three of us lingered over cups of coffee after breakfast. 'But I would think the chances of that are pretty slim. The best we can hope for is to present as rounded a picture as we can.'

Amanda had arranged visits over the following few days to local newspaper offices and television stations to review whatever pictures and information they might have about the murder. 'Just log the main shots and general content,' I instructed her. Mags was going to make some calls to journalists and the police to see what she could find out. I had to finalise crew and equipment bookings and try and set up a meeting with the prosecutor.

'One other thing I was wondering about,' offered Amanda tentatively, as our plates were removed and we prepared to leave. I looked at her expectantly and she shifted restlessly in her seat. 'One of my best friends here is a defence attorney. She's not involved in the case,' she added hurriedly, seeing my sudden look of interest, 'but she does have good contacts. I've phoned her office and left a message asking her to find out what she can about the police evidence because I know we won't get very much out of them.' She watched me anxiously for approval.

'Wonderful,' I said simply. 'How soon can we talk to her?'

Amanda visibly relaxed and allowed herself a brief smile. 'She's frantically busy and I haven't actually spoken to her yet, but her secretary said she'd squeeze us in if we could make it around three this afternoon.'

'Fine.' I began moving towards the lifts. 'I'll probably just have a sandwich in my room for lunch, so let me know whenever you think we need to leave.'

At two fifteen, Amanda tapped on my door. I picked up my jacket and we set out to visit her friend. Mags had gone off to meet a local television reporter who claimed to have the inside track on the story and none of us had seen Joe all morning.

'Her name's Lois Zimmermann,' Amanda told me as she steered the big hire car through the lazy afternoon traffic. 'Her office is on the Kansas side of the city.' Shortly afterwards, we arrived at an imposing red brick building on a wide street near the courthouse.

Lois Zimmermann rose from her desk as we entered, waving one hand to indicate a couple of expansive cream leather sofas set at right angles to each other near the large window. She was about six feet tall, with a slender, graceful build. Her long face and strong features were softened by fine skin and pale blonde hair cut in a soft bob reaching to her shoulders. Her smartly cut dark suit, cream silk shirt and expensive-looking shoes completed the image of a successful lawyer. She was holding a tiny dictating machine, but after murmuring a few more words into it she placed it on her desk and rushed over joyfully to hug Amanda.

'It is so good to see you!' she enthused.

While Lois ordered coffee for us, I glanced round her office. It, too, spoke of financial success. Copper metal shutters bracketed the windows and Native American paintings in shades of brown, cream, burnt amber and sienna adorned the walls, which had been taken back to the original brick. The furniture was a mixture of discreet and tasteful modern pieces and highly polished antiques. One of these was a large partners desk which took up one end of the room.

'Well, I'm not involved in this case, as you know,' Lois was saying, 'but I do have some good contacts in the police department.'

'I remember,' broke in Amanda with an arch smile. 'Wasn't there somebody you used to date?'

'Yeah, well.' Lois looked embarrassed and waved one slender hand dismissively. 'Whatever it takes . . . Now.' She leaned forward in her leather chair opposite us. 'According to my source, they've got a pretty good case against this guy. Firstly –' Lois began ticking points off on the fingers of one hand – 'the sister-in-law, who is divorced, and the niece had gone out for the evening and Malcolm Laurie and his wife were alone in the house. There were no outgoing calls made after that until the murder was discovered. No one else was seen leaving or entering the house around the time of death – remember it wasn't that late, only about eight p.m. The people across the way still hadn't pulled their drapes and were sitting in their front room. They saw the sister-in-law drive off, then her daughter was picked up by her boyfriend and once they'd gone there was no one else.

'Now, you could argue that the killer could have sneaked round the back way and –' she paused to take the cup of coffee her assistant was handing her – 'there was in fact some sign of forced entry at the rear of the house. Although all the doors and windows were locked, one pane had been broken on the patio doors. But the police think that was just to make it look as if there had been a break-in.'

Abruptly, Lois rose and crossed to her desk, returning with a small notebook which she consulted. 'Let's see. Yes. In fact, in their eyes, that just incriminated Laurie further because the glass had been broken from the inside. A real amateur attempt at a cover-up.'

She flipped over several pages. 'The cops also found a footprint in the mud just outside the patio door, size thirteen

Nike Air running shoes, but all three of the guys the lawn service sent over the day before to do the yard have size thirteens, so it looks as if they can rule that one out as reliable evidence.' She looked up, grinning. 'Welcome to the land of giants.' We all laughed.

'Apart from that,' Lois continued, 'there is the forensic evidence. Mrs Laurie was battered with a chunk of flintstone which was in the room where she was found. There were some smudged fingerprints on it, and at least one of them has been identified as the husband's. He also had his wife's blood on his hands and clothes.'

Lois laid her notebook on the coffee table in front of her with an air of finality. 'So there we have it. He's got motive, opportunity, there's forensic evidence, no other suspects, the attempt to fake the break-in . . .' She held her arms wide in a gesture of defeat. 'What can I say?' Sounds to me like the guy's guilty.'

There was silence. Amanda had been taking notes throughout, but now she stopped.

'Were his clothes spattered with blood,' I asked, 'or could he just have become smeared with it when he discovered his wife's body?'

Lois looked dubious. 'I don't think they could tell. There was blood everywhere, apparently. A lot of it. And his clothes – he was wearing pyjamas and some kind of robe, I think – were soaked in it.' She glanced at an elegant gold watch on her wrist, then got to her feet. Amanda and I also stood up.

'I'm sorry,' Lois said. 'I have another meeting in a few minutes.'

'You're a pet!' Amanda leaned forward and kissed her friend's cheek. 'Come and have dinner with me tonight.' She turned to me questioningly. 'There's nothing special I have to do for work, is there?' I shook my head.

'I'd love to. I'll call you later.' Lois was already shepherding us towards the exit. I lingered behind in the long hallway, pausing to examine a particularly beautiful pen and ink drawing of a group of Native American women. The other two waited for me by the exit, talking in low tones. After a few moments, I became aware of a different note in their voices. They appeared to be arguing. Suddenly Lois spoke loudly. 'Goddamn it, Amanda! Are you out of your mind? Why did you come back? Don't you know you're playing with fire?'

I spun round in time to see Amanda shrug and turn away. There was a self-conscious silence as I walked towards them. Lois smiled at me with automatic courtesy as I passed her, then turned back to her office, slamming the door shut behind her.

Amanda sat in silence all the way back to the hotel, in spite of my attempts to make small talk. We joined the others for a drink in the bar before dinner. Joe had spent the day touring the city and doing some more relaxing in sidewalk cafes. He was in an uproariously good mood, however, and entertained us all with his stories and his mimicry of the outraged tones of the maitre d' of one restaurant he'd tried to enter that day, dressed in his usual worn jeans.

We were beginning to realise that Kansas City ran on a different schedule to the one we were used to. Most people seemed to get up at dawn or just after and were in their offices by seven thirty or eight. Lunch was any time between eleven and twelve, while the evening meal was eaten around six. By the time we had finished dinner it was almost ten thirty, and we decided that if we were going to keep up with the local regime, then we should all retire to bed.

As my head hit the pillow, it was as if I fell off the edge of the planet and I slept heavily and dreamlessly. I have vague memories of trying to pull myself to the surface at some point, drawn by some unfocused sense of urgency, but I gave up and slipped back into oblivion.

And then I was floating only a few feet below consciousness. Something tugged at me, torturing my peace of mind, until I floundered awake and propped myself up groggily. I shook my head to clear the fog of sleep, then lolled across the bed and switched on the lamp. The warm shaded glow helped to bring all my senses back into focus. Suddenly I became aware that someone was weeping.

In the adjoining room, Amanda was crying, deep, rending sobs that rose and fell in long cadences. Pulling my knees up to my chest, I laced my arms round them, resting my chin on top. I had no idea what to do. I hated the thought that I knew another person was suffering while I deliberately did nothing to help, not even offering sympathy. But who knew why she was weeping? It could be something devastating, or something trivial. I'd already had a glimpse of how highly strung she could be. Perhaps it was simply her way of letting off steam.

But I found it unnerving. There seemed to be so many unanswered questions surrounding her. Why had she had to leave Kansas City in such a hurry without taking even her clothes? And why, for that matter, had she come back? What was she involved in that Lois seemed to think was so dangerous? Who were the people she had been spying on in the restaurant? And last but not least, why, oh why was she so unhappy?

Sighing, I lay back down on the pillows, turning on my side to cut out some of the noise and trying to compose myself for sleep. Amanda was an articulate woman, even if she did seem to be rather neurotic. I would just have to accept that if she wanted my help, she was perfectly capable of asking for it.

I lifted my head off the pillow and listened one last time.

The sobbing seemed to have abated, to have taken on a more even, softer rhythm, less spasmodic, as if she, too, were drifting off to sleep. I curled up into a ball and pulled the blanket up to my chin, suddenly feeling the chill of the air conditioning.

Chapter Four

I woke at 5 a.m. again the next morning, far too early to go for breakfast. Feeling restless, I pulled back the curtains and slid open the glass doors, stepping out on to the small balcony. A grey dawn light pervaded the atmosphere, tinged with pink pearl on the eastern horizon. The air felt comfortably cool and a delicate breeze played fitfully across my skin. On the other side of the creek with its accompanying six lanes of roadway, the shops and restaurants of the Plaza were still and empty. A solitary figure walked slowly along the pavement.

Idly, my gaze strayed to follow a blue sedan as it crossed the bridge on the right-hand edge of the Plaza and turned into the hotel parking lot. For a second, it didn't register. Then I leaned forward, watching as Joe and Amanda emerged and walked towards the foyer, arms linked. I shook my head helplessly. Only a few hours ago, in the middle of the night, Amanda had been sobbing in her room. Now she was returning from an outing with Joe at a time when most people were still asleep, or at least just waking up. What was going on? If it was simply that they were having an affair, why the secrecy? Why the pretence of ignoring each other in public? And what part did Joe play, if any, in Amanda's distressed state of mind?

Unless it affected their work, I told myself, it was none of my business. Resolutely, I pulled on my swimming suit and headed for the pool. But when Amanda and then Joe joined us for breakfast a little later, I could not help watching them closely for the smallest signs of an understanding between them, some explanation for what I had seen. They barely acknowledged each other.

We had a busy day ahead of us so I pushed these thoughts to the back of my mind. Amanda had arranged a meeting with Beth Anne McGregor, the dead woman's sister, at her home. We would also get a chance to talk to Malcolm Laurie while we were there. He had been let out on bail and was staying with his sister-in-law. After a brief discussion over breakfast, the three of us set off.

It took about half an hour to reach our destination, a leafy residential area north of the city. Here there was an atmosphere of contrived charm. The roads were not laid out in a grid pattern but curved and twisted like those of an English country town. One street split in two round a spreading oak tree. The houses were large and there was an air of understated wealth about them, but when we arrived at the address Amanda had written down, I was surprised. It was not what I had expected.

Beth Anne McGregor was a millionairess several times over. I had assumed she would live in a mansion. But her home was a sprawling one-storey house built of gold-coloured brick with a steeply sloping red-tiled roof, much like the others in the neighbourhood. It was substantial, but it was hardly imposing. A number of mature oak and maple trees encircled the house and as we got out of the car I could hear birds chirping.

The doorbell was answered by a young Filipino maid, dressed in a plain black dress and wearing white lace-up shoes. When I told her who we were, she stood aside, holding the door wide so that we could enter. 'Mrs McGregor is expecting you,' she said in heavily accented English.

Stepping over the threshold, I found myself in a spacious

circular hall, the walls of which were covered in deep rose-pink silk. The floor was white marble. Glancing around, I noticed three pairs of doors made of light oak set into the walls at regular intervals. Ornate gilt side chairs and a couple of elegant bureaux were the only furniture.

At that moment, the doors directly in front of me opened and a small, wiry woman in her mid-forties appeared. She had the competent air of someone who was used to making all her own decisions. She was also immaculately groomed, and wore a peacock-blue silk dress and expensive kid shoes. Her hair was dyed a golden blonde and she was tanned and fit looking, but her face was heavily lined as if she had spent too many years in too hot a sun. Her eyes were a vivid blue. She stepped forward and greeted us with the smile of a practised hostess.

'Welcome to my home! I am so glad to see you!' She shook hands with each of us in turn, beaming as she introduced herself. 'I'm Beth Anne McGregor – although you can just call me Beth if you like.' Her voice was low and husky and she had what I was beginning to recognise as a Midwestern twang.

She led us through the doors by which she had entered into a spacious sitting room, predominantly cream in colour but with touches of silvery blue in the curtains and the two large sofas flanking the open fireplace. There was a smell of new paint. The wall opposite the door was almost entirely glass and looked out on what seemed to be a woodland dell, complete with delicate pastel-coloured wild flowers nestling under the trees.

She motioned us to sit down as another Filipino maid, this one wearing a frilly white apron over the black uniform, laid a tray of glasses with an insulated metal pitcher on the vast square coffee table in front of the fire.

'Can I offer you some homemade lemonade?' Beth inquired politely, then in response to our nods she began to pour the pale cloudy liquid into glasses and hand them round. As she did so, I took the opportunity to study her more closely. She had a kind face, I decided. She had never been a beauty, or even especially pretty, but now that the hostess smile had slipped and was replaced by a frown of concentration, I could sense a profound weariness behind the bright façade and see hurt in her eyes as she passed me a glass of lemonade. There was something very wise and patient about the set of her mouth, something long-suffering and steady about her gaze.

When we had all been given our drinks, she shifted back into the luxurious drift of the deep sofa opposite us and sighed. 'Well, you want to interview me, is that right?' She glanced from one to the other of us, seeking a response. Amanda pulled out her notebook.

'That's right,' I spoke up.

Beth bowed her head, considering, then lifted it again slowly, as if shouldering a burden. 'I'm ready,' she said.

But before Mags could ask the first question, Beth began to talk. 'This was where it happened,' she gestured round the room. 'And –' she half turned to indicate the glass doors behind her – 'that was where the murderer came in.'

'How do you know?' Mags interjected quickly. 'I understand the police think the glass was broken from the inside.'

For a fleeting moment, Beth looked confused. Then she rallied. 'Well, I know they say that, but I don't agree with their conclusions. I mean, he had to have got in somehow. Either Marlene could have let him in or maybe, and this is what I think could have happened because, believe me, I have lain awake so many nights trying to understand all this and make sense of it.' A tearful note had crept into her voice. But then she seemed to get a grip on herself before continuing in a more normal tone.

'You see, perhaps the killer had one of those sucker things, you know, like you get to clean a blocked drain, and he held the pane with that so that when he broke it, the glass stayed attached to the sucker and then he dumped it on the ground outside.'

I gazed at her with interest. It was a possible explanation, although not a very obvious one.

'So you don't believe your brother-in-law is guilty?' Mags kept her voice neutral.

Beth shook her head vehemently. 'No, sirree. No way. I've known Malcolm for fifteen years and he is a gentleman through and through. There aren't many of them around these days but, believe me, he's one of the few. No one could have loved Marlene more than he did. Why, do you think I would have him under my roof if I thought for one instant he had killed my little sister?' Beth gazed at us with an expression of pained outrage in her eyes.

'So if Malcolm didn't do it, who did?' Mags asked.

Beth slumped back in her seat. 'I have no idea. There are so many strange people around these days. The police would rather have a convenient suspect than hunt for a needle in a haystack, but I'm afraid that's what they're gonna have to do. Because it definitely wasn't Malcolm.'

'Your sister arrived about ten days before her husband, isn't that right?' Mags was back-tracking to the questions we had planned to ask at the beginning of the interview.

'That's right. Our mother died a few months ago and we had to finalise her affairs. We drove to our farm in western Kansas and cleared out the family home. It was a very distressing time for both of us.' There were no tears in Beth's eyes as she said this but her mouth was set in a straight line as if she was holding back her emotions. 'We came back to Kansas City and Malcolm joined us here the night before my sister's death.'

'Can you tell us what happened that evening?' Mags asked quietly.

Beth heaved a sigh and looked upwards for a moment. 'Well,' she began slowly. 'It was a Sunday and the maids always have that night off. I had arranged to play bridge and there was no one to take my place so I didn't want to let the other girls down and I decided to go even though I had guests. Anyways, I thought it would be nice to leave Marlene and Malcolm to have a little privacy together. Lola's got a den of her own in the basement where she always hides away. Lola's my daughter. She's seventeen.' Tears welled in Beth's eyes but she ignored them defiantly, swallowing hard and carrying on.

'We all had supper – Malcolm barbecued some steaks and we had them with salad and baked potatoes with sour cream. Then I left for my bridge game. That would have been about seven.' She took a deep breath. 'I came home early because I didn't want to leave my guests on their own too long.' She paused and when she continued, her voice had shifted down a gear, as if she were far away inside some distant, unreal memory.

'The front of the house was in darkness apart from the security lamps. I drove into the garage and entered the kitchen. There were no lights on there and I could hear a strange sound, like someone was choking, only very quiet, coming from the next room – this room, in fact. I walked in here and found Malcolm, dressed in his P.J.s and a tartan robe, on his knees beside Marlene's body. He was weeping. That was the sound I'd heard. He was holding Marlene in his arms and she was bleeding and he had her blood all down the front of his robe.'

Beth turned her head away as if to evade the memory. 'I don't know how long I stood there. I just couldn't make any *sense* of it. I couldn't believe it. I couldn't accept that I'd gone out for a normal evening and come home and found this carnage in my house.' She looked at us with a pleading look in her eyes, as if begging us to understand.

'So what happened?' I asked quietly.

Beth closed her eyes wearily, then opened them again. 'Lola came home. I didn't find out till later but she'd been out with her boyfriend, Pete. He dropped her back here and she walked in and saw everything and started screaming. She just screamed and screamed. And that sort of brought me out of it.'

Beth looked up at us with an air of resignation. 'So I called the police and they were here in a couple of minutes. They tried Marlene's pulse, but she was already dead.' There was a pause, before she added, 'I was so stunned, I couldn't take it in. It didn't hit me till several hours later and then I just fell apart.'

No one spoke for several moments, as if we wanted to let these images fade away before proceeding.

Then Mags asked, 'Were any of the outer doors unlocked?'

Beth shook her head emphatically. 'No, Ma'am, they were not. I made sure to close up before I left and they were still locked when I came back.'

'Could they be opened from the inside without a key?' I interjected.

Beth glanced in my direction. 'Yes. All the doors could be opened by turning a handle on the inside.'

'Did you see anyone loitering in the vicinity of your house as you drove up?'

Beth shook her head again. 'No.' She had clearly answered that question many, many times before.

'And was there any sign that anyone else had been inside the house apart from members of your family?'

'No, Ma'am.' There was a pause. 'Oh, there was one thing. Marlene had poured a bourbon and soda for herself and one for someone else. It hadn't been touched and the police didn't find anyone else's fingerprints on it.'

Mags turned towards me enquiringly.

53

'Did you know or even suspect that your sister might have been having an affair? I asked.

Something in Beth's face changed, but her emotions were too much under control for me to be able to detect how she felt.

'To my knowledge, my sister had never considered adultery. Not at any time during her marriage,' she answered stiffly.

'Then I think that's all we need to know for now.' I rose to my feet and thanked Beth.

'I'd be happy to take you out to western Kansas and show you around,' she offered unexpectedly. 'We could stay overnight at my mother's house. The new people don't take it over for another few weeks.'

'That would be great!' I enthused. 'How soon d'you think we could go?'

She considered for a moment. 'How about tomorrow? I could pick you up at your hotel around seven.'

'Wonderful.' I smiled happily at her.

Beth stood up and stretched awkwardly. 'You know,' she said suddenly, 'I really don't believe Malcolm killed my sister. I really, truly don't, and I want you to believe that too.' She gazed intently into my eyes as her own filled with tears. 'I have refused to do any more interviews with the media here because they've distorted everything I've ever said, but I decided to speak to you because you're British and I thought you might stick up for Malcolm and tell his side of the story.' She took a step nearer. 'You will, won't you?'

I smiled sympathetically. 'We'll try to present the facts as fairly as we can and give everyone a chance to put their case.'

Beth pulled back a little, nodding. 'I was sure you would.' She patted my arm distractedly as she turned away. 'Now, you want to meet Malcolm, don't you? I thought you could speak to him in the library because it has a nice English feel to it and he doesn't like being in this room any more.'

She beckoned us to follow her through a door to the left. We found ourselves in a long corridor running parallel to the front of the house. I was beginning to realise that Beth's home was much larger than it had appeared from outside. Doors opened off on either side of the hall, but Beth headed for an imposing carved archway at the end, through which could be seen dark wood shelves stacked with leather-covered tomes.

As we entered, someone rose from a wing armchair which had been placed facing the large stone fireplace. His back was to us, but I had an impression of a tall man with sandy hair streaked with grey, his shoulders thin and stooped.

He turned and I realised this was Malcolm Laurie, but so changed from the photographs I had seen as to be almost unrecognisable. His face was gaunt and haggard, the eyes pained and bewildered. Clearly he had lost a great deal of weight; the blue striped shirt he wore fitted him but the expensive hand-stitched suit hung off his shoulders and had obviously been made for a much larger man. He did not smile or say anything as he held out his hand while Beth introduced us.

'He could be interviewed in this leather chair when you come back to do your filming because it's so masculine, don't you think?' Beth guided Malcolm back into his seat and moved behind him, placing her hands on the studded back. She was like a mother fussing over her child. 'And I'll have Maria light the fire,' she continued nervously, not waiting for my reply, 'because I thought that would create a warm sort of family atmosphere.' She stopped and gazed at me anxiously.

I nodded. 'That would be fine, just as long as it doesn't get too hot for Malcolm.' I looked at him questioningly but there was no response.

'Oh, I'll have the central air going good,' Beth jumped in. 'It should be fine, don't you think, hon?' She bent solicitously over Malcolm. He fixed his eyes on her with the look of a drowning man. I could not help recalling the figure in all those photographs of him before the murder. Then he had been large and powerfully built, strong-jawed and muscular, a man whose face was held taut by confidence and conviction. Now his features were slack, the muscles withered, his eyes bewildered. I had come here convinced by the evidence I'd been given that he was his wife's killer. Now, confronted by the man himself, I suddenly had doubts.

'I can't believe what's happened.' He began the interview in a low, distant voice, devoid of emotion. I could see Mags gathering herself, searching for the right, careful words to put to this shattered man.

'Malcolm, the police claim they have evidence that you are the murderer.' Malcolm lifted his head and fixed pain-ridden eyes on her. 'They say that your fingerprints were on the weapon which killed your wife.'

There was a long pause. Malcolm seemed to be thinking slowly and it occurred to me he might be under sedation. Then he nodded. 'Of course they were. The killer used an old Indian axehead. This whole area belonged to them and the farmhands are always finding relics of their way of life. Beth has a whole collection of Native American artefacts in the family room and I was looking at them earlier that day because I'm really interested in the history. Of course my fingerprints would be on them.' There was a hint of derision in the last words, as if some of his old spirit was seeping through the fog of inertia.

A question occurred to me. 'On the night of the murder, you say you were asleep. Why didn't you wake up when your wife was attacked? There must have been screams, some sort of commotion.'

He laughed painfully. 'I'd taken a sleeping pill. I don't adjust to the time changes as well as I used to and I was shattered. I thought if I could get an early night and sleep through till morning, I'd be right as rain. Instead . . .' he looked down abruptly at the gnarled hands which clawed at each other on his knee.

'So you heard nothing?' Mags prompted.

He shook his head with an air of exhaustion. 'I didn't wake up until afterwards. I have a vague impression of being disturbed, of something turbulent in my sleep.' He looked up at us sadly. 'But I couldn't say whether that was just my own nightmares or restlessness or if I actually heard the murderer.'

'But you woke up eventually?'

'Yes. Around nine thirty. I had a raging thirst. I lay for a while, trying to gather the energy to go for a drink. I heard nothing. The house was completely silent. I finally got out of bed, put on my dressing gown and walked into the kitchen and poured a glass of iced water from the fridge. That was when I noticed the clicking noise, coming from the family room next door. I walked through . . .' He paused, looking away, the only sign of emotion in his face a sudden tensing of the muscles round his eyes and mouth. 'And I saw my wife lying face down in front of the fire.' He looked up at Mags, bewildered again. 'I couldn't understand at first what she was doing there – if she'd fallen or perhaps gone to sleep. I walked towards her. The floor in the family room is made of terracotta tiles with rugs over it. I was walking across the tile when my foot slipped on something sticky. I looked down and there was a dark liquid on the floor. But I still didn't understand. I bent down to touch Marlene's shoulder and turned her over and it wasn't her. It was some monstrosity and I was . . . confused, I suppose. She was still bleeding but her face was gone and there was just blood and bone. It didn't make sense. Then I was sick.'

There was a long silence. A single tear travelled down one gaunt cheek. He was shaking convulsively. Swallowing hard, he continued, 'I tried to dial nine, nine, nine. I wasn't thinking.

Then I remembered it's different here but I couldn't recall the numbers . . .' He was weeping now. 'I couldn't remember what they were. Of course I should have called the operator but I wasn't capable.' He closed his eyes and said, his voice soft, 'So I held Marlene in my arms. I don't know how long it was before Beth arrived and she took over. The police came.' He looked at us hollowly. 'That's all. I didn't kill my wife. I couldn't. I can't answer any more questions.' Feebly he hauled himself out of his chair. 'You must excuse me.' The last words were automatic, born of a lifetime's habit of politeness and consideration.

I watched as he left the room with the slow, laborious gait of a much older man. Beth gazed after him with tears in her eyes. There were a few awkward moments of silence. Nothing I could think of to say seemed appropriate after what we had just heard. In the end, I muttered a few words of thanks to Beth and then we, too, left.

'My God,' Amanda breathed as we drew away from the house. 'That man is completely destroyed.'

'It's hard to believe he's guilty,' I agreed thoughtfully.

But Mags was not so easily swayed. 'I think he did it,' she said candidly. 'On impulse. And now he's devastated by what he's done.' She turned sideways in her seat so she could face us. 'I've interviewed people like him before. Ordinary people where a combination of circumstances came together and they blow. In his case it was the collapse of his entire life. The farm that had been in his family for centuries was about to go down the tubes, the wife he adored was leaving him, he would be broke, he wouldn't have a job and, last but not least, he may have suspected that Marlene was having an affair in spite of what Beth said. He'd always been a ladies' man himself. I'm sure his ego would have found such a betrayal the final indignity. If she stayed with him, all his troubles would be over. If she left, he was done for.

'I think there was enough there to make any normal person crack. And in that situation, the more decent they are, the more they're appalled at what they've done and the more likely they are to block it out. They get themselves into a state of mind where they genuinely have no knowledge any more of what they did and they come across as innocent because in a sense they are.' Mags made a wry face. 'You know what they say about there being no guilty men in jail!'

'There is all the circumstantial evidence,' I agreed uncertainly.

'And how.' Mags ticked them off on her fingers. 'No sign of anyone else in the house. His fingerprints on the weapon. No sign of forced entry. The botched attempt to make it look like a break-in.' She spread her hands wide. 'I rest my case.' Her expression softened. 'Although I must say I wish he wasn't guilty. He does seem like a decent sort of man.'

Amanda cleared her throat. We looked at her expectantly. 'The thing I don't understand,' she said tentatively. We waited.

'Yes?' prompted Mags impatiently. 'What don't you understand?'

'The clicking.' We stared at her for a moment.

'Shit.' Mags hit her forehead with the palm of one hand.

I groaned. 'Of course. The clicking noise. All that other stuff was so overwhelming we forgot to ask about that.'

Chapter Five

'Oh that. It was some film. In the projector.' Beth's tone of voice on the phone was dismissive. 'When we were clearing out my mother's house, Marlene found some of her old student movies. They'd never even been taken out of the wrapper they were sent back from the labs in. She thought it would be kinda neat to bring them back to Kansas City and watch them with my daughter. That's what she was doing the night she died. I guess they weren't too good because she'd burnt them. But the projector was still running and there was a piece of film left in it which was flapping against the top of the machine. That's what the noise was.'

'What were the films about?' I was suddenly curious.

'Oh . . .' There was obvious reluctance in Beth's voice. 'I don't really know. I never saw them. The person you really need to talk to is my daughter Lola. She's at the Art Institute about five minutes away from your hotel right now. She's working on one of her sculptures, I think. Why don't you go over there? I'll give her a call on her mobile phone and tell her you're coming.'

'Great. I wanted to have a word with her anyway. Thanks, Beth. Talk to you later.' I was about to hang up.

'Wait. There was something I forgot to mention when you were here. Some friends of mine are hosting a fundraiser tonight for Malcolm's defence because it's going to cost him a lot of money he doesn't have. I was wondering if you people would like to come along. You could talk to some of his supporters and maybe take some pictures if you wanted to. I don't think anyone would mind.'

'We'd love to,' I said. 'I'll have to check with Joe, our cameraman, but if he's willing I'd probably like to do a bit of filming. The idea of holding a party to raise money for legal fees is not something we're used to and it would be good to show it in our documentary.'

'Fine. I'll have someone drop by with your invitations and the address.' There was a pause. 'People will be dressed a little bit smart. I don't know what you've got with you to wear, but you can always borrow something of mine or Lola's if you get stuck.'

'Thanks, Beth,' I said warmly. I was beginning to realise that Beth spent most of her time looking after other people. 'I'm sure we can come up with something but I appreciate the thought. We'll see you later.'

I got directions from one of the elegant young men behind the reception desk in the hall and set off. The Kansas City Art Institute was only a few minutes' drive away, as Beth had said. It was in an older part of town, surrounded by a mix of historic wooden or rough stone houses which had been lovingly restored, the elaborate carvings on the eaves and porches picked out in rich colours.

The institute itself was enclosed in a mellowed red brick wall. Turning in through the open wrought-iron gates was like entering another world, immune and protected from the rush and clamour of the city outside. A motley collection of modern concrete and graceful old brick buildings were set around rolling lawns shaded by large trees. Beth had said Lola would be working in the outdoor sculpture area and when I stopped and asked for directions, a slim girl with clouds of tawny curls round her face pointed out a high brick wall, above which could just be seen several rusting gantries and pulleys.

I parked my car and walked round one end of the wall which acted as a screen between the genteel buildings of the institute and an area that looked like a cross between a construction site and a junk yard strewn with various large metal and stone objects, some of them loosely wrapped in plastic. The only other human present was a young woman who stood contemplating a misshapen lump of clay set on top of a pallet.

Assuming this must be Lola, I picked my way across the rubble to introduce myself. She was taller than her mother and more athletic looking, with blonde frizzy curls falling over her shoulders. Her skin was lightly tanned, which made the large grey-blue eyes stand out, and she had even features which added to the overall impression of prettiness. She wore fashionably revealing clothes, a halter top from which her breasts threatened to spill out and shorts which exposed her long, shapely legs.

'What can I help you with?' She flicked a stray frond of hair back from her face with one large, capable hand. 'I know all about your documentary. Mom told me.'

'I'd just like to hear your side of what happened that night.'

She wiped her hands down her shorts, leaving a residue of grey clay. 'Well, after Mom left, Auntie Lenie – that's what I called her when I was a baby so it's always sort of stuck – well, Auntie Lenie was asking about what I was doing at the Art Institute and she looked at my pictures and all and some collages I did and she thought they were pretty good . . .'

Lola had pulled on a pair of thin rubber gloves, of the type a surgeon might use, and now she paused to lean into a large red plastic garbage can. She emerged with a chunk of greyish clay which she proceeded to knead and mix with sand as she spoke.

63

'Anyways, Auntie Lenie suggested we look at her old student films. I know it is wrong to speak ill of the dead, but they were B-O-R-I-N-G. The first one was just of the outside of the Art Museum – you know when you take one frame every so often and then you play it back at normal speed so the clouds rush by and the light changes real fast.' Lola rolled her eyes. 'She said they were all influenced by Andy Warhol, for Chrissakes! I thought oh my, I've got to get outta here fast! So I pretended I needed to go to the john and I took the phone in there with me and flushed the toilet and dialled Pete's number real quick and whispered –' Lola affected a look of agonised urgency – ' "Call me back quick!" I told him he had to rescue me because Auntie Lenie was making me look at all her student films from fifteen years ago and I was bored stupid.' She laughed as she began to mould the lump of clay.

'So I get back to the sitting room and the phone rings and I pick it up and say –' Lola now assumed a look and tone of exaggerated surprise – ' "Why hello, Pete, sure I'd love to go to dinner with you . . ." ' She dropped the act and added in her normal voice, 'Of course he hadn't actually asked me to dinner but I was *desperate*! And then I said, "But I can't, my Auntie Lenie's here – Oh, you've got reservations? At the Vanderbilt House? Oh, what a pity!" ' Lola was overacting so outrageously that I found it hard to believe that Marlene could have been taken in.

'Well, of course Auntie Lenie is –' Lola's face fell – 'was such a honey and she immediately said, "Well, we can look at these another time. Why don't you go with Pete?" So he came and picked me up and we went out about seven thirty and that's all I know until Pete dropped me off around ten and then the police came and that was it.'

I thought this over for a few moments. 'Did you see Malcolm at all after your mum left?' I asked.

Lola shook her head without looking up from what she was

doing. 'No. He'd taken a sleeping pill to help with the jet lag,' he said. 'I heard him snoring when I passed his room when I went to change.'

'Did your aunt mention she was expecting any visitors?'

'Uh-uh.' Lola was beginning to sound bored. 'Don't you think this looks really like her?' she asked, indicating the lump of clay. I stared at it then at her blankly. 'Auntie Lenie,' she explained. 'I thought I'd do a bust of her for Mom. I think she'll really like it, don't you?'

Then suddenly her expression changed and her eyes widened as if an idea had just struck her. 'I forgot. I meant to say something to you. When Mom told me about your programme and all, well, I wanted to ask . . . You see I'm sort of flunking out here and Mom thinks I should do a vacation project like Auntie Lenie did and then maybe if I did a real good job they'd let me come back in the fall. And I was thinking I could do a video of you making a film. Don't you think that's kinda neat – making a film about making a film?' Lola looked at me, her face suffused with delight, as if this was the first time anyone had ever thought of that.

I only just managed to stop my horror at her suggestion from showing on my face. The last thing I wanted was a second crew or even just another camera operator getting in the way of what we were doing.

'That's a very interesting idea,' I lied, then added truthfully, 'but the problem is that we're not allowed to include anyone in the production who isn't employed by our company. It's because if you had an accident at the location, our insurance wouldn't cover you and they're terrified you'd sue them.' Lola's face clouded over and she pouted, ready to argue, so I added quickly, with a leaden feeling that I would live to regret it, 'But of course we will be filming in a number of public locations, including some properties belonging to your family and friends, and if you choose to show up, I couldn't actually stop you.' I smiled to try and defuse the unwelcoming tone of my words.

Lola's face cleared. 'Why, thank you. That'll be really bitchin'.' Inwardly I groaned. Having Lola lurking round the edges of our crew with her camera was going to be a pain in the neck.

I had just risen to take my leave when another question occurred to me. 'You mentioned the film of the Art Museum. What else was there?'

Lola frowned and she shook her head slowly. 'Nothing much. I only saw one other. She'd filmed the sky. That was all. Just clouds moving and stuff. There were another two reels that I didn't see, but I think it was all the same kind of thing – all time-release footage.'

'Hi there!'

We both spun round to face the speaker. A smallish, slightly built man dressed in a business suit had entered the yard and now stood viewing us a little uncertainly. I guessed him to be in his late thirties, an unremarkable looking person with a pale complexion, ash-blond hair, and a slightly anxious air about him.

With a whoop of joy, Lola flung her arms round his neck. 'Pete! I wasn't expecting you.' She turned to me, her face radiant. 'This is my boyfriend, Pete Ottinger. He's Mom's accountant.' She caressed his face teasingly. 'I have to be real nice to him or I don't get my allowance.' She nodded in my direction. 'This is Bel Carson – you know, the British film-maker Mom was telling you about.'

'Hi.' He flushed slightly and held out his hand to me. 'This is a real pleasure.'

'You must be the person Lola went out with the night her aunt died,' I said.

He looked sombre. 'That's right. Although I'm afraid I can't help you much with the details. I only wish I'd gone into the house with Lola instead of dropping her off like I did.' He grimaced unhappily.

'You didn't see anything suspicious, then, as you were leaving?'

He shook his head. 'No. Everything was just as normal. I didn't see a thing and I knew nothing about what had happened until Lola called.' He sighed. 'It was just so dreadful.'

I nodded sympathetically. 'There's just one other thing, Lola.'

'Yeah?' She gazed at me, eyebrows raised.

'Did your aunt ever mention any other men in her life apart from Malcolm – any boyfriends or lovers?'

Lola looked mystified. 'No. Absolutely not.'

'OK.' I smiled at her. 'I just wondered if she might have found it easier to talk to you because you're younger. Thanks anyway. I must be going.' I waved goodbye. As I picked my way across the yard, I could hear Pete admonishing his girlfriend.

'Now, Lola, I'm here to take you to get something to eat. I spoke to your mom ten minutes ago and she said you'd skipped lunch. That is not . . .'

I emerged from the yard and found a shady tree on the sloping lawn to sit under, grateful to get out of the heat. Leaning back against the uneven bark of the trunk, I closed my eyes, mulling over what Lola had just told me.

The assumption seemed to be that Marlene had viewed her student films, decided they were rubbish and burned them herself. But wasn't it possible that they had contained something her killer didn't want anyone else to see? I thought about that for a while, then dismissed the idea. It was difficult to imagine what fifteen-year-old home movies could have to do with her murder.

As soon as I got back to the hotel, I phoned Joe's room and told him about the fundraiser that evening. My request that he do some filming was tentative – he would have been within his rights to refuse, since he was officially still on holiday. But as usual he was perfectly agreeable and easy-going and in fact seemed quite enthusiastic about the prospect of observing millionaire Americans at play.

We agreed to meet for a drink around six in the hotel bar. This was a large room opening off the foyer with floor-to-ceiling windows overlooking the hotel forecourt. When I arrived, Joe and Mags were already there. All of us had found something in our luggage which was smart enough for the reception – although some of us were more elegant than others. Mags had on a long, clinging, sleeveless frock and Joe had found himself a pair of stylish khaki slacks and a blue silk shirt. It was the first time I had seen him in anything except torn jeans and I had to admit he looked very handsome. I wore an ankle-length cream linen dress. Just sitting in the bar caused it to wrinkle and I reflected ruefully that I would probably look like a dog's dinner by the time I arrived at the fundraiser.

I realised no one would be looking at me, however, when I saw Amanda sweep into the room. She had put on the most beautiful silk dress I had ever seen. It was a swirl of hyacinth blues and lilacs, given depth by touches of plum and delicate streaks of pale pink. It made her eyes seem the exact shade of cornflowers, deep and liquid.

But it wasn't just the colours which caught the attention. The fabric wrapped across her breasts then clung to her hips before falling in soft folds almost to her ankles. As she walked into the bar, the wrap skirt flew open a little, revealing a glimpse of long slender legs. It seemed as if every man in the room was watching her.

Joe grinned with amusement as she approached. 'You girls certainly know how to make an entrance.' He chuckled glee-fully. 'I want to warn you that I will not fight anyone in defence of your virtue. If any of these hot-blooded males –' he glanced around the room – 'decide to make a grab for you, you're on your own.'

'Thank you, Joe,' said Amanda drily as she sat down. Joe made a comical face at her before disappearing towards the bar to fetch us drinks.

'I love your dress,' I said.

'It's gorgeous,' agreed Mags.

Amanda looked down and smoothed out an imaginary crease with quick, agitated movements. 'Me too. It was one of the few things my husband ever gave me that I liked. I just happened to be wearing it the night I left.' Mags and I stared at her in amazement. We had been working closely with Amanda for almost two weeks now and this was the first time she had mentioned her husband. It was on the tip of my tongue to ask her more about him but she had turned her head and was craning to look out at the forecourt, indicating only too clearly that the subject was closed.

She swung one leg up and down restlessly and I noticed she was wearing the navy kid shoes she had bought on the Plaza. Suddenly, one of them flew off. It spun through the air and landed in the lap of a businessman sitting nearby. Blushing furiously, Amanda retrieved the soft pump and slipped it back on.

Mercifully, Joe returned with our drinks at that moment. An hour later we set off in a taxi for the address given on the invitations which had been left for us at the reception desk. The fundraiser was being held not far away in an area known as Mission Hills. This, I realised as we drove into the neighbourhood, was exactly the sort of milieu I had imagined Beth would live in. Imposing mansions, complete with turrets and battlements, fountains and magisterial gateways, were set back from quaintly curving streets behind rolling lawns and landscaped gardens.

The house belonging to Beth's friends was a low stone building with a sweeping driveway on one of the quieter side roads. When we arrived, the surrounding streets were lined with large cars parked along the verge. The front door was open and we were greeted rapturously by Beth as we entered.

Within minutes, Mags and Amanda had disappeared into the throng and Joe and I were swept by the flow of people out on to the expansive lawns at the back. Coloured lanterns were suspended from the branches of the trees around the edges and well-groomed men and women stood on the terrace, chatting in groups. Several had dark mahogany tans which must have been acquired during the winter in some more exotic location, but many of the younger women had pale complexions to go with their minimalist designer frocks. A few of the men wore white tuxedos, but most were dressed simply in smart suits. Waiters wearing dark trousers, white dress shirts and cummerbunds moved smoothly amongst the crowd, bearing silver trays of drinks.

I had a hurried discussion with Joe. 'General shots of the crowd and whatever you can get of Malcolm Laurie himself and Beth,' I muttered, anxious to draw as little attention as possible to what we were doing. 'And try and catch anything that suggests how *rich* this lot are – gold, diamonds, Rolex watches, the lot.' My gaze travelled over the throng milling about on the lawn. 'And a sense of how much fun they're having – I bet they don't give a damn about Malcolm.'

I followed Joe at a discreet distance, allowing him to mingle as unobtrusively as possible. Occasionally, when I spotted something of interest, I would slip up behind him and tap his shoulder, whispering in his ear. When it grew dark, Joe took some more dramatic shots of the house from the garden, lit up like a jewel box with silhouettes of the guests as they moved in front of the lighted windows and open doorways. After about an hour and a half of intermittent filming, I felt we had as much as we needed.

'That's a wrap,' I told him. Since his insurance wouldn't allow him to leave his camera unattended, Joe kept it with him and decided to position himself at one of the white garlanded tables on the lawn and stay put. I went in search of drinks for both of us and to check up on the others.

I pushed through the crowds towards the terrace and the large reception room where the bar was set up. Just before stepping inside, I glanced back towards Joe. He was no longer alone. A blonde woman in a slinky white gown had joined him at our table and I could see quite clearly from here that he was smiling at her winsomely.

Feeling amused, I turned back into the fray. As I did so, I caught sight of Lola through a gap in the press of people. She was hurtling across the room towards Pete, who had apparently just arrived. He reached out to catch her, stumbling a little under the onslaught as she kissed him passionately. When she finally stood back and moved to the side, one arm still wrapped round him proprietorially, I noticed that his pale skin was flushed with embarrassment. I was intrigued that this was the man Lola had chosen. He could not have been more different from her.

Turning round, I headed for the bar which had been set up in a corner of the room. After ordering a glass of red wine for Joe, I noticed a waiter opening a bottle of champagne. I couldn't resist and accepted a tall flute for me and took another one for Joe. So I was clutching three brimming glasses as I turned to make my way back outside.

A tall man with brown curly hair was standing with his back to me, blocking my way. I paused, holding my drinks aloft, and was just about to ask him to move to one side when he suddenly burst out laughing, leaning back as he did so.

Paralysed with horror, I watched helplessly as the red wine

poured over his creamy linen jacket. Even from the back, it had the sort of perfect fit and drape that suggested it had cost an awful lot of money. The jacket's wearer turned round. With a sick sense of foreboding, I looked up into a friendly freckled face with myopic blue eyes behind gold-rimmed glasses. Evidently he was still unaware of the wine stain on his back because he began apologising to me.

'I'm so sorry! Did I hurt you?'

Numbly, I shook my head. I opened my mouth to confess, but before I could say anything he continued, 'I noticed you earlier when you were filming. Someone said you were a director. That must be a really interesting job.'

I nodded, trying to steel myself to break the bad news.

He held out his hand. 'Sorry. I haven't introduced myself. I'm Carl Scott. Oh, right, I see you're not in a position to shake hands but I'm pleased to meet you anyway.' He smiled.

I found my voice. 'You're going to wish you hadn't met me in a minute when you find out what I've done.' By now, his companion could see the damage. Without a word, he slid Carl's jacket off his shoulders, then held it up for him to see the florid stain across the back.

'I'm really sorry,' I murmured humbly.

His friend scowled at me but Carl merely looked amused. 'I hope you feel really guilty,' he said.

'I do,' I replied.

'Good. I love guilt,' he continued happily. 'I can do a lot with guilt. I think you now *owe* it to me to have dinner with me tomorrow evening. How about I pick you up around seven?'

I stared at him. 'Certainly not,' I blurted. I hadn't gone out on a proper date with anyone since Jamie had died. 'I hardly know you.' Inwardly I cringed. I sounded disgustingly prim.

Carl grinned even more broadly. Behind him, his friend was dabbing ineffectually at the stain on his jacket.

'Hey! I've introduced myself. *I'm* the one who doesn't know who *you* are.'

I found myself laughing. 'I'm Bel Carson. Are you a friend of Beth's?'

'Uh-uh. At least, not a close friend. My dad is representing her brother-in-law in this murder trial. You're British,' he added. 'Are you something to do with this television programme they're making?'

'That's right,' I began. But at that moment, a commotion broke out in the room behind us.

Turning to see what the noise was about, I spotted Amanda through a gap in the crowd on the far side of the large room. She was screaming incoherently, tears streaming down her face.

I shoved the three glasses I was carrying into Carl's hands and caught a brief glimpse of his startled expression before I dived into the crowd and began pushing my way through. When I finally emerged next to Amanda, she was weeping hysterically. Pete had appeared and had an arm around her, as if to restrain her, and was saying urgently, 'Amanda, this is just plain stupid. There's nothing you can do.'

Amanda lifted a tear-stained face and stared fixedly across the room. I followed her gaze. Standing about ten yards away was the tall, muscular man I had seen at the restaurant on the Plaza. He was dressed in a white tuxedo which set off his brooding dark looks to perfection. Cowering against him was the slim auburn-haired woman who had been with him that day. She wore a stunning emerald-green evening gown, complemented by a heavy gold chain and locket round her neck. A livid scratch, obviously recent, was scored across her throat.

'What's happening?' I looked questioningly from Pete to Amanda but neither answered me. Pete merely shrugged helplessly and tightened his hold round Amanda's waist, as if he feared she might lunge at the other couple.

Then Joe showed up. He took the situation in at a glance. Passing his camera to me, he put an arm round Amanda, wrenching her out of Pete's grasp, and began elbowing his way towards the exit. 'I'll get one of the taxis waiting outside,' he called over his shoulder to me.

I glanced round. Mags had appeared at my side, her face very pale.

'Let's go,' I said in a low voice and she nodded assent. I turned to leave, but found my way blocked by a pleated white dress shirt. I looked up into Carl's face. He appeared concerned.

'Everything OK?' he asked quietly, then when I nodded and started to move past, he caught my arm. 'Listen. I'm a doctor in the ER at St Dominick's Hospital. I usually work nights, so if you ever feel like some emergency treatment, stop by.' He tucked a small white card into my shoulder bag.

'Thanks,' I murmured. 'I'm sorry about this. I don't mean to be rude but I must go.'

'I understand.' He patted my shoulder lightly as I edged past.

When Mags and I finally reached the waiting taxi, we found Joe sitting grim-faced in the back with Amanda slumped next to him, eyes closed after her bout of hysteria. As soon as we had slid into our seats, the driver pulled away from the kerb. No one spoke during the journey back to the hotel. When we got there, Joe lifted Amanda out, then supported her into the hotel and through the foyer, oblivious to the curious glances of a few lingering guests.

In silence, we travelled up to the fifth floor, where Joe deposited Amanda on her bed. She had calmed down considerably during the journey home, and now regarded us with tired, reddened eyes.

'What happened?' I asked gently, feeling that she was sufficiently recovered to answer questions.

Amanda bit her lip, before replying, 'I must apologise for my behaviour. That dark-haired man is my husband. I hadn't seen him since I left Kansas City several months ago. It upset me – plus I'd really had too much to drink. I'm sorry. It won't happen again.' She pursed her lips and looked away, evidently unwilling to say more on the subject.

'Will you be all right?'

She nodded. 'I just need some sleep. Don't worry about me. I'm fine,' she said, before turning her back to us and closing her eyes.

We all retreated to the corridor. Joe would not meet my eye. 'See you in the morning,' he said briefly and hurried off towards the lifts before I could say anything. Mags and I watched him disappear round the corner.

'Well!' said Mags, shaking her head. 'Would you like a cup of tea?' Without waiting for my reply, she led the way to her room, on the other side of mine. Neither of us said anything until she had boiled water in her little travelling kettle and poured out steaming cups of Earl Grey. We sank into the two armchairs on either side of the small table by the window.

'What d'you think?' Mags asked eventually.

I was silent for a moment. Even though Mags is one of my best friends and I would trust her with my life, I had said nothing to her about Amanda's weeping and late-night jaunts with Joe, partly because I didn't know how seriously to take them, but also out of respect for Amanda's privacy. The only thing I had told her about was the incident in the restaurant on the Plaza.

I made a face. 'I have no idea. I'd almost persuaded myself that that first time I saw her she was just having a bad attack of nerves. Now I'm not so sure. But I can't decide whether I would be interfering if I said anything, or whether it's my duty to sort it out.'

'I suppose the thing is, it hasn't affected her work – yet,' Mags reasoned.

'No,' I agreed uncertainly. 'But it was a close thing tonight. That woman with Amanda's husband had a bad scratch on her throat. And it looked to me as if it was Amanda who did it. We were there at the invitation of the people we're going to be filming so it's entirely possible that we could have doors slammed in our faces because of it. My impression at the time was that everyone wanted to play it down and I don't *think* there'll be any repercussions, but we can't afford any more incidents like that.'

'It just seems to be her husband that gets her upset, doesn't it?' commented Mags.

I nodded then closed my eyes and leaned my head back. 'I don't know what to do. I mean, we've both gone through emotional traumas when it's been a struggle to hold things together.' I looked at Mags for her agreement. 'Everyone has a right to deal with grief in private. Maybe I should be more understanding. It's not affecting her work, like you say, and if we can just keep her away from this man, perhaps it'll all die down.' I spread my arms helplessly. 'I'm reluctant to force a showdown because if I end up having to send her back home and then arranging for someone else to replace her it'll mean days of lost time.'

Mags smiled sympathetically. 'I wouldn't have your job for anything.'

'Well, I wouldn't feel too smug about it,' I commented wryly. 'You're going to be in charge for a couple of days. I'm going with Beth tomorrow to recce Rapid Falls, the place where Marlene grew up in western Kansas, remember?'

'That's right. I'd forgotten.' Mags made a face.

I stood up and stretched. 'I'm sure it'll be fine. And Joe seems to have some influence over her. We just have to hope the worst is over.' I grimaced as I walked out the door.

I realised how tired I was as soon as I got back to my own room. Minutes after climbing into bed, groggy with exhaustion,

I passed out. But a few hours later, I woke again with a start. I must have heard something in my sleep, some noise that had registered somewhere in my subconscious, because without pausing to think, I immediately got out of bed and crossed to the window, filled with the certainty of what I would see.

I slid behind the lined curtains, then pulled aside the heavy nylon net drapes until the night lights of the Plaza were visible on the other side of the creek. The streets were quiet, almost deserted. I shifted my gaze to the parking lot. I could see our hired car where we'd parked it close to the building so someone could hear if the alarm went off. Two figures had stepped from the darkness. As they passed directly beneath the light, I saw clearly that one of them had long flowing red hair while the other had a blond crewcut. Transfixed, I watched as Joe and Amanda got into the vehicle, backed out of the parking space and drove off into the darkness.

Chapter Six

Early the next morning, I packed my overnight bag for my trip to Rapid Falls and went down for breakfast. The others were already there. Mags and I exchanged looks as Amanda and Joe carried on an animated conversation. We were getting used to this double existence that the other two led, behaving as if what occurred during their off-duty hours belonged in another life. No one made any reference to the reason for our sudden departure from the fundraiser the previous evening, or to Amanda's hysteria. The only signs of strain were a slight tension in her manner, a feeling that her gaiety was forced and a weariness about her eyes. It was as if it had never happened.

Amanda broke into my thoughts. 'Guess what I found out at the party last night?' she asked a little too theatrically. 'Who do you think is paying the bill for Malcolm Laurie's defence *and* put up half a million dollars in bail?'

'Beth,' I volunteered at once.

'His sister-in-law,' said Mags at the same time.

'Oh.' Amanda looked crestfallen. 'You knew already.'

I shrugged. 'Who else could it be? He doesn't have any money, we know that, and his farm's mortgaged to the hilt. I suppose some of his friends back home could have forked out, but there aren't many people around who've got that kind of money. I just assumed it would be Beth, since he's staying with her.'

Amanda frowned. 'But don't you think it's strange? He's supposed to have murdered her sister.'

'She doesn't believe he's guilty,' reasoned Mags.

'Yeh,' Joe chimed in, 'and if you look at it from her point of view, if he's found not guilty, he gets the wife's lolly and can pay Beth back, and if he's convicted, she gets the money anyway, since she's Marlene's nearest relative.'

Mags and I looked at him with new respect. Up until now, there had been no indication that Joe had taken any interest in our research into Malcolm's case.

'I couldn't have put it better myself.' Mags grinned at him.

That conversation was still on my mind as I waited for Beth outside the hotel just after seven. It had already occurred to me that the alliance between Malcolm and his murdered wife's sister could be interpreted in lots of ways, not all of them innocent, and Amanda's words had reminded me of it. Could their collaboration have extended to murder? I wondered. But I found that idea hard to accept. There was something too open – too *genuine* about Beth, about both of them really. I could just about find it credible that Malcolm had been pushed to the limit by his wife's behaviour and had committed a crime of passion. But I had no sense that either he or Beth was capable of duplicity and the cold-blooded scheming that would have been necessary to plan such a murder.

Beth arrived to pick me up in a huge cream-coloured Lincoln which made her seem diminutive as she sat behind the wheel. The large prow of the car dipped as she steered the big vehicle out of the forecourt on to the street. 'The journey will take about five hours,' she announced. 'We want to get there before it starts to become really hot because even with the air conditioning and the tinted glass it can be pretty uncomfortable in here.'

Already there was a steady stream of cars heading into town, but Beth's bejewelled hands deftly guided the Lincoln through the traffic and on to Interstate 70 going west, in the opposite direction from the main flow of commuters. As soon as we were clear of the city, Beth set the cruise control to regulate our speed automatically and took her foot off the accelerator. 'All I have to do now is point us in the right direction till we get there,' she commented.

There was a heavy mist lying close to the ground this morning, obscuring much of the terrain on either side. Occasionally, trees would loom up a few yards from the road, only to recede into oblivion behind us.

'That'll burn off soon,' Beth assured me, as if she had read my thoughts. For the most part we travelled in silence until we had left behind the cluster of small towns – Bonner Springs, Lawrence, Topeka – which were strung along the highway in this more populated corner of the state. By that time, the mist had evaporated as Beth had predicted, leaving only a slight haziness in the air and revealing low hills and valleys, their contours softened by leafy trees and shrubs.

Soon the terrain opened out and there was only mile upon mile of undulating grasslands as far as the eye could see, broken only occasionally by a cluster of farm buildings half hidden in a windbreak of trees, or the patiently nodding pumps which kept the pipelines of Kansas oil flowing beneath the surface. From time to time, the existence of some small community would be announced by the appearance of a water tower against the horizon, the name of the town stencilled on its side. With their globular bodies and stilt-like supports, the towers looked like a new species of giant straight-legged spider.

But if the landscape was nondescript, the skyscape was vast, rising in an overwhelming arc above us. When I looked back, we were being pursued by a relentlessly burning sun.

'It's going to be another hot one,' Beth murmured.

'I was just thinking,' I said, 'the terrain here is so numbingly predictable that it's a bit like being in the desert. It's the sky that becomes important.'

Beth gave a delighted chuckle. 'Well, aren't you the observant one. That's what I always tell visitors from out of state. We have the most incredible sunrises and sunsets here. They just explode across the heavens. And at night, if it's clear, you can see the stars from one end of the planet to the other, it seems like. And you know,' she continued, taking her eyes off the road momentarily to look at me, 'when we have storms – and we really do have storms like nothing you've ever experienced, I'll bet – you can see them coming in for hours and when they hit, they hit big. It's like they take over the sky and we are just tiny insects with nowhere to hide down here. Oh my word!' She suddenly swerved to avoid a pick-up truck which had appeared out of the blue while she was talking.

'You know,' she resumed when the danger was past, 'that was what Marlene was trying to film for her project that summer. She was trying to show the Kansas sky in all its moods. She filmed it, you know, one frame at a time. And then when she projected it back at normal speed, it would all look as if it was happening fast.' She was suddenly silent, her lips pursed together.

'Did she get her project finished?' I asked.

Beth shook her head. 'No,' she said sadly. 'She didn't. That was the summer she met Malcolm. She lost interest after that.'

'How did they meet?' It was a question I had forgotten to ask before, although it had been nagging away at the back of my mind. From the very first time I had seen the photographs of the slim, fashionable young woman and the staid older man, I had felt them to be an incongruous couple.

'Well, now.' Beth sounded as if she was settling down to tell a long story. 'It's not as strange as some people might think.' She cast me a swift, sideways glance. 'A lot of US beef ranchers used to go over to Scotland to buy cattle to improve their breeds. That doesn't happen so much nowadays but twenty, thirty years ago, it went on a lot. So they'd buy bulls for breeding or sometimes whole herds. And Malcolm and his father had some of the best Aberdeen Angus in the world.

'Now my daddy and my uncle both had cattle ranches and they bought livestock from Malcolm regularly. And my daddy invited Malcolm to come stay with us when next he was over. The first time he visited, Marlene was away at camp, but he came back the next summer. Couldn't stay away, he said.' Beth's voice had softened.

'Marlene would have been nineteen that summer. She'd just finished her freshman year at the Art Institute.' A little sigh escaped from her lips. 'My daddy always sort of *indulged* Marlene and she was real spoiled. He let her study to be an artist instead of doing home economics or something more useful to a farm girl.' Beth shrugged. 'It was always all or nothing with her. That summer she came home from Kansas City all fired up about her vacation project – she was going to film the sky, like I told you. It was the only thing she talked about and all she thought about, or did, for that matter, for the whole of the month of June. She was convinced she'd be a famous artist. Then it all stopped when she met Malcolm. After that she focused the whole of her energies and hopes on him.'

Beth's voice became dreamy. 'Malcolm was such a good-looking man. He was so tall and well-built, and he had this thick, dark gold hair and deep blue eyes and he was foreign; I suppose that was part of it for us because neither of us had been anywhere except Denver and Kansas City and once to New York for the weekend. He was in his late thirties, a handsome man in his prime, you might say, and ready to find him a wife. Marlene was beautiful. I got my looks from my daddy but she took after my mother and she was so pretty. The instant Malcolm laid eyes on her, he was smitten, you could see that. And Marlene.' Beth gave a tight smile. 'Well, Marlene was flattered that this older man was paying her attention. There was something so, so gallant and courtly about the way he treated her.

'And then he showed her a picture of his home.' Beth laughed softly. 'It looked like a mansion to us so Marlene's imagination sort of filled in the blanks and she decided if she married him she would be a grand lady in England. When he proposed after two weeks, she accepted. It was the sort of thing she would do, make a snap decision like that, her mind full of romantic ideas.'

Beth shook her head slowly and it was several moments before she spoke again. 'In a way, I was surprised it lasted as long as it did, but I think that was purely because Malcolm let her have whatever she wanted. He would do anything to keep her, it seemed to me.'

She paused as she steered the Lincoln round a truck pulling a trailer loaded with a tottering pile of hay. 'Of course, the thing was,' she continued with bitter humour, 'when she got to the UK, she found the house was huge all right, but it didn't have central heating, it was damp, half the floorboards were rotten, the kitchen was like something out of the ark and Malcolm didn't have the sort of money she thought he did.'

'But Marlene was rich in her own right, wasn't she?' I asked.

Beth shook her head, glancing in the rear-view mirror. 'No. We were land rich but cash poor. And what there was, was all my daddy's, and he was very old-fashioned. He believed a woman should be looked after by her husband, that he should provide her and their children with a home and she shouldn't need anything from her father. He also didn't believe in divorce. He thought it was modern nonsense. Women getting uppity. So no, Marlene didn't have any money of her own till after Mom died.' She paused, then added very quietly, 'And that was just for a few weeks.'

'So will Malcolm inherit all of it?' I asked, watching Beth's profile intently.

Her jaw tightened. 'Not all. But a lot. My mom's will put some of it in trust for us girls. So that will come to me.'

I looked at Beth with renewed interest. 'Did he know that at the time of Marlene's death?'

Beth shrugged. 'I have no idea.' She glanced at me. 'You have to understand that Malcolm showed no interest, and I mean *no* interest, in how much money my sister was going to inherit. You might have thought that would have been the first thing he would have asked about when he arrived because we had just come back from talking to my mom's lawyer in Rapid Falls and from clearing out the house and putting it on the market, so it was really the first time we'd had any sort of idea how much her estate was worth. But he didn't say a word. He's a real gentleman.'

Shortly after this conversation, we stopped for a cup of coffee, then continued at a more leisurely pace. Occasionally there would be a flurry of pick-up trucks and automobiles around the access ramps and exits signposted for various small towns, but for the most part we travelled due west on wide, virtually empty roads.

After about three or four hours' driving, we pulled off on to a two-lane road and drove north and then west again. I noticed that every half mile or so there would be a dirt track set at right angles to the one we were on, often with one or more mailboxes marking their entrances. The land seemed to be divided up into a grid by this system of roads.

About one o'clock, when the sun was drilling heat into the earth around us and it was becoming uncomfortable, I noticed a signpost announcing that Rapid Falls was only ten miles further on. Seconds later, Beth turned off the tarred road we were on and we began to bump along a rutted path. We drove for several minutes, heading towards a small clump of trees.

The car dived under the overhanging branches into deep shade. Before us was a low, modern-looking ranch house, freshly painted white. All along the front was a screened-in porch, the railings almost concealed by bushes which grew along the line of the foundations. There was a thick lawn of coarse grass.

'This is it.' Beth parked the car in the drive which went up the far side of the house and turned to me with a smile. Slowly we got out, stretching stiffly. The heat closed round me like a damp woollen blanket, so that I found myself gasping for breath. Although we were standing in the shade, I could feel sweat begin to trickle down the back of my neck. My T-shirt had stuck to my skin and I tugged at the hem, flapping it to let air circulate around my body.

Beth was hauling a small cooler from the boot of the car, followed by a canvas holdall. I grasped the handle of my overnight bag, adjusting it on my shoulder before reaching down to pick up the cooler. I could hear the chink of glass as I walked with it towards the house.

Beth unlocked the screen door and we stepped on to the porch and from there through another outer door into the house. The interior was blessedly cool and I could hear the low thrum of the air conditioning. Beth fixed us both drinks – something alcoholic for her and iced water for me.

Around three o'clock, we ventured out for a tour of the area. All around the small oasis of trees, kept green and flourishing by irrigation, the land stretched flat as far as the eye could see.

'It's always windy out here,' commented Beth as our hair whipped into our faces.

'What's over there?' I asked, nodding towards a building just visible beyond the trees.

'Oh that!' Beth looked pleased by my question. 'That's the original farmhouse that my great-granddaddy built. I was born there and spent the first ten years of my life in that house, but once my daddy started making some money, Mom wanted a new home that was modern and had air conditioning and all. Nearly all the farm wives around here wanted that. So we moved into the other one just after Marlene was born. We can go take a look at it if you like.' She gazed at me questioningly and when I nodded with enthusiasm she turned left through the trees, away from the modern ranch.

'What will happen to it now?' I asked as we emerged from the windbreak of trees and walked across furrowed dry earth, baked to dust by the heat. I could feel the warmth rising up from the ground.

'Oh,' Beth sighed. 'It's gonna have to be torched in a couple of weeks' time. It's getting to be pretty dangerous and the farm manager said he chased off some kids who were playing out here a few weeks ago. So we need to do something soon. We cleared all the rubbish we didn't want out of the new house and stacked it in there because getting rid of trash is a real problem out here. It's so far to the dump and everything has to be hauled there.

'Of course,' she continued with an arch grin, 'if the EPA – that's the Environmental Protection Agency – got to hear about it, then I suppose they might get a little bit upset. But there ain't nobody out here's going to tell them diddly so I guess that's that.'

As we drew near to the house, I could see how derelict it had become. Most of the paint was gone, revealing grey and rotten planks of wood. The building was of a very simple design, square with a door on the left side and two windows ranged along the front, with the same plan on the floor above, except there was a third window over the door. There was evidence everywhere of work done by craftsmen. An elaborately whittled frieze decorated the eaves and the porch. Posts had been turned on a lathe, window and door frames were carved, and a few coloured panes indicated that the front door had once had stained-glass panels. Now it was secured by a heavy padlock, the broken glass was backed by panels of wood and the windows were boarded up.

We crossed the porch, taking care to avoid rotten or loose planks. Beth produced a key and unlocked the padlock, pushing open the door. A strong smell of decaying wood met us as we entered the house. To the left was a broken-down staircase with several of its treads missing. Faded, brittle wallpaper hung down in great swathes and light cascaded from the high stairwell, as if part of the roof was caved in.

I paused for a moment and listened. Timber creaked as the wind assaulted the decaying structure of the house and infiltrated the cracks in the walls. It was like being in a forest listening to the trees swaying in the breeze overhead.

Beth had wandered through a large wooden archway to our right into a long room dominated by a huge stone fireplace at the far end. When I followed her, I noticed thirty or forty bulging black rubbish bags piled up along the walls, interspersed with broken bits of furniture and debris. I picked my way across the oak floor towards the fireplace. Three or four up-ended logs encircled it as if in readiness for a meeting of dwarves and there were still ashes and a few charred pieces of wood in the iron gate. A length of slate served as a hearth and several spent matches lay strewn on it beside a couple of candles, once ornately shaped but now melted to globs of wax round the wicks.

'Has someone been living here?' I asked.

Beth shook her head. 'When Marlene was a teenager it used to be a sort of clubhouse for all her gang. They would come here and drink beer, which wasn't allowed, and I know for a fact that they smoked pot. It seems so long ago. My daddy knew what they were up to but he never told. Mom would have hit the roof if she'd known about it but Marlene could always charm Daddy against his better judgement.'

She stood stock still, her face a mask of sadness. 'It was quite an emotional time for Marlene and me when we came out here to clear Mom's house,' she continued in a faraway voice. 'We knew we were literally destroying our links to the past, returning to the prairies what our ancestors had taken from them. It was so sad.' She spun round to look at me. 'Marlene got really upset. In the end, she staged some little ceremony by herself. I was sort of hurt that she didn't include me but I suppose she and I were never close. She said she was at a sort of crossroads in her life. She wanted to say goodbye to the past and be ready for the new.'

'What did she do?' I was curious.

Beth shrugged. 'Oh, I think she just collected together some of the bits and pieces that meant something special to her, things that conjured up memories. She said that when the house burned them, the ashes would mingle and the spirit of her past life would be purified and rise to the heavens.' Beth gave a wry smile. 'Marlene was always one for the grand gesture.' She was silent for several moments. 'Of course, the irony is that she thought she was marking the end of an era, when really she was saying goodbye to her whole life.' Beth's voice was almost inaudible. 'It was only a few days after that that she died.'

Abruptly, she turned and lead the way back through the arch into the hall leading to the rear of the house. We passed a doorway to what might have been a dining room once, the walls panelled with oak. But that was as far as we could go. A makeshift barrier had been set up and beyond it we could see a gaping hole in the rotting floorboards.

'It's probably better to cremate this place decently, rather than let it die away like this,' said Beth. Suddenly it was as if she could no longer bear to be here. With quick steps, careless of the rotten floorboards, she headed for the front door. I picked my way after her as swiftly as I could, emerging into the dusky evening light.

'Time for supper,' announced Beth. 'Anything else can wait till morning.'

We walked back across the dirt field towards the new house. Then, after eating a simple meal of baked potatoes, cheese and salad, we carried a bottle of wine for me and one of bourbon for Beth out to the screened-in porch. There we sat and watched a glorious sunset of burning reds and vivid pinks and listened to the buzz and chirrup of thousands of insects.

After a while, Beth said, 'You know, I feel so guilty about Marlene. I was always so jealous of her. She seemed to have everything I wanted – she was beautiful, my daddy doted on her, she didn't have to do chores every day before school the way I always did, she got to go to college to study art, and then she got Malcolm. I hated her sometimes.' There was a catch in her voice.

'Everyone feels guilty when the people they love die,' I said in an attempt to offer comfort. 'I know I did.'

Beth sighed. 'But then when she was gone, it felt like it was my fault. And I'd lost her before I ever really knew the person she was.'

I was silent for a while, then I said, 'You just have to let it go, Beth. It doesn't sound as if Marlene made it easy for you either.'

'I guess.' I could hear the chink of ice as she raised her glass and took a long sip of her bourbon. 'Do you have any family?'

'No,' I replied quietly. 'I was orphaned when I was nine. I had a foster sister but she died in tragic circumstances a few years ago. So I'm a bit like you, really.'

'I'm sorry to hear that, Bel.' There was genuine concern in Beth's voice. 'Are you married?'

I laughed awkwardly. 'Widowed. I know this is sounding like a real sob story, but I don't feel that way about it. I've had a lot of happiness in my life. More than most people.'

Beth reached out and patted my arm gently. 'Well, I think it must take a great deal of courage to deal with all that, whatever you say.' She drank some more and when next she spoke, I noticed that she had started to slur her words a little. 'I wasn't really married, you know.'

Automatically I turned to look in her direction, but all I could make out was her profile against the luminous night sky.

She laughed softly, evidently sensing my shock. 'Oh, I thought I was at the time. We all did. There was I, the ugly duckling, a real Cinderella, slaving away, making breakfast for the farm hands every morning and doing chores and cleaning, but nobody wanted me for a wife, it seemed. Then Travis arrives out of the blue to help my daddy manage the farm. He is so good-looking I don't even imagine he'll notice me. But he does. I could hardly believe it. It was every dream I'd never dared to have come true.' She paused and took another sip of bourbon. It occurred to me that it must be rare for her to be able to relax without being anxious about the welfare of those around her. Tonight she had only herself to worry about.

'We had a big family wedding and everyone was so happy for me. We moved into a little house we had built for us on the back pasture – it's gone now – and I was happy.' Her voice cracked. 'For the first time, I was happy. I didn't feel like I deserved it. Then I got pregnant and had Lola. Then . . .' There was a long pause, before she continued in a tight voice. 'Why then Travis's wife, his real one, showed up one day wanting money. He and my father had a meeting about it. Mom and I could hear them shouting at each other but we didn't know what was said. Next day, Travis was gone. And I wasn't anyone's wife any more.'

'Didn't you think of marrying again?' I asked gently.

Beth let out a strange, bitter laugh. 'D'you know the really funny, awful thing about all this?' I could see her head turn to me in the darkness. 'Even when I was supposed to be married to him, Travis didn't really pay me much mind. He was always out with the boys – and the girls, too, I've no doubt. And once Lola came along, I was left home with the baby on my own so much, I was dying with loneliness inside. Then Malcolm came to stay with Mom and Dad. And he was so nice, such a gentleman. We got along so well, it was like talking to my twin. He was kinder and more considerate to me than my own husband. And when he left, he asked me to go with him. Really he did. Oh, I thought about it. I wanted to go so much. But I couldn't. I was married – so I thought – and I had a baby to think about and my parents to help out with the farm and so many other people I had to take care of before myself.' I could hear the tears in Beth's voice. 'So I said, "No. I'd have to think about it."'

'The next year he came back and by then Travis had gone and I was all alone. And I hoped, oh, I hoped he would ask me again. But of course he didn't.' Her voice broke and she was silent. When she finally spoke again, it was in a dead, flat tone.

'After a while, I gave out that I'd gotten divorced although of course I hadn't because I didn't need to. I never changed Lola's birth certificate that says her parents were married so she never knew any different. I just concentrated on bringing her up and then my daddy got sick, so I looked after the farm for a bit, until we got a good manager. Then Mom needed a lot of help. So one way and another there was never much time to think of myself.' She laughed bitterly. 'How about you? Have you thought of remarrying?'

Perhaps we were both getting drunk, or perhaps it was a bond forged by our shared suffering, but suddenly I found myself saying things to Beth I had only ever contemplated in private.

'No,' I said. 'After Jamie died, I was grief-stricken. But when the worst of the pain and feelings of loss were over, I suddenly felt him there, with me, so to speak. At times, it was as if I could hear his voice, telling me not to be so stupid about something I was upset about, or comforting me the way he did when he was alive. His personality sort of balanced mine. I always got wound up about things but he was never really bothered very much about anything. I managed to pretend he wasn't gone, not really. I held him safe inside where he could never ever die. So I've been sort of tied to that memory. Anyone else was unthinkable – unnecessary, really.'

I turned to Beth in the dark. 'But something's happening, Beth. I don't know what it is, but I'm scared. All the things are gone that cushion me, that cocoon me from my real situation, that maintain the fiction that my life hasn't really changed. But it has, Beth, it has. That's what's so painful. All of a sudden, I feel alone. I have friends, good, kind friends, but it's not enough. The heart of me is empty. And it's my own fault.'

'You shouldn't be so hard on yourself, Bel.' Beth's voice floated towards me gently. 'Coming to terms with grief can be a long process. Lots of people, perhaps most people, are alone. I've sat here many times over the years, staring out at the Kansas wheat fields, the flatlands that stretch for hundreds of miles, and it all seems so empty and lonely and I've felt that everything I've ever had, except Lola, has turned to dust. It makes me wonder what point there is in all this. But I guess for me the point is Lola. I still have someone to love. And you will too.' She gave a sad little laugh. 'We can all take opportunities or turn our back on them. I guess in a way we create our own destiny.'

There was a scraping of wood on wood and I watched her silhouette as she rose to her feet. 'It's getting late and this is getting serious. I think we should turn in for the night. It'll seem better in the morning.' I felt her hand touch my shoulder lightly. 'Don't worry. Your time will come. And so will mine. Someday.' She turned, fumbling with the catch on the screen door, then led the way inside.

Chapter Seven

I got back to the hotel in Kansas City late the following afternoon. There was a message from Carl. I tried unsuccessfully to get through to him. Then, after dumping my luggage, I knocked on the door of Mags's room.

'How have things gone?' I asked as soon as I entered.

'Fine. Everything seems to be back to normal. No more tears or upsets although Amanda and Joe still try to act like there's nothing special between them. We've spent the past two days talking to prosecutors and police and trying to track down potential witnesses. I think I can sum up our conclusions in one phrase.'

'And what's that?'

'He's guilty,' she said with a shrug of resignation. 'He has to be.'

I phoned Amanda and asked her to join us. She walked into the room with a sunny smile, and I noted with relief that she seemed relaxed and confident. I just hoped it would last.

The three of us spent the next few hours going over our research, discussing potential contributors to the programme and trying to work out a rough filming schedule. Malcolm Laurie's trial was due to begin next week, starting with jury selection, which could last several days or even weeks, and Mags had pulled off a coup by obtaining permission for us to film in the courtroom whenever we liked. I had decided to skip the first couple of days, but since Malcolm and possibly Beth would be tied up from Monday onwards, I had arranged to record interviews with them both the following day.

It was after six thirty by the time we completed sorting out our arrangements. I stood up and stretched. 'What is everyone doing for dinner tonight? Does anyone fancy eating out?'

'I'm not joining you this evening,' Amanda said quickly. 'I'm meeting a friend for supper. We're going to some new place that's opened called the Happy Hangout,' she continued hurriedly as if to forestall any questions. She rolled her eyes. 'Sounds wonderful, doesn't it? But apparently the food's fantastic and it's the in place at the moment.' She rose to her feet and swiftly gathered her files together. 'See you all tomorrow.'

When she had gone, Mags said, 'I told Joe we'd meet him in the bar in half an hour. I thought he'd be getting bored of his own company by now, but he seems to be quite happy wandering around by himself all day.'

I went back to my own room and took a shower. That revived me after the draining heat of the day and the long drive back from western Kansas. I dried my hair, applied a token amount of grey eyeshadow, mascara and red lipstick, put on a long, flowing sleeveless dress and headed downstairs.

Mags was already sitting in the bar just off the reception area, nursing a drink. Shortly afterwards, Joe – the short bristles of his hair still damp – joined us, wearing a dark blue shirt, chino slacks and black Doc Martens. On to the chair beside him he tossed a cream linen jacket and a tie with a large penis printed on it. Joe had been having a running battle with the maitre d', who didn't think guests should eat in his dining room in casual attire.

'That'll get you far,' I commented drily.

'It's a tie.' Joe grinned gleefully. 'It meets the regulations. It'll be wanton discrimination if they don't let me in.' Within minutes, he was charming the female bartender into making up some exotic concoction he'd read about somewhere, with the result that a pitcher chinking with ice and full of some lemony looking drink arrived at the table. It was delicious – light and tangy but with a kick to it that would send us into orbit, Joe assured us.

'Where's Amanda?' he asked suddenly, looking around the room as if he had only just realised she wasn't there.

'She's not eating with us tonight,' Mags volunteered. 'She said she was going out for dinner.'

Joe stiffened. 'She didn't say anything to me. What's she doing?'

I was a little taken aback by the ferocity of his response. 'She's meeting a friend. I . . .'

But Joe wasn't listening. He had leapt to his feet after my first words and raced from the room. Perplexed, Mags and I watched as he moved swiftly across the foyer to a small alcove on the far side where there was a house telephone. At that moment, the lift doors immediately opposite where we sat parted and Amanda emerged, unnoticed by Joe, who had his back to her.

She caught sight of us as she crossed the foyer and took a detour to pause for a few moments at our table. She looked stunning. The golden-red hair had been brushed out in its full glory around her head, her skin seemed somehow luminous and her eyes were shining. She had on the same beautiful silk dress and elegant navy pumps we'd seen her wearing before.

'You look fantastic. Is this something special?' I smiled at her.

She shook her head dismissively. 'No, no. It's just an old friend. I won't be late.' She glanced round nervously and suddenly froze. Following her gaze, I saw Joe emerging from the phone booth with a deep frown on his face. He was heading for the lifts and evidently hadn't seen Amanda yet.

'I must be going. 'Bye.' Amanda spoke hurriedly. She made

a move towards the main exit. A shout echoed through the foyer.

'Amanda!' Joe was racing across the reception area, his progress impeded by an elderly woman with a walking frame and a crowd of excited teenagers. Amanda broke into a run. There were a couple of taxis parked at the entrance and she veered towards them. Joe leaped over the back of a sofa, shouting at the top of his voice. 'Amanda! Stop! Stop!'

A dark blue cab slipped smoothly up to the kerb and Amanda moved towards it. But Joe had almost reached the exit.

'Excuse me, sir!' One of the undermanagers stepped smartly into his path. Joe cannoned into him. Amanda ducked inside the cab, slammed the door and was off, her head down, deliberately ignoring Joe as he thrust the other man aside and propelled himself through the heavy swing door.

He came to an abrupt halt and stood watching the departing taxi helplessly. Then he let out a loud moan, threw back his head and spread his arms wide. The undermanager had followed him out and was remonstrating with him about jumping over the furniture and knocking down other guests. Joe didn't pay any attention. Before the tirade had stopped, he spun on his heel, walked back to our table and collapsed into a chair.

'What's wrong?' I asked anxiously.

'Nothing,' he muttered. He shook his head, an angry expression on his face. 'Absolutely nothing.'

The mood of the evening had changed dramatically. Without anything being said, the idea of going out to eat was dropped and shortly afterwards we moved upstairs to the hotel restaurant. In spite of the efforts of Mags and me, the conversation flagged and we ate most of our dinner in silence. Joe seemed preoccupied and worried. We were seated next to a window overlooking the front of the hotel and he kept craning to look down into the forecourt. By nine it was dark, and each time the headlights of a car approached the entrance, he would lean forward, cupping a hand up to the glass to peer out. But Amanda did not return and his mood of despair never lifted all evening.

Finally, around ten, he excused himself, saying he was tired, and went up to his room. Mags and I moved back down to the bar for liqueurs. For the next hour we discussed possible explanations for the drama we had witnessed.

'Are they having an affair or what?' queried Mags incredulously. 'Because if they are, they've kept it pretty quiet, is all I can say. I usually pick up on anything like that in two and a half seconds.'

I shook my head. 'I've no idea. I've said already that I think there's something funny going on between those two but I can't work out what it is.' I paused, debating with myself. 'This relationship they appear to have – whatever it might be – didn't just spring up overnight. I'm sure they knew each other from before and that working on this project was part of a plan to get them back here. But what that plan is and what exactly they've got in mind, I can't imagine.'

'Ah, well.' Mags yawned. 'It'll doubtless wait till tomorrow. Either it will all become clear, or it won't.'

We returned to our rooms and, in spite of my anxiety, I fell into a deep sleep. But I awoke early the next morning feeling tense and decided to go for a swim. The air was comfortably warm, without the searing heat that would come later, and the water, when I slipped into it, felt languid and soft.

I began a leisurely breast-stroke, dipping underwater, raising my head only for occasional rhythmic breaths. It felt good. All the tensions of the last few days, the unresolved questions about the relationship between Joe and Amanda, the muscle aches of the long car journey from western Kansas, flowed away from me as I gradually increased my speed. Underwater everything was virtually silent, the light filtered, the outside world far away.

By the time I emerged, I felt so wonderfully relaxed that I could hardly walk without staggering as I made my way back to my room. The pool was on the basement level at the back of the building away from the main thoroughfare and public areas. So it came as no surprise that the lift going up was empty. It stopped at the ground floor, however, and I moved aside to make room for the two people who got in. I kept my head down as I did so, conscious of the fact that I resembled a drowned rat, quietly dripping water on the floor with my hair plastered to my skull. But as soon as the lift door closed again, I noticed a palpable air of unease.

'Morning, Bel.' My head shot up and I gazed straight into Joe's grey eyes. He hadn't shaved and he looked exhausted, but he was trying to smile nonchalantly. His torso was bare except for a jeans jacket and he was wearing a pair of crumpled, muddy tracksuit bottoms.

By now, I knew without looking that the woman standing next to him would be Amanda. She kept her gaze on the floor as she cowered beside Joe. She had been crying; there was a trail of mascara down both cheeks and a large weal swelled under her left eye. Both arms were bruised and scratched.

I recognised the outsize T-shirt she wore as one I'd seen on Joe. The Levis she had on were clearly several sizes too large, so I assumed they belonged to him as well. Only the shoes were her own, although the navy pumps which I had so admired were now torn and caked with mud.

Joe cleared his throat nervously. 'Been for a swim? How was it?'

I jerked my attention back to him, at the same time becoming conscious that we weren't moving.

'Have you pushed the button?' I asked, ignoring his question. I leant forward and pressed the number for the fifth floor and the lift moved off smoothly.

Joe laughed awkwardly. 'God, we could have been here all day. Thank goodness you noticed.' There was silence.

I took a deep breath and looked directly at Amanda. 'What's happened? How did you get hurt?'

'She fell.' Joe answered for her hurriedly. He paused a moment, as if searching for words. 'We went for an early morning stroll in the park and she tripped over a branch.' He smiled, as if that would help to convince me that what he was saying was believable.

The lift came to a halt and the door slid open. 'See you downstairs in an hour,' Joe said a little too brightly, pulling Amanda after him out of the lift. I followed them down the corridor as Joe half carried her to the door of her room, unlocking it before he helped her inside.

I returned to my own room filled with a pervasive sense of foreboding.

On impulse, I telephoned Martin as soon as I had showered and dressed. He interrupted a meeting and came on the line at once.

'How's things?' He sounded very breezy. Quickly I filled him in on our progress on the documentary. He was elated that we had obtained permission to film in the courtroom.

'There's something I wanted to ask you,' I said when I had finished my work report.

'What's that?'

'You know you said you had to hire Amanda because the word came down from on high.' There was a grunt of agreement on the other end of the line. 'Well, could you find out for me who exactly pulled the strings to get her on the job?'

'Awww, Bel.' Martin sounded exasperated. 'That's water

under the bridge. Forget it. You said yourself she's been doing good work.'

'She has. It's something else that's bothering me. I can't explain exactly what at the moment because I'm not sure I understand it myself. But it would help me to know how she got this job. I just have a gut feeling it's important and it could explain a lot of things.'

'OK.' Martin's tone was indulgent. 'Take care. Everything else fine?'

'Sort of,' I replied darkly. 'I'll let you know if we hit any trouble.' After perfunctory goodbyes, we hung up.

I went down to breakfast and found Mags sitting alone. As I ate hurriedly, I filled her in on the latest developments. She was as concerned as I was. There was no sign of Joe and Amanda.

Under the circumstances, I wouldn't have been surprised if they hadn't shown up for work, or had at least been very late, but when we emerged from the lift just before seven o'clock, they were sitting side by side in the foyer, Joe's hair still wet from the shower, and wearing clean, pressed clothes.

But for the first time, the effects of the strain they must be under were showing. Amanda was wearing a long-sleeved shirt, which hid the scratches on her arms, but her make-up could not completely disguise the bruising on her face. She looked exhausted and slightly dazed. When she saw Mags and me approaching, she rose to her feet without a word and hoisted her big leather satchel on to her shoulder as if she hardly had the strength to carry it.

Joe, on the other hand, seemed tense and full of nervous energy, his responses to questions or requests almost too quick. He was trying to appear bright and cheerful, but it was clearly an effort.

I had hired two local freelancers to join the team – a thin, stringy-looking sound recordist in his thirties called Evan and a younger camera assistant by the name of Lewis. They arrived promptly at seven. Both of them seemed extremely quiet and reserved and after shaking hands with all of us they lapsed into silence. As I led the way outside to the vehicles, I reflected that this was not an auspicious start to our first day of filming.

After consultation with Joe, I had hired a mini-van which would be used to transport the gear and the crew. Amanda, Mags and I would travel in the car. After a hurried discussion about our destination and the best route to Beth's house, we set off in convoy.

There was a traffic jam on the main approach to the bridge we had chosen to cross the river, and to my intense irritation we were reduced to crawling along. I was in the passenger seat next to Mags, who was driving, and I had just turned to say something to her when I felt a blast of air on the back of my neck. It was rather unpleasant, with the full force of the wind funnelling along the river channel. Turning to find out what had caused it, I flinched back as an object flashed by close to my face. When I looked again it was in time to see something hurtling over the low stone parapet between the metal struts of the balustrade. Amanda had opened one of the rear windows and thrown a large brown paper package into the river.

Without a word, I turned back around in my seat and looked resolutely ahead. Instinctively, I felt that the situation with Amanda was so fragile that anything I said might provoke an outburst. I took a deep breath. One way or another I had to get everyone through this first day of filming. What would happen beyond that was anyone's guess.

Beth and Lola were waiting for us when we arrived, the former wearing an elegant grey silk dress with a long pleated skirt, her hair sculpted into a bouffant style. She seemed slightly tense but typically was more concerned for our welfare than her own. On her orders, the maids brought coffee and doughnuts which all of us, except Evan, politely declined, and then they showed us to a small room in the left wing of the house, where we could leave our equipment.

Lola hovered alongside me chattering excitedly about her own project. More than ever I bitterly regretted allowing her to use us as the subject of her film. It was one more distraction in an already fraught day.

I had agreed to leave the interviews till last because Malcolm had said he would prefer to talk later in the day, when he had had a chance to see how we operated and had got to know us better. So while Amanda and Mags chatted to Beth, the rest of us started work outside. Lola set up her small video camera at a distance. To my intense relief, it turned out that she would be working alone without any of her fellow students to act as a crew.

We took shots of the house from every angle, front and back. Then, after a brief pause for cold drinks, we moved inside. Malcolm was nowhere to be seen. The bedroom where he claimed to have slept while his wife was being murdered was situated at the end of a long hall, some distance from the family room. It was extremely neat and impersonal. Clearly no one occupied it now.

'Can I have a shot from the killer's point of view, walking from the bedroom to the family room and then wandering all over the house?' I asked Joe. In response, he took the camera off the tripod and hefted it on to his shoulder, recording the route that the murderer might have taken that night. By then it was noon and I decided to break for lunch before starting on the interviews with Beth and Malcolm.

I had been prepared to take everyone to a nearby restaurant to eat, but Beth had organised a buffet meal for us in a small summerhouse at the rear of the house. It was situated in the shade of a couple of large oak trees and felt cool and breezy. Malcolm was already seated there, reading a newspaper. He tossed it on to an adjacent chair and rose to greet us. As before, his manners were perfect but distant, as if he was being polite and welcoming from habit but he himself was far away.

Beth had laid on a banquet. There were heaped bowls of fresh seafood – flown in from the Gulf this morning, she told us proudly – and the maids produced a seemingly endless parade of salads and exotic cheeses. It was a wonderful treat and we all began to relax.

The first day of filming is always a relief to me, and I suspected it was the same for the others. This project had been the focus of much anxious preparation and now at last we had an outlet for our nervous energy. There was a lot of joking around as we let off steam.

'Joe would make eyes at anything,' Mags announced to the assembled party with a sidelong glance at him. 'He gets bored if he can't flirt. I mean –' she shrugged helplessly – 'if there's no one else around, he'll have a go at the furniture.' She turned to him, her eyes dancing with mischief. Joe chuckled good-humouredly.

Even our hosts seemed to unwind a little and enjoy our company. Some sign of life had flowed back into Malcolm's demeanour. He seemed to take on definition, character, as his face became more expressive and showed glimpses of emotion. Towards the end of the meal, Beth began to recount racy gossip about leading socialites in the city. Watching her, I caught a glimpse of the person she could be when her life was not overshadowed with tragedy and she was not weighed down with looking after others.

During a lull in the conversation, when everyone else was busy helping themselves to more food, I saw Beth lean across and stroke her brother-in-law's hand gently. He smiled at her. It was an intriguing relationship between a man accused of murdering his wife and the dead woman's sister.

Only Amanda remained aloof and preoccupied. She ate almost nothing and after a while I noticed that she had withdrawn from the main group a little and had picked up Malcolm's discarded newspaper, holding it as if to put a barrier between herself and the rest of us.

All too soon, it was time to start work again. I rose to my feet and thanked Beth for her generous hospitality, then began walking back towards the house, flanked by Joe and Evan. I was aware of some commotion behind us, but I thought nothing of it, until I heard Malcolm shout, 'Watch out!'

Spinning round I was just in time to see Amanda collapse on to the grass. She lay without moving, her skin grey and her lips bloodless. Instinctively, all of us rushed to her aid. Malcolm was on his knees, feeling her pulse, while Beth gently stroked her hair back from her face.

'What happened?' I looked at Malcolm questioningly. He seemed nonplussed.

Beth answered for him. 'She got up to go inside. Then she just sort of stood there for a few seconds swaying and the next thing was she passed out.' Beth was clearly alarmed.

Joe stepped forward. 'Let's get her inside. She needs to lie down.' Quickly, he picked Amanda up and strode towards the house. Beth hurried ahead, calling to the maids.

As we entered the cool shade of the family room, Amanda opened her eyes. Joe laid her down on one of the big sofas.

'Angelina, call Dr Evanston at once,' Beth instructed the maid who had just entered.

Amanda stirred on the couch and tried unsuccessfully to raise herself to a sitting position. 'No. I don't need a doctor.' She fell back on to the cushions. 'I'm fine,' she murmured weakly. Her eyes were dark hollows but a faint flush of colour had returned to her lips and face. 'It's the heat. I don't deal with it very well.'

Beth had disappeared but now returned with a glass of water. Amanda sipped it slowly.

'You're sure you don't want to see a doctor?' I asked dubiously.

Amanda shook her head. 'No. Absolutely not. This has happened before. I'm fine.'

'OK,' I conceded reluctantly. Beth left the room, shouting to the maid to cancel the message to the doctor.

'Look, I'll call a taxi to take you back to the hotel,' I said. 'Would you like one of us to go with you?'

Amanda shook her head again.

'Then we'll get on with these interviews and return as soon as we can,' I decided.

Mags put a comforting arm round Amanda's shoulders. 'Don't worry. We can manage without you for one afternoon. I've got all the stuff we prepared and you briefed me really well, so it shouldn't be a problem.'

By the time the taxi arrived ten minutes later, Amanda was looking a little better and insisted on walking unaided out to the car. As soon as she was gone, we began to set up for the interviews with Beth and Malcolm, reasoning that the faster we got those done, the sooner we could get back to check on Amanda.

In spite of the upset, everything proceeded smoothly. We had worked out questions in advance and Mags was an experienced television journalist, adept at responding to nuances in her interviewees' replies and following up on new leads as they cropped up.

Beth argued eloquently for her brother-in-law's innocence, and Malcolm came across as a decent man, beset by events beyond his worst imaginings and emotionally devastated by them. He talked movingly of his profound sense of loss at the death of his wife. Together their testimony would counter the impact of the circumstantial evidence. On a personal level I was pleased that it might help Malcolm's case, but as a programme maker I was also appreciative of the fact that it would introduce an element of tension and doubt into the outcome of our documentary, making it less predictable.

It was after five before we finished and could begin to pack up. I spoke to Beth about filming the ranch house in Rapid Falls and we agreed to make the trip on Monday. She wouldn't be needed in court while the jury selection was in progress. I thanked her and we left as quickly as possible. I was anxious to get back and check on Amanda. Joe, Evan and Lewis drove the van round to the back of the hotel to unload the equipment on to the freight elevator. Mags and I swung our car into the parking lot at the front.

Entering the lobby, I noticed a noisy group of people on the far side, near the lifts. As they drew closer, I could make out two or three cameramen and reporters holding radio hand mikes. They were walking backwards as they covered a tight knot of policemen surrounding several men in dark suits who were making slow progress towards the exit, ignoring the journalists and pushing the television crews aside. Following behind them was the hotel manager, wringing his hands in agitation.

Openly curious, Mags and I stood to one side to let them go by. As they reached the exit, they began to thin out into ones and twos, in order to pass through the door. That was when I caught sight of Amanda. She was at the centre of the group, handcuffed to a woman police officer, and she was crying. At that moment, she looked my way. There was an expression of pure panic on her face. I saw her lips move as she tried to say something to me, but her voice was drowned out by the clamour of the reporters crowding round asking questions.

Before I could do anything, she had been led out to a waiting police car and pushed unceremoniously into the back seat with her guard before being driven away. The other officers in the group quickly leapt into various vehicles and disappeared also, leaving a trio of disgruntled television crews.

I turned to Mags. She was gazing after the departing cars with a shocked expression on her face.

'What's going on?' She looked at me helplessly.

'I don't know,' I replied, equally bewildered. Then with sudden inspiration I said, 'I'm going to call Lois.' I broke into a run, dodging the armchairs and sofas in the lounge area, heading for the small alcove on the far side of the reception desk where vending machines and the telephones were located. I fumbled in my shoulder bag and, with shaking hands, withdrew the small buff business card that Amanda's friend Lois had given me.

'She's in a meeting,' bleated the secretary who answered the phone.

'Then interrupt her!' I shouted. 'Just say that Amanda is in serious trouble. Got that?'

The woman on the other end sounded justifiably offended. 'Please don't shout, Ma'am. I can hear you perfectly well,' she admonished me primly.

'Just hurry!' I yelled even louder.

Lois came on the line five seconds later. 'Amanda, what's wrong?' She sounded breathless.

'It's Bel,' I said quickly. 'Lois, Amanda has just been taken away by the police. She was handcuffed.'

There was a split second's silence, followed by an anguished groan. 'Oh my God! I was scared this would happen!' There was another brief pause during which she seemed to get a grip on herself. When she spoke again, she sounded strained but businesslike.

'Who carried out the arrest? Was it the Missouri police?'

'I don't know,' I stammered. 'I'd no idea there were two different forces.'

'Separate jurisdictions,' she said tersely. 'Where was she arrested – at the hotel?'

109

'Yes.'

'Then it's Missouri. Thanks for letting me know. You did the right thing. I'll be in touch.' She hung up.

I replaced the receiver and turned round. 'She said she'd been expecting something like this,' I said in response to Mags's questioning look.

'But why?' she asked incredulously. 'What's Amanda done?'

'God knows. Let's go up to my room and call the police and ask them.' I turned to leave the little alcove. Ranged along the outside wall was a row of vending machines. The last two in the line dispensed newspapers – one of them the *Kansas City Star*. Underneath a banner headline proclaiming 'Johnson County Woman Murdered' was a photograph of the redhead I had last seen alive in the company of Amanda's husband.

Chapter Eight

'Christ!' Mags had followed my gaze and was staring at the newspaper. She turned to me, her green eyes huge. 'Now what?'

I tried to gather my thoughts. 'We'd better find Joe first and then call the police.'

As we emerged from the alcove, a flashlight suddenly flared in our eyes and we both flinched away from it. The photographers and news crews, frustrated in their attempts to shoot Amanda, had evidently been tipped off that we were her friends. Lowering my head, I grabbed Mags by the elbow and began pushing my way through the throng, steadfastly refusing to answer any of the questions being thrown at us. It was strange to be on the other side of the camera, and while I sympathised with my American colleagues' desire to get the story, I desperately needed peace and quiet to come to terms with what had just happened.

We had almost reached the lifts on the far side of the foyer when Joe appeared through a plain wooden door leading from the rear of the hotel. He stared at us, surrounded as we were by reporters and television crews. Then he sprang into action, shouldering his way through the crowd and putting an arm round each of us. Within seconds he had propelled us into the nearest available lift, blocking the entrance with his large frame, until the doors had closed and we were on our way up. I breathed freely for the first time in several minutes.

'What the hell's going on?' Joe turned to me in alarm. There was no way to break the news of Amanda's arrest gently. His face went chalk white when I told him and for a moment I thought that he was going to collapse. But he merely swayed dizzily for a few seconds before pulling himself together.

'Where is she?' he managed to say.

'That's what we're planning to find out,' I answered.

The other two accompanied me to my room, where I phoned the Kansas City Missouri Police Department. The officer who answered was polite but would tell me nothing.

'I hope she's all right,' I said worriedly after hanging up.

'Lois will see to that.' Mags tried to reassure me. Joe had sunk into one of the armchairs, his face grey, and was watching us silently.

I looked at the clock on the bedside table. 'It'll be after one in the morning at home,' I said. 'I wonder if I should call Martin.'

Mags shook her head. 'Leave it another day. We don't know for sure that she's been arrested for murder. It could just be for –' she scanned the wall behind me for inspiration – 'for unpaid parking tickets from when she lived here . . . or something.' I looked at her sceptically.

'No. I'd better give him a ring. There's nothing he can do, but I don't want him to find out about this from a press report, rather than from us.' I glanced sharply at Joe. 'Before I do that, however, I need to know what you know about all this, Joe.'

An alarmed expression flickered across his face, to be replaced almost at once by a more neutral, guarded look.

'Absolutely nothing,' he stated firmly. 'I know as little as you do.'

I gazed at him levelly. 'But what about this morning?

Amanda looked as if she'd been beaten up. What had happened?'

Joe stiffened but his voice was firm as he replied emphatically, 'Amanda had an accident, that's all. I went to help her.' He looked up at me, his grey eyes luminous. 'She's done nothing wrong, nothing at all, that I'm aware of.'

I shrugged and turned away. I did not know whether to believe him or not.

Martin was still awake when I telephoned his home number. Briefly I informed him of what we had witnessed and the little we had been able to surmise.

He let out a groan when I finished. 'Oh my God! This is a nightmare! Have you been able to speak to her?'

'No,' I replied shortly. 'I've contacted a friend of hers who's a lawyer and she's doing whatever she can. I think all we can do is wait.'

'I feel so helpless this far away,' Martin muttered. 'And I blame myself. I should have listened to you and Mags when you said Amanda was unsuitable.'

'No use dwelling on that now,' I answered drily. 'Look, there's nothing you can do at the moment. I'll try and find out what's going on and keep you informed.'

Martin agreed, sounding very subdued on the other end of the line as I said goodbye and hung up. Then I stood deep in thought for a moment, head bowed.

'I think I should go down to the police station,' I announced abruptly, looking up at the others. 'I know they wouldn't tell me anything on the phone, but maybe they'll be more forthcoming in person.' I reached for my bag. 'At least I'll be doing something. Anyone coming?'

Mags nodded and Joe jumped to his feet. Emerging from my room, we glanced around us fearfully in case there were reporters lurking in the corridor. It was empty. Joe led the way towards the freight elevator at the rear of the hotel and we descended to the basement garage where the crew van was parked. Within minutes we were heading downtown.

It took some time to reach the police station because we made several wrong turnings and had to ask directions twice. When we finally got there, we parked and walked through the main entrance. We found ourselves in a lobby which had the look of institutional buildings all over the Western world – barely furnished and clean in a perfunctory sort of way. A middle-aged woman, with permed grey hair and round glasses obscuring a nondescript face, greeted us from behind a glass partition.

I tried cajoling, pleading, being pathetic, threatening her with exposure on primetime network television in the UK, everything I could think of, to persuade her to let us see Amanda or at least give us some information, but to no avail. She was polite but adamantly noncommittal. The only comfort she could offer was that Amanda did have her attorney with her and she insisted that all their prisoners were treated well. Reluctantly we returned to the van and drove in silence to the hotel, parking in the basement garage and returning to my room the way we had come.

None of us had thought to buy a newspaper and we were reluctant to venture down to the lobby again in case our colleagues in the media were still lying in wait for us. So we settled for watching the news on television. The report was brief and to the point. Sharon Donovan, the live-in girlfriend of Kansas City cardiologist Harlan Kingsley, had been battered to death the previous evening. Dr Kingsley had also suffered head injuries but had been released from hospital. A late bulletin announced that his estranged wife, Amanda, had been arrested in connection with the murder. No further details were given.

There was total silence in the room after I turned the television off. Joe kept staring at the screen, a look of devastation on his face. I could think of nothing more we could do to help Amanda, so at my insistence we ordered a meal from room service. But we hardly touched it. Joe, in particular, seemed unable to eat a thing. Morosely, he picked up a forkful of spaghetti and lifted it to his mouth. After a second's pause, he replaced it with a clatter on his plate. 'I keep wondering about Amanda,' he said when we both looked at him. 'She'll go mad if they lock her up.'

We sat considering this in silence. Eventually we gave up trying to force the food down and drank cups of tea instead. We discussed how we would cope with our production schedule. I had already arranged more interviews for the following day, this time with Malcolm's legal defence team followed by senior police officers involved in the case. It was too late to cancel them now.

'I suppose we should carry on as best we can until things become clearer,' I decided without much enthusiasm.

Around ten, I phoned Lois's home number but I got the answering machine and had to content myself with leaving a message asking her to call me back as soon as possible. Somehow it seemed ominous that she hadn't already done so.

Finally, Mags and Joe dragged themselves off to their own rooms and I got ready for bed. Before I climbed between the sheets, I opened the sliding glass door and stepped out on to the balcony. It came as no surprise to see Joe drive off in the van, heading towards downtown. It brought a question I had been trying to avoid all evening to the front of my mind. If Amanda really had committed murder, what part had Joe played in it?

I was wakened at five the next morning by the phone ringing. When I answered, Lois said, without any preamble, 'Could you come to my office around noon today? I really need some help.'

'Fine,' I stammered. She hung up.

I went down to the pool for a swim, but this time it didn't

115

make me feel much better. I suspected that nothing would, except the release of Amanda. I was haunted by the memories of her heart-breaking sobs and dogged by guilt that I had done nothing to help. Perhaps if I had, none of this would have happened.

Returning to my room, I showered and changed, then went down to the restaurant for breakfast. This time I made myself eat; I had a long and difficult day ahead of me. Mags arrived, immaculately groomed and ready to appear on camera, but I could tell she was tired in spite of her carefully applied make-up. Joe merely sat staring bleakly out of the window, drinking black coffee.

We were joined by Evan and Lewis in reception and drove off in convoy to our first location, the defence lawyer's suite of offices near the courthouse in Kansas City, Kansas. As soon as we arrived, I set about selecting a location for the interview. I decided on the law firm's library, with its acres of leather-bound legal tomes in the background, and supervised the setting up. But I found it hard to keep my mind on the job. I could tell that all of us except Evan and Lewis were simply going through the motions. Joe had to send Evan back to the van twice for things he had forgotten. He looked haggard but when he glanced up once and caught my eye, he gave me an encouraging wink. I smiled back, but I was wary. There were too many unanswered questions surrounding Joe's part in Amanda's predicament. I was no longer sure I could trust him.

We finished the interviews with the defence team around eleven thirty. I had told the others about my appointment with Lois and after a few whispered words with Mags, I slipped out, leaving them to pack up and find somewhere to have lunch. Retrieving the hired car, I launched into the traffic with only a dim idea of where I should be going. But it turned out that Lois worked just a few blocks away.

I was shown into her office at once. She looked as if she had been up all night. She wore no make-up and her face was pale and drawn with dark shadows under the light blue eyes. Her movements were jerky and a little uncoordinated, as if she was only just keeping her nervous tension under control.

'Thanks for coming,' she said shortly, moving from behind her desk to join me on the sofa. She rubbed her reddened eyes with one hand as she continued. 'Amanda has been charged with the murder of Sharon Donovan. I had her sign a waiver so she's now under the jurisdiction of the police on the Kansas side and I'll be representing her.' She looked at me wearily. 'The thing is, I'm already overloaded with cases, so I need all the help I can get. The police must have some pretty strong evidence to go ahead and press charges but I don't know yet what it is.'

'Don't they have to tell you?' I asked.

Lois grimaced. 'Oh yes. Eventually. But they're not going to hand it over on a plate. I'll file a motion in court on Monday morning for what we call "discovery" so it will be forthcoming. But that's two days away and the sooner I know what's going on, the better. Can you tell me anything?' She gave me a searching look.

I shrugged. 'Very little. I saw her leave for dinner around seven and then I met her coming up in the lift the next morning with Joe. Both of them looked very dishevelled and Amanda had bruises on her face and seemed upset. That would have been about six. That's it.'

Lois shook her head despairingly. 'Amanda's date that night was with Harlan. She admits she went back to the house with him afterwards to pick up some of her stuff. She says he tried to rape her but she knocked him out and got away. Then she called Joe to pick her up. She claims she didn't even see Sharon, let alone kill her.'

'How did Sharon die?' I asked quietly.

Lois shuddered. 'Beaten to death. Whoever it was smashed her skull with something. I'm not even sure what the murder weapon was yet.'

'What about Harlan? Where was he in all this?'

'Oh, poor Harlan claims he was unconscious when it happened,' Lois replied with a snort of derision.

There was a moment's silence. 'Do you believe Amanda?' I asked.

'I have to.'

'Well, if she didn't do it, who did?'

'I don't know. All I have to do is convince the police that it wasn't Amanda. But if you want my guess, I'd say it was that fucking husband of hers!' Lois uttered the last words with such vehemence that I was taken aback. But after a few moments, she continued in a controlled, level voice.

'Harlan was violent towards Amanda all the time they were married. Several times she took refuge with me, but he always talked her into going back. It seemed she couldn't stay away from him, no matter what. I'd almost given up because I thought she'd never leave – except in a coffin. Then six months ago he beat her to a pulp. She refused to press charges, but I gave her the money to go home and she left. I thought that was it. When she turned up that day with you, I was devastated – and angry as hell with her.' Lois buried her face in her hands, so that her next words were muffled. 'I just knew she wouldn't be able to stay away. I just knew that something terrible would happen.' There was a long silence.

'Can I see Amanda?' I asked.

Lois stretched her neck and rubbed the muscles at the base of her skull. 'Eventually. She has to go through a procedure called classification at the jail. It takes about twenty-four hours. After that, they'll assign her visiting times.'

'What happens next?'

'There'll be a hearing to discuss bail.'

'Does that mean she'll get out?'

'Probably not.' Lois grimaced. 'The prosecution will be against it because it's a serious crime and she's a foreign national with very little to tie her to this area and stop her taking off for Canada, for example, even if they do take away her passport. I'll argue that it is inhumane and unnecessary to lock her up for however many months it takes to get the trial over with. Either way, the outcome will be the same. Amanda will stay in custody because even if I do persuade the judge to allow bail, it will be set at something like a quarter, maybe half a million dollars. She doesn't have that kind of money. She wouldn't even have the ten per cent she'd need to pay a bondsman to get her out.' She turned to me, looking suddenly hopeful. 'I don't suppose your company would come up with the money?'

I shook my head. 'I doubt it. This isn't their responsibility. Amanda didn't get arrested because of something to do with her job.'

Lois nodded in understanding and rose to her feet. 'Well, I must get back to work. I've still got all my other cases to take care of.' We moved towards the door.

'What happens if she's convicted?' I paused on the threshold, hardly daring to hear the answer.

'Well, they're going for murder one because they say this was a premeditated, violent killing,' Lois answered slowly. She took a deep breath. 'The good news is we don't have the death penalty in Kansas.' She bit her lip. 'The bad news is we have what we call "hard forty". That means that if convicted she will be sentenced to forty years in prison with no prospect of parole or early release.'

I stared at her. 'Forty years? She'll actually serve the whole forty years if convicted?'

Lois nodded.

'She'd be sixty-eight before she got out.'

Lois nodded again. 'That's why I need all the help I can get. They've got a couple of star witnesses and I'd really like to know fast what they have to say. Anything you can find out will be most welcome.'

'I'll do what I can,' I promised, before she closed her office door, leaving me standing in a state of shock in the hallway.

I don't know how long it took me to gather myself together, but as soon as I did I headed back to the car, got in, then sat with my head in my hands trying to take stock and put my thoughts in some sort of order. I reached for the mobile phone which we had hired with the car and dialled the number of the handset which Joe had in the van. Mags answered at once. I could hear Joe's voice in the background and the sound of traffic.

'Bel,' Mags said, her voice tense. 'What's going on?'

Quickly I told her what I'd discovered. 'It's not looking good,' I concluded. 'I'm going to see if I can find out anything that'll help. D'you think you can manage the police interviews without me this afternoon? Joe knows the sort of thing I want.'

'No problem.' There was a sudden crackle of interference. '. . . Do anything stupid, will you?' she was saying.

'Never,' I assured her.

There was another ferocious outburst of clicking and zinging on the line before it went dead. I returned the phone to its holder.

Right, I thought to myself. Start at the beginning.

The Happy Hangout was on the edge of a sprawling shopping centre near one of the older suburbs. It was basically a long, rectangular building, with a second, smaller oblong joined to it at a right angle in the middle. Every attempt had been made to disguise its utilitarian and essentially commercial architecture. It had been given a roof of red tiles, steeply slanted and overhanging the sides

120

to provide deep, quaint-looking eaves. Although there were large plate glass windows all along the main part of the building, the smaller section, where the entrance and waiting area were, had miniature panes with whirlpools of coloured glass, as if they had come from some Hollywood version of an ancient monastery.

My feet echoed on the terracotta tiled floor of the entryway as I approached the hostess, who was smiling invitingly where she stood by the cash register. The entrance to the restaurant was roped off.

'We're not open for dinner until five,' she announced politely. I hadn't really thought through how I was going to handle this, so on the spur of the moment I blurted out, 'Actually, I just wondered if I could have a word with one of your staff who was working here last night?'

The young woman frowned. 'Is this business or are you a friend or a relative? The manager doesn't really allow us to talk to personal contacts during working hours.'

I looked at her carefully, toying with various stories which might persuade her to let me through. Finally I settled on telling the truth.

'One of my friends was here for dinner with her husband last night. It's important I talk to whoever served them,' I said.

There was a look of dawning comprehension in the hostess's eyes. 'Oh, I know who you mean! The police were here earlier. It was Jessica who waited on them. Are you English?' she inquired eagerly.

'British,' I answered impatiently. 'Do you think she would talk to me? It's really important.'

'Oh!' The hostess's face creased in a wide smile of genuine pleasure. 'My mother comes from Coventry. I'm hoping to go over there in the fall to meet some of my cousins.'

I chatted for a few minutes, passing on the few bits of

information I knew about that part of the country, shamelessly exploiting her interest in order to persuade her to fetch her colleague for me. Finally, she said, 'I'll tell Jess you're here.' She paused awkwardly before adding, as if to justify her change of heart, 'We're not busy at this time and the manager's gone out, so perhaps I could cover for her for a few minutes.'

I thanked her profusely, then restlessly paced around the empty, spotless waiting area. The wall opposite the windows was flanked by a long glass counter containing desserts which patrons could purchase in their entirety on the way out. I surveyed them dully. Apart from the apple tart, which at least looked as if it contained chunks of real fruit, they all appeared to be confections made for visual appeal – deep mounds of dark chocolate custard topped with cream engineered into an enduring froth, or elaborately layered gateaux which I knew would taste of nothing but sugar.

'Can I help you, Ma'am?' I turned to face a stocky woman of about twenty-five, wearing a uniform of red checked dress and frilled white apron with its connotations of picket fences and good old-fashioned home cooking. Her straight brown hair was scraped back from her tanned oval face and tucked under a gingham mobcap. But the uncompromising stance, shoulders squared and feet apart, as well as the sensible white leather lace-ups she wore, belied the twee girlishness of the outfit.

'Maggie said you were asking for me.' Her brown eyes surveyed me steadily.

I nodded, rapidly coming to the conclusion that this was a woman who shot straight from the hip and who would sense in two seconds when someone was trying to con her. 'I believe you may have served one of my friends and her husband when they ate here last night.' I paused, but nothing in Jessica's expression gave anything away. 'My friend is in trouble with the police and it would help if I could confirm her where-abouts last night.' My eye strayed to the hostess who was back at her post by the cash register and was trying to look as if she wasn't listening to every word.

Jessica's eyes narrowed. 'Are you from the media?' she drawled coldly.

I shook my head. 'No. I do work for a British television company – so does my friend. But the last thing I want is to get any more publicity for this.'

She eyed me intently for a moment, then nodded decisively. 'OK. But you better not be lying to me because if I find out you are, you'll be real sorry.' She turned and led the way past the hostess who gave us her automatic smile. 'I have a job to do so I can support two kids plus go to college and I can't afford to lose it. You can talk to me while I work.'

We crossed the silent, empty restaurant, whose vast floor space was broken up by tall plants and coloured glass partitions. Jessica reached a booth set against the plate glass window on the far side and picked up a damp cloth and a yellow spray bottle of cleanser. There was a faint smell of ammonia as she began energetically dousing the table with liquid and mopping it with the rag.

'What d'you want to know?' she asked without looking up.

'Just what you saw that night.'

Jessica's shoulders slumped momentarily and she paused in her cleaning, as if gathering herself for an unwelcome task. She sighed, then moved on to the next table as she talked.

'I know who you're talking about. I remembered them real well when the cops showed me the pictures. For one thing, they were so good-looking. They both could have been movie stars and –' Jessica looked up at me with a mixture of envy and admiration in her face – 'she was wearing the most *gorgeous* silk gown. I have never seen anything so beautiful! Especially not in here. Most folks' idea of dressing up for dinner in this place is to put on a clean pair of jeans.' She rubbed furiously at the table in front of her, polishing the wood to a dull sheen.

'I kept hanging around whenever I could, just to look, just to sort of soak up the *glamour*.' Jessica paused again to look up at me with such longing in her eyes that for a split second I could imagine her life, an endless round of waiting on customers, struggling to look after her kids and clean the house, and trying to study when she was dead tired, in the hopes that one day she could escape from all this. No wonder she was drawn to Harlan and Amanda. They must have presented a tantalising glimpse of what she ached to have.

Jessica turned back energetically to her cleaning. 'You'd think that two people who were that beautiful would *have* to be deeply in love with each other,' she continued. 'It would be like looking at your mirror image. Anyway, I took their orders but when I came back with the drinks, they seemed to be having an argument. They stopped till I left, but I noticed the woman – well, her hand was on the table and it was shaking. Quite definitely, it was shaking.'

Jessica picked up the bottle of cleanser and the cloth and walked to the service station shielded by a couple of wooden screens. She returned with an armful of cutlery and some red checked paper place mats and began laying them on the tables.

'It just seemed to get worse,' she went on. 'Each time I returned to the table, they were angrier and angrier – no, that's not quite correct.' She paused, turning towards me and pointing a fork in my direction. '*She* was getting more and more upset, but he stayed as cool as a cucumber. He was even smiling at one point.' She shook her head in wonderment as she bent to her task again. 'God, he was so beautiful!'

After a few moments I prompted her. 'How did you know she was upset? Was she crying?'

124

Jessica nodded. 'Yeah. I noticed there were tears in her eyes. She wasn't sobbing or anything. It was more the shaking. She was holding on to the table like this.' She demonstrated, clutching the bevelled edge so tightly that her knuckles went white. 'And her whole body was *vibrating* as if she was going to explode or something – take off into the stratosphere maybe, I don't know.'

She finished setting the tables and sank down on the edge of one of the banquettes. 'There was a sort of a lull when I wasn't busy for several minutes – no one saying "Ma'am! Ma'am! Can I . . ." None of that. So I was stood over there at the serving station watching them. They didn't notice me. I saw him take a photograph out of his inside coat pocket –' Jessica mimed his movements, as if that would help her recall the events which followed – 'and he handed it to her with a smile. I caught a glimpse as he passed it over. It was a picture of a woman with short red hair – the one who was murdered, I guess. She just looked at it for about three seconds, then ripped it in two and threw it on the table.

'She stood up –' Jessica had got to her feet, acting out this drama – 'and she sort of hissed at him, real low, but I'd moved closer when I saw what was happening so I heard her say, "It's about time that bitch learned to keep her hands off what belongs to me!" Then she just sailed out of here, nearly knocking me over.' Jessica took a step back, as if recoiling from an imaginary blow. 'And then he throws money on the table and follows her. I saw them arguing for a few minutes outside – he seemed to be pleading with her and he had hold of her arm, but she shook him off and cut across the parking lot towards the shopping centre. And that was it.'

I thought for a moment. 'What did the man do then? Did he follow her?'

Jessica screwed up her mouth as she considered my question.

'I wouldn't say *followed*. Not exactly. He got in his car and drove out maybe a minute later.'

'But in the same direction?' I persevered.

She shrugged dismissively. 'Well, there's only one way you can go outta here. So yes. In the same direction.' Her gaze shifted beyond me and a professional smile of welcome appeared on her face. 'Well, hi,' she said. I looked round. The hostess was showing an elderly couple to one of the booths which Jessica had just set with mats and cutlery. I glanced at my watch. Five o'clock. The first customers for dinner. Everyone ate early out here. The restaurant would start to fill up soon.

'I have to go,' Jessica said briefly. 'I hope you can help your friend. If you need anything more you know where to find me.' She made a move towards her customers.

I thanked her and walked out into the baking heat, crossing the dusty parking lot to my car. No wonder the police considered they had a good case. Jessica was intelligent and articulate and utterly convincing in what she said. Her account of events built up a clear picture of Amanda's feelings towards Sharon. She had even threatened the other woman for taking what Amanda considered belonged to her. She would have a tough time talking herself out of that.

Chapter Nine

The mobile phone was ringing as I got into the car. It was Mags.

'The police want to talk to all of us. They've been looking for us all day but of course no one knew where we were. I can tell you how to get to their headquarters and we'll meet you there.'

My mind was racing as I headed across town. Should I volunteer what I knew of Amanda's and Joe's nocturnal activities? Should I tell them about our encounter in the lift the morning after the murder? How far should I go to try to protect my colleagues?

I was still wrestling with this dilemma as I pulled into the parking lot in front of the police station and parked next to the crew van. I came to a rapid decision. I would answer their questions truthfully, but I wouldn't offer any information they didn't directly ask for. At the back of my mind a little voice reminded me that this was what was known as not telling the whole truth but I shut it off angrily. The police didn't need much help anyway, I rationalised. It looked as if they had the makings of a cast-iron case already.

The police headquarters were situated in a low building of brown brick with semi-circular steps leading to the entrance. It was icy cool inside. I crossed the waiting area to a glass window behind which sat a grey-haired man wearing the blue police uniform shirt. I explained why I was there and after a few minutes' wait, a locked door to one side of the room clicked open and I was beckoned inside.

The two detectives who questioned me were friendly and polite, and I found it hard to steer a path somewhere between telling the truth and not incriminating Amanda – or Joe. Most of the time I gave them straightforward answers, but when they asked if I'd noticed my colleague behaving suspiciously, I fudged the issue by replying that I had known her for only a short time. They seemed to know all about the incident at Beth's fundraiser. I shrugged that off by saying that Amanda had been drinking and that anyway she was always a bit highly strung. I didn't tell them about the package I'd seen her throw in the river.

It was hard to judge whether the police were satisfied with my answers or not, but they allowed me to leave. Mags and Joe were sitting waiting outside when I emerged, not talking, lost in their own thoughts.

'How'd it go?' Mags asked as soon as we left the building.

I spoke under my breath. 'I told them most, but not all, of what I know.'

She nodded. 'Me too. It's like some sort of nightmare. I keep thinking any minute now we'll get to the end credits and we'll know we were in a movie.'

'I wish.' I glanced at Joe. He was striding towards the crew van, a grim expression on his face.

'See you at the hotel,' he muttered without even looking in our direction.

On the way back, I filled Mags in on what I had discovered at the diner.

'Christ!' she exclaimed when I finished. She leaned back in her seat and closed her eyes. 'I was convinced the police must have made some kind of mistake, but it doesn't sound like it. We have to tell Martin. This is serious.'

When we reached the hotel, Joe was nowhere to be found, so we went up to my room. I checked my watch. It would be about one a.m. in the UK. 'We may as well call Martin in the morning. It's the middle of the night now,' I pointed out, secretly relieved that I would not have to break the news to my boss just yet.

I dialled Lois's office number. She answered at once. 'Any luck?' Quickly I told her what I had discovered. Her reaction was not quite what I expected. 'I'm sure I could talk our way out of that one and I'm equally sure the police would know that. Shouting at someone in a restaurant is not the same as battering his girlfriend to death. They must have something else. I'm supposed to get all their evidence on Monday. I'll talk to you when I know more. 'Bye.' There was a rustle of clothing as if she were in the process of hanging up, then I heard her voice again.

'Oh by the way. Amanda's visiting hours are from nine to nine fifty Monday morning and one ten till two on Saturday. She'd like to see you. She's in the Johnson County Jail in Olathe.' The line went dead. As I replaced the receiver, I noticed a red light blinking on the telephone.

At that moment, Mags returned from her own room, carrying her kettle and teabags. 'Well?' she asked, seeing my face.

'Nothing. I can visit Amanda on Monday morning,' I replied despondently as I dialled the number to retrieve my messages.

There was only one, from Beth, to say she'd seen the news and asking if there was anything she could do to help. I returned the call while Mags brewed up some tea. One of the maids answered, but Beth came on the line moments later.

'Oh, this is just such terrible news!' she exclaimed. 'I had no idea Amanda was Harlan's wife. I'd never met her till she showed up last week with you. That poor girl!'

'You know Harlan?' I could hardly keep the surprise out of my voice.

'Oh, yes. Since he was a baby. He's another one from Rapid Falls,' Beth replied. 'I used to see him quite a bit at parties when he first moved to Kansas City, but we've never been what you'd call close. Look, the reason I called you was to ask if there's anything I can do. The Lord only knows I can imagine what you're going through.'

'Thanks, Beth,' I said gratefully. 'We're a bit in the dark ourselves at the moment. But I'll let you know.' I said goodbye and hung up.

Mags sank on to the bed next to me. 'There must be something we can do. I can't stand the thought of just hanging around waiting for bad news.'

I nodded, staring morosely out of the window. I turned to Mags. 'Why don't we go and talk to Harlan's neighbours? Maybe we could find out something from them.'

Within ten minutes we had got Harlan's address from the phone book and were heading towards the affluent neighbourhood where Amanda used to live. I parked about a block away and we sat in the car for several minutes, surveying the scene. Unlike the newer suburbs, which had street after street of expensive homes all built on essentially the same plan, this was a neighbourhood of older houses, all completely different. Small wooden houses with steep roofs and porches stood side by side with sprawling bungalows or stucco, Tudor-style homes. The only thing they had in common was that they were all built on large plots with sweeping, unfenced lawns.

It was very quiet. The only sign of life was the sprinklers playing in several of the gardens. Almost every property had at least one large shady tree and these provided a leafy screen on either side, stretching to the end of the road. We got out of the car and approached Harlan's home.

'I wonder if he's there.' There was a sudden note of panic in Mags's voice.

But the house looked deserted and the yard surrounding it was cordoned off by barriers and lengths of yellow tape. We stood looking at it for a moment. It was an ordinary two-storey white painted house with a garage. It was hard to believe a young woman had been brutally murdered there only two days before.

I shivered. 'Let's get started. You take this side and I'll do the other.'

Mags nodded and set off across the grass towards the brick bungalow just visible through the bushes to the right of the crime scene. I turned to the house immediately opposite.

One of the things you learn working in news for so many years is to be quite brazen about sticking your nose in where you're not invited and accosting anyone, anywhere. Knocking on the doors of complete strangers didn't embarrass me – or Mags – in the same way that it might have someone normal.

So for the next hour, we trailed from house to house up and down the street, trying to find someone who had seen or heard anything suspicious the night of the murder, but to no avail. Occasionally, we would catch sight of each other and shrug despondently. By the time I had completed the trawl of my side of the road, the sun was setting. Deep shade enveloped the front gardens as I returned to the car disconsolately to wait for Mags. I had seen her being invited into the home of an elderly couple about five minutes before, and I had a feeling she might be a while.

None of the people I had spoken to had had any useful information to impart. All of them seemed to be acquainted with Amanda and to be sympathetic to her predicament, but no one seemed to know her well. On the night of the murder, they were either asleep or watching television in some back room, or, like the woman in the house opposite, out of town.

Unless Mags had more luck with this last couple, we had drawn a blank.

There was a tap on the car window. Turning, I could just make out the neighbour who lived across the road from Harlan and who had been visiting her daughter in Tucson at the time of the murder. She was mouthing something to me very emphatically, but I couldn't make out the words. Quickly, I rolled down the window.

'Go and see Patsy McFee round the corner at 3603 Helmut. I just remembered she was looking after my yard for me while I was out of town. She might be able to help you,' she said. I stared at her in surprise, but before I could even thank her, she turned on her heel and headed back towards her house. At that moment, I spotted Mags hurrying in my direction.

'Nothing,' she gasped breathlessly as she flung herself into the passenger seat. 'That last couple just wanted to know my life history and to tell me theirs.' She took a deep breath. 'How about you?'

I started up the car and cruised to the next intersection, turning on to Helmut.

'Same thing, except that the neighbour across the road has just told me to talk to someone down here.' I leaned forward, peering at house numbers. 'That's it.' I pulled over to the side of the road. An elderly woman stood with her back towards us in the front yard, in the process of moving a green hosepipe which sprayed slender filaments of water across the lawn. We got out and approached her slowly.

'Excuse me,' I said. Laboriously, she straightened up and turned to see who was speaking. She couldn't have been more than four feet six and I guessed her age at somewhere around seventy. Grey wispy hair was pulled back into a bun at the nape of her neck, and bright dark eyes gazed at me with open curiosity.

'Can I help you with something?' she inquired politely.

There was a strong Midwestern twang in her voice. She stood waiting patiently for my answer, arms akimbo and feet planted firmly on the ground, wearing a washed-out shirt and faded denim dungarees. As I gazed at her, I had a feeling that the West was probably won by women like this.

Quickly I explained who we were and what we were after.

The woman's face changed. She didn't give her name in return or offer to shake hands.

'You a reporter?' she asked abruptly.

I shook my head emphatically. 'No. We're not here representing any of the media. We're colleagues of Amanda's. We're trying to help her.'

The elderly woman cocked her head on one side, considering me closely. Then she nodded slightly, reaching a decision. 'Well, you've got the same British accent as her, I'll give you that. I'm the one you're looking for all right. Ellen Maybury called me not ten minutes ago to see if I might know anything. Come on in and visit a while.' We followed her up broad wooden steps at the front of her house, waiting as she pulled back the aluminium screen door and pushed open the white wooden one beyond.

Inside it seemed dark. Patsy felt her way across to a low table and switched on a lamp. Then she lifted a sleepy grey cat from its place on the sofa. The cat walked away, its tail in the air, complaining loudly.

'Now sit down,' urged Patsy. 'Can I get you anything? A glass of ice tea or something? I don't have any beers or anything like that in the house if you're drinkers.'

I shook my head, sinking into the gold brocade couch covered in clear plastic which squeaked with every movement I made. 'Some tea would be nice,' I murmured.

'What kind of tea? If you want hot tea then you'd better come on through to the kitchen and make it yourself 'cause I don't think I can do it the right way to suit someone English,' she replied in a headlong rush of words.

The thought of a nice cup of tea made with boiling water seemed suddenly irresistible. 'OK,' I said, getting to my feet with a smile. 'I'll make some for us all.'

She led the way through an arch into an old-fashioned kitchen. Plain wooden units painted pale green lined the walls and the counter was covered with something that looked like grey linoleum. Without a word, Patsy opened cupboards and placed teabags and a container of sugar in front of me. From the fridge came a carton of milk. Then she disappeared through another archway leading to a dining room. I heard the creak of hinges before she re-emerged carrying three delicate pink china cups, saucers and plates. 'These belonged to my dead Auntie Gertie,' she announced, laying them down on the counter next to the other things.

I set about filling the kettle and brewing tea.

'My name's Patsy McFee,' she announced suddenly. Mags and I shook hands with her. Patsy's palms were calloused and her skin dry to the touch.

'Amanda, Mags and I were working on a television programme about Malcolm Laurie,' I began. 'You know, the British man accused of killing his wife.'

'I read about that.' Patsy had dragged a low stool out from a corner of the room and hoisted herself on to it. 'Seemed a real shame. She looked like a pretty woman. My folks used to have a farm out at Rapid Falls – long time ago, though. I'll take two sugars.' She nodded in the direction of the container as I poured out the tea. 'There's some cookies in that jar over there.' This time she indicated a ceramic model of a house with a roof that doubled as a lid.

Mags and I said in unison, 'No thanks.' Then I leaned back against the counter, holding my cup. Outside it was now almost dark and the kitchen was lit only by the glow from the lamp in the sitting room and the last embers of a burning sunset which reflected off Patsy's glasses. 'We're trying to help Amanda prove she's innocent,' I said.

'Well, I certainly hope you can because she's a real fine little lady. But I don't think I'm gonna be much help to you.' There was genuine regret in Patsy's voice.

I was filled with a sense of foreboding. 'Why not?'

'Well, I heard nothing, nothing at all until about eleven. I couldn't sleep and I remembered I'd promised Ellen Maybury that I'd water her flowers while she was gone visiting her daughter. So I was on the front porch of her house right across the street from Harlan's when I heard a screen door and then I saw Amanda running down their driveway.

'She was wearing that pretty silk dress that Harlan gave her for their second anniversary. It was bloodstained and she had blood on her hands and arms and there was some on her legs and spattered on her shoes as well, like she'd walked through a pool of blood.' Patsy shook her head sorrowfully. 'I called out to her but she took off running down the street. And that's all. I didn't see or hear another thing until the police sirens.'

'Are you sure it was Amanda? Remember, it was dark, and I noticed you don't have much street lighting around here.'

Patsy sipped her tea thoughtfully before answering. 'I'm pretty sure. I didn't see her face, because of that red hair of hers falling forward, but the woman was about her build, and had her hair and wore her dress.'

'But couldn't it have been another woman wearing a similar dress?' Mags broke in.

Patsy smiled sadly. 'No, it could not.'

'But even designer clothes are mass produced these days,' I argued. 'And if there's a fashion for a particular style or colour, then half a dozen companies will manufacture dresses that look alike. Couldn't you have been mistaken?'

Patsy regarded me with an air of deep pity. 'No, darlin', I

couldn't. You see, that dress was unique. And the reason I know that is because Harlan got the silk on a trip to Hong Kong and he gave it to me to make up. He had a photograph from a magazine for me to follow. I'm retired now but I used to work as a seamstress and I still do bits and pieces for friends. I'd made several pretty gowns for her already so I knew she was a size eight. He wanted it to be a surprise for their second anniversary, like I said. There was no way anyone else had a dress like that.'

I looked at Mags. She shrugged in resignation. I knew she was thinking the same thing I was. Patsy's account was utterly credible.

We left soon afterwards and drove back to the hotel in gloomy silence. 'Well, I don't give much for Amanda's chances,' was all Mags said as we walked into the foyer. She glanced at her watch. 'Nine o'clock. Let's get something to eat.'

We walked across the room towards the main staircase leading to the first-floor dining room. Just as we reached it, a tall figure stepped smartly in front of me, blocking my way.

'Bel Carson?'

'That's right.' I looked up into the dark, brooding face of Harlan Kingsley. He was dressed casually in an open-necked cream shirt and chinos and seemed remarkably calm and collected for a man whose girlfriend had so recently been murdered, apparently by his wife. The only indication of his recent trauma was a dramatic-looking dressing which was taped to one side of his head where the hair had been shaved off.

'I wonder.' He spoke hesitantly, his voice low. 'Do you have a moment?'

'Of course,' I replied automatically, wondering what he could possibly want with me. His gaze strayed to Mags, who was eyeing him critically. 'In private, if that would be possible.' His manner was tentative.

'I'll go on up to the restaurant,' Mags spoke up before I could say anything. 'I'll wait for you there.'

As she mounted the stairs and disappeared round the bend, Harlan turned to me. 'Would over there be all right, or would you prefer the bar?'

'This is fine.' I led the way across to a small group of armchairs set out in the middle of the room. I sat down. 'What can I help you with?'

Harlan gave me an intense look and I was suddenly vividly aware of the sexual magnetism which he exuded. It was almost predatory and it put me even more on my guard. 'You must forgive me,' he said in a soft, intimate voice, 'but I saw your picture in the newspaper, so I know you're a friend of Amanda's.' He sighed helplessly. 'Lois won't talk to me and I need to know how she is.'

I stared at him, trying to assess whether his concern was genuine or not. I couldn't tell. But instinctively I decided to give away as little as possible.

'Obviously this is a distressing situation,' I commented, sticking to generalities, 'and being in jail can't be pleasant.'

'But what about her mental state?' He leaned forward and touched my hand. His eyes were brimming with concern.

I felt confused. There was something odd about his behaviour. With an effort, I pulled my thoughts together. 'She's finding it hard, of course, but she's remaining calm and pinning her hopes on being released very soon,' I replied carefully.

He sighed and said in broken tones, 'I know how she is. This must be torture for her. I can't bear to think of her suffering all alone and locked up like that. I feel so responsible. I knew she was jealous, but I thought those were idle threats. I had no idea . . .' He stopped, apparently overcome. 'If you see her,' he said eventually, gazing deep into my eyes, 'tell her I love her and to call me if there's anything I can do.'

I stared at him, trying to digest his words. There was something inappropriate about his reactions – they were too controlled, the emotions too orchestrated. It made me uneasy. I found Malcolm's bewildered confusion more believable than this odd response, with no hint of grief or even anger that Amanda had apparently killed his girlfriend and destroyed her own life into the bargain. It was, I reflected, as if he were speaking a foreign language. He'd learnt the broad dictionary definitions but he was missing all the nuances that made sense of the words.

He rose to his feet, handing me a card which he had extracted from his wallet. 'If she needs anything, or if I can help you in any way, or if you'd just like to talk to me any time, this is my office number – or you can reach me through Pete. I'm not living at home at the moment for obvious reasons.'

'Pete?' I queried sharply.

Harlan frowned. 'Pete Ottinger. I thought you'd met. He's my accountant.'

'I didn't know you knew him.'

Harlan laughed, his anguish of a moment ago forgotten. 'He's one of my oldest friends. We grew up in the same town in Western Kansas – place called Rapid Falls.'

'That's where Marlene Laurie was from, isn't it?' I asked quickly.

'That's right.' He suddenly looked sombre. 'We all knew each other pretty well. Pete and I were a couple of years older, but there weren't that many young people in town, so we all sort of hung out together. Poor Marlene. That is such a tragedy.' He wiped a tear from his eye.

'And Sharon, too,' I added, keeping my eyes fixed on his face. 'It must be dreadful for you.'

Harlan nodded, apparently too overcome to speak. He swallowed hard, then visibly pulled himself together, before repeating, his voice breaking with emotion, 'Well, please give my love to Amanda and tell her to get in touch.' He gave a little farewell wave and walked out of the hotel with all the measured dignity befitting the recently bereaved.

'What was that all about?' asked Mags tartly as soon as I joined her in the restaurant.

I rolled my eyes. 'Your guess is as good as mine. But I tell you, that guy is seriously creepy. He turns emotions on and off like they're on tap. I don't think he knows what a genuine feeling is. But the really interesting thing is he knew Marlene Laurie. She and Sharon were both bludgeoned to death. It makes me wonder if he could be linked to her murder in some way.'

Mags looked dubious. 'I don't see how. No one's even suggested he had anything to do with her.'

'He could have been this lover we've never been able to track down.'

'We can't even find evidence to implicate him in Sharon's murder, never mind one he's got no connection with at all,' Mags pointed out reasonably. 'I don't think growing up in the same town as Marlene all those years ago exactly makes him guilty of killing her.'

I nodded, sighing. 'You're right, I know. I just took an instant dislike to him. I suppose I'd better try and turn my mind to more immediate concerns. We're supposed to be travelling out to western Kansas the day after tomorrow to film the place where Marlene grew up. I think we should keep to that schedule because, apart from the fact that we need to try and finish this job regardless, the old family house is going to be burnt down pretty soon and I'd like to get some shots of it before it's too late.'

Mags nodded. 'I think you're right. You don't really need me to be there, though, do you? It's mostly pictures for voice-over, isn't it?'

'Yeh,' I agreed, 'plus a bit with Beth showing us round the house and talking about her sister and Malcolm. I can get by without you. I suppose that way at least there's one of us here to keep an eye on Amanda in case there's something we can do to help.'

'That's what I was thinking. I also thought we should have a word with the hotel management. We should really stop holding Amanda's room. I could pack up her stuff while you're away and get the porter to move it into one of our rooms.'

'Fine. I'll talk to them just now.' I rubbed my hands across my face tiredly. 'I thought I'd go and visit Amanda on Monday before I leave. Beth has offered to take me to western Kansas so I can probably leave you our car. Joe and the crew will have the van.'

'Done.' Mags stood up. 'I'm completely knackered. See you in the morning. Don't forget to call Martin.'

I wandered downstairs to the reception desk to cancel the booking for Amanda's room, then spent the next ten minutes reassuring the undermanager that there would be no further dramas.

'I do understand your problems, but I hope you appreciate ours.' He sniffed with a hint of injured dignity. 'This *is* a major hotel and we prefer it if the police have no reason to be here – ever.'

I finally escaped and was crossing to the lifts when I spotted Joe sitting in the far corner of the bar. He had a glass in front of him and he was staring glumly at the lights of the Plaza in the distance.

I sat down opposite him. He turned round and I was shocked by the change in his appearance. He looked haggard – ill almost; his skin was very pale and there was an air of utter exhaustion about him. He tried to smile.

'Bel. Like a drink?'

I shook my head. 'There's something I wanted to ask you.'

He nodded resignedly, as if he had been expecting this.

'Joe,' I began carefully. 'You knew Amanda before you came on this job, didn't you?'

Joe smiled sadly. 'I knew you suspected something. Amanda and I lived next door to each other when we were kids. We've been best pals since we were three. She's the sister I never had.' He looked out of the window again quickly, but I had caught a glimpse of tears. He rubbed his eyes with the palm of one hand.

'And it wasn't any accident that you both landed up on this job, was it? You planned it, didn't you?'

Joe nodded, all pretence gone. 'That's right. Mandy had unfinished business to take care of here, but she was so broke she could hardly afford to eat, never mind buy the plane ticket. And she wouldn't let me give her the money. So when we heard about Malcolm Laurie we came up with this idea. I had a word with Benny Upperton. I shot that film for him that got a bunch of awards so he was willing to listen and I suggested this documentary. Then I said he had to hire Mandy as well. So that's what happened. We thought if you knew about us being friends you wouldn't give her the job.'

I waited, but he said no more. 'Was the unfinished business anything to do with Sharon?' I finally asked quietly.

Joe shook his head emphatically. 'No! Absolutely no! Mandy didn't even know Sharon existed till she got here.' Then, fixing me with a look of desperate intensity, as if willing me to believe him, he added, 'Mandy's pretty flaky a lot of the time, I know, but that's to do with the life she's had. You haven't had a chance to really get to know her, but she's a good person at heart. She could never kill anybody.'

'The evidence is looking pretty bad.'

Again he shook his head forcefully. 'I don't care how much evidence they stack up, it's wrong! Mandy didn't kill that woman.' He turned to me with a look of anguish. 'Lois says she could get forty years. Christ!' He seemed lost for words.

I took a deep breath. 'Where did you go to on those late-night jaunts of yours?'

For a second, Joe looked at me with a mixture of shock and alarm, then the shutter came down. 'That's private,' he said stonily. 'And it has nothing whatsoever to do with the murder.'

I stared at him for a moment, but I could see he would tell me no more. 'OK,' I conceded, then leaning forward I added, 'Listen, Amanda's allowed a visitor on Monday morning. I was going to go, but perhaps you'd rather speak to her.'

Joe shook his head. 'It would tear me up, seeing her in jail. You go. I've spoken to her on the phone a few times. She can call me whenever she likes. Oh . . .' He fumbled in the pockets of his jeans and produced several twenty dollar bills. 'Would you take this? If you hand it over at the jail, they'll put it in an account for her so she can buy toothpaste and stuff and make phone calls. She doesn't have a bean.'

I nodded, stowing the money carefully in the back pocket of my wallet. 'That reminds me, did she say if they've allowed bail?'

A sour look came over Joe's face. 'Oh yes, they've set bail,' he said, a sharp edge of bitterness cutting through his words. 'Half a million dollars. She can get a bondsman to put up the money if she can hand over ten per cent to him, cash. That's fifty thou. She doesn't have 50p.' He shrugged. 'I offered to see if I could raise what she needs, but she wouldn't hear of it. They might as well have not given her bail at all.'

Without another word, he rose unsteadily to his feet, and left the room.

Chapter Ten

The next day was a Sunday, and since most of the people we might have wanted to interview were unavailable, and offices and libraries were shut, I had decided we would have some time off. I stayed in bed till mid morning, sunk in the oblivion of sleep. We had been working hard and the events of the past few days had taken their toll, so we had made no firm plans about how to spend the day, tacitly agreeing that we would see how we felt.

I had just drifted luxuriously to semi-consciousness and was trying to summon the energy to call room service and order coffee when the phone rang. Reaching for the receiver, I mumbled, 'Hello.'

There was a brief pause before a male voice asked, 'May I speak with Bel Carson, please?'

'You're speaking to her,' I answered, wondering who on earth this could be. The voice was vaguely familiar.

'Hi! This is Carl Scott. Remember me?'

'Of course,' I said, propping myself up on the pillows. A thought struck me. 'How did you know where to find me?'

'Oh, I hired a private detective,' he replied nonchalantly.

For a split second, I believed him.

But in response to my shocked silence he added hurriedly, 'No, not really. I phoned Beth and asked her.'

'Oh.' I was lost for words.

'Look –' there was an edge of nervousness in his voice now – 'I was wondering . . . I don't know if you guys work Sundays or what but this is my first weekend off in a month and I'd like to invite you to meet me for brunch.'

'Oh,' I said again. I tried desperately to think fast, but I was still groggy with sleep. I really couldn't come up with a good reason not to accept. 'OK.' I knew I sounded uncertain. 'What time?'

'Wonderful!' he replied enthusiastically. 'Tell you what. How about I pick you up at the front entrance to your hotel in about an hour.'

'Fine.' I was beginning to warm to this idea.

'Great. I'll look forward to it. Bye.' He rang off.

I dialled Mags's number. She sounded bright and alert when she answered. Years of getting up at dawn with her children means that she never seems to sleep late.

'I'm going out for a while,' I said, trying to sound casual. 'I'm meeting someone for lunch. I should be back by mid afternoon, but I'd appreciate it if you would check on Amanda for me.'

'Who are you meeting?' Mags asked curiously. It's one of the disadvantages of having journalists as friends. They never stop asking questions and they home in at once on anything you're trying to gloss over.

'Oh . . . just someone I spoke to at Beth's party,' I murmured vaguely.

'Not that tall man with the curly hair?'

'How the hell do you know that?' I spluttered.

I could hear her laughing. 'I was watching you. He looks very nice. It's about time,' she finished in her best maternal tone of voice.

'About time for what? I'm only going out for eggs and bacon. It's not the grand passion of the month,' I countered.

'Oh, give me a break! And wear that blue linen dress you've

got. The hotel will press it for you in a hurry if you kick up enough fuss.'

'I'll wear what I like.'

'See you later. I want a full account.' Mags was still laughing as she hung up.

In spite of what I'd said, I did telephone reception and cajole them into sending one of the maids up to fetch my linen dress. By the time I was showered and had dried my hair, it had been returned, freshly ironed.

Feeling absurdly self-conscious, I went down to reception, where I spotted Carl, wearing a pale blue oxford shirt and khaki slacks, sprawled in a chair reading a newspaper. He greeted me with a happy smile before leading the way out to his car. I felt a rush of joy when I saw that it was a convertible. I had missed my TR6 more than I'd realised and although this was some modern American model, the thought of driving with the wind in my hair again made me ecstatic.

Before we had even left the parking lot, all the stresses and worries of the past days had been swept away. We drove along sunny streets to a restaurant with an open air courtyard shaded by leafy trees. It was crowded with chattering groups of people, all immaculately groomed, but dressed casually in shorts and a variety of T-shirts or flowing summer dresses.

After a short wait, the maitre d' found us a table and we ordered a substantial brunch. When the food arrived, I realised I was starving and I ate hungrily. But after the plates had been cleared and we were left to drink our coffee, there was an awkward silence.

Up until that point, we had been distracted by things around us. On the way here we had talked about Carl's car and the weather, then discussed where to eat. Since our arrival, our attention had been taken up with finding a table, ordering our meal, commenting on the restaurant and finally eating brunch. Now we were confronted with each other.

But the silence lasted only moments. Carl, I was to discover, was indefatigably curious and he seemed to be fascinated by the work I did, plying me with questions. I was slightly taken aback. I love my job, but it's what I get up and do every day and I am always surprised that others should think it glamorous or exciting. Moreover, I wasn't used to talking much about my own life. But I found myself responding with easy familiarity, telling Carl about RTV, and my home in Britain, even about Jamie and my foster sister, Rosa. The one topic we did not discuss was Amanda and I appreciated Carl's thoughtfulness in not mentioning such a distressing subject.

Instead, he listened intently to all I had to say. Then he described his job in the emergency room of a busy city hospital. He, too, loved his work, although he often put in punishingly long hours.

'I've been on nights for the past two months,' he groaned. 'That's a killer. And your social life takes a dive, believe me!' He had been married briefly, he told me, when he was a medical student. His wife had got tired of never seeing him and he'd come home one day to find a note saying she'd gone. Since then, he'd had one serious relationship, but that had ended six months before.

The restaurant had almost emptied. I glanced at my watch. Incredibly, it was four o'clock.

'I must get back,' I said regretfully. 'I'm travelling to western Kansas tomorrow to check out one of our locations and I have several things to do before I leave.'

Carl tossed some money on top of the bill on a small plate and rose to his feet. 'Can I see you again?' he asked as we walked back to his car.

'That would be lovely,' I replied. 'I just can't say when because I don't know exactly what my schedule will be like. It never runs according to plan anyway.'

'OK,' he agreed easily. 'Why don't I give you a call in a

couple of days' time when you get back from your trip out west?' And with that settled between us, we drove back to the hotel, where he dropped me off.

Mags, predictably, was full of curiosity about my meeting with Carl. But not even she could worm very much information out of me, beyond the comment that it had been surprisingly easy and relaxed and that I'd had a wonderful time. In fact, I realised that spending the afternoon with Carl was the best thing I could have done, because I felt ready to face all the problems confronting me with renewed vigour and equanimity.

Mags had spent the day reading by the pool. Joe had disappeared on some venture of his own, leaving a note to say he wouldn't be back till later that evening. There was no news of Amanda.

'D'you think you'll manage OK while I'm gone?' I asked anxiously, when Mags had finished her account of the day.

'Oh, sure.' She was dismissive. 'I can always call you or Martin if anything unexpected crops up.'

We spent the early part of the evening going over our plans for the week. Then we went down to the dining room for a light supper before retiring for the night.

'But it wasn't me!' I could see the vehemence in Amanda's expression behind the thick glass wall between us, but her voice coming through the screened metal grille was thin and reedy, reduced to something less than human. It seemed to make a mockery of her anguish.

I glanced round me self-consciously. It was nine o'clock the following morning and I was seated in the visiting room of the Johnson County Detention Center. A row of three plastic chairs, separated from each other by transparent partitions, faced a glass wall, on the other side of which were the prisoners, seated on metal stools bolted to the floor.

It felt very exposed. All around us were glass walls. Beyond the area in which Amanda sat, I could see a guard watching us from a window of one of the control rooms. I was also uncomfortably aware of the camera high on the wall to my right. I realised with a shock how much I took my privacy for granted – and how violated and vulnerable I felt when it was taken away like this.

I leaned forward, closer to the window. Scratches on the painted frame showed where thousands of visitors had pressed against the glass before me.

'But Patsy McFee saw you running away! She recognised you. You had on the dress she made – something unique, that no one else has!' I said, equally emphatic. For a moment Amanda slumped, apparently overwhelmed.

She looked dreadful. There were shadows under her eyes and she appeared to have lost weight, although it was hard to be sure since she wore the prison uniform of baggy neon orange slacks and loose top. Even her hair seemed to have dulled and the delicate pallor of her complexion had shifted to a greyish green. But it was the expression on her face that disturbed me most – as if the whole facade of the adult I knew had crumbled, exposing a terrified, bewildered child. She seemed diminished and dehumanised, beyond reach behind these glass barriers, even her voice unable to get through clearly.

Perhaps sensing that, she put one hand up to the window, trying to make contact, and her words sounded faint through the metal grille. 'She must have been wearing a dress *like* mine, but it couldn't have been the one I had on that night because mine was in shreds.' She gazed at me with an agonised expression.

'Didn't Lois explain?' she went on. 'I walked out on Harlan after years of abuse. I was terrified of him but he lured me back to the house that night by promising to return some of my personal things, photographs of my mother, plus her wedding ring and a locket with a picture of me as a baby that she wore all the time. It was all I had left of her. It wasn't even valuable but he kept it because he knew it meant so much to me.'

Amanda swallowed, as if the effort to project her voice, to try to convince me through this wall of glass that she was speaking the truth, was almost too much for her. But she began again.

'When I arrived in Kansas City I phoned him up but he said he'd burnt the photographs and sold the jewellery. I was frantic. I couldn't believe he'd do such a thing. I phoned him again the next night and the next. He was playing with me, I knew that. The only way to deal with it was to walk away.' She paused, looking at me piteously. 'But I couldn't do that. Then I finally got him to admit that he did still have them. But he would only hand them over in person.'

She sighed, an eerie sound that whispered through the metal grating between us. 'Once I was in the house, he locked the door and tried to rape me. My dress was ripped apart. I only got away because I hit him with a chunk of sculpture – he's got a collection of modern pieces and I think it was one of those. Then I climbed out of the window. But I was practically naked and I'd left my bag behind so I hid in the woods at the back of the house. Just before dawn, I saw a man jogging. I called out to him and asked him to phone Joe. And he came and got me. That's when you saw us. I put my shoes and the rest of my clothes in a bag and chucked them in the river. That's the whole story.' She stopped and bowed her head, exhausted.

'Then who was this other woman?' I asked.

Amanda raised her head very slowly, as if lifting a great burden. 'I don't know. I can't explain it. I have no idea who killed Sharon.' She gestured with her hands for emphasis. 'I was *glad* he was in love with her because I thought it meant he might leave me alone. I didn't want to kill her.'

'But the waitress at the restaurant saw you tear up Sharon's photograph.'

A look of acute frustration flashed across Amanda's face. 'I can explain that! Harlan handed me that photograph on purpose. It was all part of the torture – not because it was Sharon,' she added quickly, 'but because she was wearing my mother's ring and her locket. She had them at Beth's party, too. The things I treasured most in the world. The things I yearned to have that he wouldn't give back to me. And this woman was wearing them as if they were trinkets.

'I lost my temper and ripped the picture up and said something about her keeping her hands off other people's property – something like that. But it was *Harlan* I was angry with really. Not her. I knew she probably didn't understand how important they were. She may not even have known they belonged to me.'

'Time's up.' I hadn't even heard the Sheriff's officer enter the room.

I turned back quickly to face Amanda on the other side of the glass wall. 'Don't lose hope,' I said urgently. 'You've got Lois and all of us rooting for you. You'll be out soon.'

Amanda smiled wanly and put a hand up to the glass again. It was as if she craved contact with another human being. I placed my hand opposite hers. Such an agonised look came over her face that I thought she would burst into tears. Instead, she rose unsteadily to her feet. I watched her follow the other prisoners out of the visiting area, shuffling in her black, prison issue canvas slippers. She looked very frail. It occurred to me that, whether or not she was guilty, if we didn't get her out of here quickly, it might soon be too late.

I was in a subdued mood when I returned to the hotel, where I found Beth waiting for me with Mags. In order not to

150

waste precious filming time, I had arranged with Joe over breakfast that he and the others would go on ahead and start taking general shots of the countryside in western Kansas and then hang around Rapid Falls, trying to capture the flavour of small town life. It was hardly an ideal way to direct a documentary, but it was the only hope I had of juggling my professional duties with trying to help Amanda. It would have been impossible without Joe's whole-hearted support, but he understood what I was trying to do.

Fortunately, Lola's interest in filming us at work had not extended to making a trip out to western Kansas. That, she had explained to me in lowered tones which her mother could not hear, would be B-O-R-I-N-G.

In spite of my offer to share the driving, Beth was insistent that she take the wheel, so I settled back in the soft luxurious seat, preparing myself for the long journey ahead. During the first couple of hours I said very little. My mind was on Amanda. I had called Lois as soon as I had wakened to report on my efforts of the previous day.

She had groaned when I described what Patsy McFee had seen.

'How credible is she?' she demanded as soon as I finished.

'Very,' I replied succinctly. 'I'd believe her if I was on the jury.'

'That's all I need,' she muttered softly. Then, speaking more loudly, she added, 'I was hoping I could argue that what happened in the restaurant is inconclusive, and plant reasonable doubt in the prosecutor's mind – and the jury's too if it comes to that – that someone else could have entered the house after Amanda left and murdered Sharon. But you're telling me they have a credible witness who can put Amanda at the scene at the time of death, behaving in a suspicious manner and covered in blood.' She sighed. 'That will be hard.'

Lying back in the passenger seat, I struggled with the

problem of Patsy's testimony. There were only two possible explanations – either Amanda was lying, or Patsy saw someone else who looked like Amanda. But that seemed so improbable. Setting aside the question of how she got hold of a dress like Amanda's, how could another woman with the same red hair, in identical clothes, just happen to run down the drive at that moment? There were too many coincidences.

Not for the first time, it crossed my mind that Amanda might in fact be guilty, but that she might be suffering from some form of hysterical amnesia. It was easy to imagine anyone – never mind someone with a history of mental instability – denying their guilt in the face of a threatened forty year incarceration.

I shifted restlessly in my seat, my eyes closed behind my sunglasses, and tackled the questions raised by the possibility that it had been another woman Patsy had seen. What about the dress? It was handmade – so it was possible that a second one could have been made just like it, if the same fabric and pattern were available – but that was a big 'if'. For that to be true, it had to be someone who knew Amanda and had seen the dress before. Could Sharon have had one like it? Or was it possible that Harlan had had an identical present made by another seamstress to give someone else – perhaps another mistress?

We cruised relentlessly westward past scenery that seemed never to vary. Grasslands rolled away as far as the eye could see, interspersed only with a few arthritic trees or bushes wherever there was a creek or a small pond.

I turned to Beth. 'Did Harlan have any other girlfriends apart from Sharon that you know of?'

'Harlan has always had other girlfriends,' she said drily. 'You'd have to be a bit more specific than that. D'you mean girlfriends when he was living with Amanda or while he was with Sharon? I don't know much about his personal life the last few years, but I have heard the gossip.'

'Girlfriends with red hair.'

'Aaah.' Beth took a deep intake of breath. 'Now you're talking. Harlan has a thing for redheads – doesn't matter what they look like, he homes straight in on them. Of course, the only ones that last longer than a one-night stand are the beauties like Amanda and Sharon. But I couldn't tell you how many he's had – or still has, for that matter.'

Another dead end. I gazed out of the window at the grey-green of ripening fields of wheat flashing by.

'Of course,' Beth continued, 'Kelly was the first. It all started with her.'

My head snapped round. 'Kelly? Who is Kelly?'

Beth glanced sideways in my direction. 'Didn't Amanda ever mention her? No?' She shook her head in disbelief. 'Well, maybe she didn't know, of course. Harlan might not have told her about Kelly.'

'Well, who is she?' I could hardly contain my impatience.

'Kelly was Harlan's first great love. She grew up near Rapid Falls and they went to the same high school, only she was a coupla years younger than him. Everybody knew they were sweet on each other but they fought like cat and dog. She was real tempestuous, you might say, and Harlan had a pretty explosive temper, so there was always some drama going on between them. Harlan went off to college but they still saw each other during the vacations.

'Then one summer, the same summer that Marlene met Malcolm, they had a falling out and Harlan broke it off. That had happened so often before, but this time, for some reason, Kelly took it to heart. That night she drove her car into the old quarry at the edge of our property and drowned.'

Beth shook her head at the memory. 'She was an only child. Her mother nearly went mad with grief. In fact, I'd say she's never really recovered.' Beth glanced in the rear-view mirror.

'After that, Harlan always seemed to go for the redheads.'

'Funny way to commemorate someone, dating people who look like her,' I commented drily. I thought for a moment. 'And it was definitely suicide? No suggestion that Harlan killed her?'

Beth hesitated. 'We-ell. That's what the coroner's verdict said. I mean, Harlan had an alibi and all. I think it was pretty conclusive. Of course, her mother sees it different, but like I said, she's a little crazy and, anyway, parents always find it hard to accept their child was suicidal but they didn't notice, don't they?' She turned to look at me questioningly.

'Two redheaded girlfriends who die tragically,' I mused. 'The only link between them is Harlan. Seems a bit of a coincidence to me.'

Beth was dubious. 'Well, I don't know about that. I think you'd have a hard time proving Kelly's death was anything but an accident. But I could take you to see her mother if you like, so you can find out for yourself.'

'That sounds like a great idea.' I reached for my mobile phone and called Joe. He, Evan and Lewis had just arrived in Rapid Falls and were having lunch. I explained what I wanted to do and why.

'Go right ahead. I can cope with this, no problem,' he assured me.

Janine Swartz lived in a small wooden frame house a few miles outside Rapid Falls. Steps leading to the porch stretched across the front and as we drove up to the lone farmhouse, the door was opened and a shadowy figure appeared behind the screen. It swung outwards when we began to ascend the stairs, revealing a tall, thin, wan woman with greying brown hair – it might once have been chestnut – wearing a short-sleeved blouse in pastel blue with maroon checked Bermuda shorts.

'I just fixed some ice tea if you'd like some,' she offered when

Beth had introduced me. Her welcome, though cordial and polite, was half-hearted. She moved listlessly.

'A widow woman with nothing to do but brood' was how Beth had described her. The light of her life had gone out, you could see that.

There was a little desultory conversation, which Beth gamely tried to keep going. When it sputtered out, there was a moment's silence. Beth cleared her throat.

'Janine, we are here for a purpose, as you may have guessed.'

Janine gazed at us through bottle-glass spectacles.

'Bel, here, wanted to talk about Kelly. Now I know it must be a real painful subject, but it could help a good friend of hers.'

There was no response.

'Janine,' I began, 'I work with Harlan's estranged wife, Amanda. She has been accused . . .'

Abruptly, Janine leaned forward to place her glass on the coffee table in front of her. 'I read all about that. Another redhead. Just like Kelly.' Then, as if someone had thrown a switch sending a vibrant current through her body, she straightened up and began speaking with sudden vehemence.

'When I heard about that girl, I thought, so he's murdered another one. Kelly didn't kill herself. She was a beautiful girl. She had everything to live for. Except for that Harlan. That's why she died. And when I read about that other girl, I thought to myself, well, this time he's killing two birds with one stone. He's probably murdered the one and the other will hang for it.'

I tried to keep my voice neutral, wary of doing anything that might provoke this disturbed woman to lose her composure completely. 'What makes you so sure that Kelly didn't kill herself?'

'Because I know my daughter. And I know Harlan. There was one night she came home after I had gone to bed. I was still awake, listening for her, and I went through to her room

155

just to make sure she was settled for the night and everything was OK. She had taken off her T-shirt and she had bruises on her arms and shoulders. Big bruises. They looked real bad and I asked her how she got them, if she'd been in an accident or something, and she just got furious and wouldn't tell me anything. But I'm sure it was him. He had a reputation for being such a violent child when he was in grade school. You can't tell me he changed all of a sudden when he grew up.'

I was silent for a moment, digesting this. An image of Amanda's bruises rose before me, and I recalled Lois's account of Harlan's violence. I leaned forward. 'Was there anything else? Anything that points to her being killed?'

Janine visibly withdrew into herself as if perhaps she expected derision. 'I don't have proof of murder if that's what you're asking, It's just something I know, that's all. They kept going on and on about the suicide note.' She paused, noticing my puzzled expression. 'You know about that, don't you?'

I shook my head.

'Well, at first the Sheriff kept saying she might have gone on a trip or be staying with friends or something and she just hadn't told me. But I knew that wasn't right. She always let me know where she was because she knew I got real upset if she didn't show up and I was expecting her.' Janine removed her glasses, revealing round myopic grey eyes, and began to polish the lenses.

'I couldn't persuade them to do a thorough search just at once – they wanted to wait and see if she called or showed up the next day. And then Harlan says he found this note that had been pushed under his door only he didn't come across it till he came home the next morning. It was in Kelly's handwriting all right, and it said she couldn't bear to live without him. If he didn't come back to her she'd kill herself.'

Janine's hands were shaking slightly as she replaced her glasses, but otherwise there was no sign of emotion, only her deadpan expression and flat voice. 'The thing is, Kelly was a real drama queen. And they was always breaking up and making up. Always. There was no date on that note. She could have written it any time.' Janine sighed and looked down at her hands, twisted together in her lap. 'But the Sheriff chose to believe it. They started the search and finally dragged the water in the quarry. When they found her they just assumed it was a suicide.'

She rose to her feet wearily. 'Would you like to see Kelly's room?'

In silence, we followed her upstairs to a small, dark landing with three doors set at intervals along its length. To our right, a window built into the gable cast a hazy light through the blinds pulled low to the sill. A green, leafy plant brooded on a small table before it. There were a few moments of complete stillness. Janine had paused before the door immediately ahead of us, as if bracing herself. Then she opened it and walked into the room beyond.

'This is exactly the way it was the day she died,' she said in hushed tones. 'I wouldn't let the Sheriff move a thing.' She stepped over to one of the windows and touched the blind so that it snapped open and the room sprang alive with light. 'I keep the blinds drawn so nothing gets faded,' she explained.

But in spite of her efforts, the room *had* faded. Life had gone. The colours were no longer vibrant, the fabric at the windows and covering the bed was limp with age. I walked into the centre of the room and looked around. Several pictures adorned the walls, of shepherdesses and cute doggies and a Snoopy cartoon. I was struck by how excessively neat and orderly everything was, not like the room of a normal teenager. It was also very feminine, with frilled lace curtains covering the windows, a ruched bedspread and a dressing table draped with matching fabric.

A red satin heart with 'I love you' embroidered across it

hung from the mirror and a few bottles of cheap perfume were arranged on the glass top. There were also a number of framed photographs. I bent forward to peer at them. There was a snapshot of four young people in fancy dress costume. In spite of the fake moustaches and brazen make-up, I could identify Harlan and Pete, plus one girl dressed like an Indian in a black wig and another wearing a long tutu. The latter had flowing red hair and I guessed it must be Kelly. This was confirmed when I turned to the second, much larger photograph. It was a studio portrait of the same young woman. She was strikingly attractive, with vivid blue-green eyes, her golden-red tresses brushed over her shoulders and with the soft innocent look of a child.

'That's Kelly,' Janine said softly. Then, as if reading my thoughts, 'She was so young, so very young to have died.' I turned and put my arm round the older woman's shoulders, squeezing gently. She reached forward and picked up the last remaining picture frame. It contained a Polaroid photograph, showing Kelly in a sleeveless top and wearing a pair of sunglasses with winged frames covered in glitter.

'That was the last picture taken of her,' Janine said sadly. 'She'd just got those sunglasses – she had them made specially for her by some fellow over by Rensville and she wanted a photograph to see what they looked like on her.' She paused for a moment, then added, 'That was taken the day she died. I never saw those glasses again. I guess they're at the bottom of the old quarry.'

She moved away from me to replace the photograph while I glanced around the rest of the room. But there were no clues to how Kelly died or why she might have committed suicide.

After a few minutes, Janine opened what looked like a cupboard door on the left, revealing a small bathroom which linked to another bedroom beyond.

'No one except me ever comes up here. I sleep downstairs

and I have my own three-quarter bath next to my room. If I have guests they sleep through there –' she nodded in the direction of the bedroom on the other side of the bathroom – 'but I always make them use the shower and toilet downstairs. I would never let anyone use Kelly's bathroom.'

'Would you mind if I looked around?' I paused, waiting for permission.

Janine eyed me up and down for a moment, then reluctantly nodded assent. She stepped forward and opened the small white painted cupboard above the washbasin. 'Don't touch anything!' she warned.

The cabinet contained bottles of hair conditioner and skin creams, lipsticks, an unopened package containing a tooth-brush, a pair of contact lenses still soaking in solution and a bottle of tablets. I noticed that the lenses were a deep aqua-marine colour, which perhaps explained the brilliant blue-green eyes I had admired in Kelly's portrait. Without thinking, I reached for the bottle and then paused, my hand in mid-air.

'May I?'

But Janine shook her head. 'Those are aspirin,' she said listlessly. 'The Sheriff already checked.' She closed the cabinet and led the way back downstairs. Halfway down, she paused to turn and look up beseechingly at us. 'You don't think she killed herself, do you?'

'Of course not, Janine.' Beth spoke in soft, comforting tones. 'Of course not. Nobody that knew Kelly ever believed that suicide story.'

We had reached the porch. After subdued goodbyes, we got back into the Lincoln and drove off down the dusty road. Turning round to wave, I saw Janine still standing on the porch, a lonely figure.

'There but for the grace of God . . .' muttered Beth, glancing in her rear-view mirror. 'I don't know but what I wouldn't go crazy myself if something like that happened to Lola.'

We drove back along the dirt track, then turned right on to the tarred road, heading towards town.

'What about Harlan's alibi?' I asked. 'How solid was that?'

'Pretty solid.' Beth made an emphatic move with her head, then glanced across at me. 'But we can go check it out for ourselves, if you like. As I recall, Harlan was in a poker game that night with some of the boys in town. Jake Rasmussen was bound to have been one of 'em and I surely know where we can find him.'

We had reached the outskirts of Rapid Falls, passing the sign riddled with bullet holes which was apparently used for target practice and which said in plain lettering, 'Welcome to Rapid Falls, 487 residents. Please drive carefully.'

The township was strung out along one main road, with a few side roads, many of them dirt tracks, crossing it at right angles. An assortment of houses was hidden amongst low trees on spacious plots of ground, sheltered from the baking sun.

Main Street itself was virtually empty of traffic and the stores looked closed, because the doors had to be kept shut to preserve the coolness of the air conditioning. Occasionally a pickup truck would trundle slowly past, eliciting a wave of recognition for the driver from the one or two pedestrians. Beth drove slowly along the three blocks of the town centre, finally parking her big Lincoln outside the police station with the nose pointing into the kerb at an angle.

She led the way across the street towards a low building covered with cream stucco, inset with rough timbers in a vaguely Tudor style. There was a Budweiser sign in the window and a big hoarding attached to the roof announcing that this was 'Jake's Beer Garden'.

The sudden dark and the shocking coldness of the interior stunned me and it took a moment to get my bearings. There was a smell of stale beer. As my eyes adjusted to the gloom, I realised we were in a very utilitarian bar room. The wooden floors underfoot were clean but pitted and uneven. Around the walls were several booths made out of dark, stained wood, the banquettes upholstered in dark red plastic. Several of these were torn and had been mended with black sticky tape. Overhead, a ceiling fan whirred and I could make out a long wooden bar stretching the length of one wall to the right. A youngish man was leaning against the far end, watching us with interest.

The bartender, a big man with muscular shoulders and powerful arms, slowly made his way towards us, drawing a rag along the top of the counter. He looked about forty, with receding hair and a weatherbeaten face, obscured by round horn-rimmed glasses, and he wore a rumpled white T-shirt and worn blue jeans.

'Hi,' he said without enthusiasm. 'What can I git you ladies?' He swiped his cloth across the bar in a circular motion, leaving a damp trail.

Beth looked coy. 'Why, Jake Rasmussen! Don't you know who this is?' Her accent had suddenly taken on the local twang.

Jake leaned a little closer, peering at both of us, frowning, then suddenly he broke into a wide grin and slapped the cloth he was carrying on the counter with a loud crack. 'Damn! Beth! You had the light behind you and I just thought you was some real smart lady from outta town.'

'Well, you were right about one of us. This here's a friend of mine from England. Her name's Bel Carson. Bel, this is one of my oldest friends. We've known each other since before we could even talk. Of course, ever since we learned to speak we haven't been such good friends.' She cast a sly glance at Jake who was looking equally flirtatious.

'What can I git for you? This is on the house.'

Beth was beaming. 'Oh, I guess I'll have some of that

161

terrible beer you serve out here.' She turned to me. 'Why don't you try one too, Bel?'

I nodded agreement and Jake pulled three glasses of pale liquid.

'Terrible stuff.' Beth had taken a good swig of hers and now she replaced her glass on the bar. 'Jake. My friend here is investigating the death of Kelly Swartz for British television and she wanted to ask you a coupla questions.' Jake looked suitably impressed. 'You were with Harlan that night, if I recall, isn't that so?'

Jake stretched out one leg and hooked it round a stool, drawing it closer so he could perch on it. He leaned forward, his beer in one hand. 'That is correct, Ma'am. I will always be real sorry that I provided that bastard son of a bitch with an alibi, but I did. We were playing poker like we always did on a Tuesday. The game started around six thirty. Harlan showed up just as we were getting going and he was with us till it ended about six the next morning.'

I frowned. 'Was it usual for him to play with you?'

Jake shook his head emphatically, swallowing a mouthful of beer. 'No sirree, it was not. That was the one thing that I always thought was suspicious – that and the fact the game lasted all night. Harlan had played with us maybe a coupla times before. But this night he showed up outta the blue.' Jake snorted angrily. 'And he kept winning. Now I have *never* trusted that sonofabitch and even at the time I figured he must be cheating but if he was he was damn good because I couldn't figure out how he was doing it.' He made a sharp sideways movement with his head and took a sip of his beer, wiping the froth from around his mouth with a big hairy hand.

'So anyways, since he was winning, he had everyone's money.' Jake jerked a thumb over his shoulder in the direction of the street outside. 'John Bartholomew had lost his entire week's wages. He *had* to stay and try to get some of it back or Kay-Lyn would have crucified him. And none of the rest of us wanted to lose all our dough so we kept on playing. On a normal night we would break up around midnight. But that time, we played till after dawn. All because of Harlan. I always thought that was real suspicious because it meant he had the perfect alibi.'

I mulled this over for several moments. 'Did he leave the room during that time at all, even for a few minutes?'

Jake's expression was wry. 'No way. He had all the money. We wouldn't have let him outta our sight.'

I was beginning to feel desperate. 'What about going to the loo – I mean the john. Wouldn't he have at least left the room for that?'

Jake smiled sympathetically. 'Nope. I don't wish to shock you ladies but we all just took a leak out the back door.'

I sighed. 'So his alibi really is rock solid.'

Jake nodded sadly. 'I wish it wasn't but it is. Whatever else he was up to the rest of the time, he was certainly with us that night. Believe me, if I could drop that guy in it, I would. Another one?' He looked at Beth, indicating her empty glass.

She picked it up and surveyed it, turning it in the light. 'Well, since you insist. But Jake, honey –' she leaned across the bar to speak confidentially – 'could I have a shot of bourbon this time? I'm not really a beer drinker.'

Jake laughed and turned with a questioning look to me. I shook my head as I slid off my bar stool. 'No, thanks.' I laid a restraining hand on Beth's shoulder as she, too, moved to get up. 'It's OK. You stay here. I'm going to go across the road to the police station and see if they'll let me look at any of the records on Kelly's death.'

Beth settled back on to her stool. 'OK, hon. But it's the Sheriff's department you need to see 'cos they deal with anything that happens out of town.' She waved me on as I paused uncertainly. 'It's OK. This place is so po-dunk that the police and the Sheriff are all under the same roof and they're real good friends. If they give you any trouble, you come let us know, but I don't think they will.'

The police station was a plain, low, yellow brick building with a short flight of steps leading to the entrance. The windows had wire mesh screens on them which kept out much of the sunlight so it seemed gloomy as I stepped inside. I found myself in a dingy waiting area, with dull, fake wood panelling on the walls, metal chairs with green plastic seats and a low pine coffee table adorned with a few curling magazines and a vase of plastic flowers.

'Can I help you, Ma'am?' A young woman, her make-up carefully applied and her blonde hair lacquered into an upswept style, addressed me from the other side of a glass partition.

'Yes.' I approached her with my most winning smile. 'I wondered if I could look at your file on a suicide that occurred just out of town about fifteen years ago?'

A wary look came over the young woman's face. 'If you'd just take a seat, I'll go ask the Sheriff.' I watched as she retreated to her desk and talked to someone on the telephone, swivelling round to look at me as she spoke.

I paced around the foyer, examining the Wanted posters tacked to the walls. There was the sound of a latch being released and a door to my right opened. A thin, angular woman in her fifties or sixties stood on the threshold. She wore bright pink and apricot striped slacks with a matching top. In the centre of her chest was an elaborate gold star and there was a heavy leather belt supporting a gun in a holster slung round her hips. Her hair was greying and tightly curled about the weatherbeaten face. Keeping the door ajar with her foot, she stretched out a hand.

'Howdy. I'm Sheriff Nita Barings. Who might you be?'

Briefly, I introduced myself and repeated my request. Her sharp, birdlike eyes watched me intently. 'I'm a friend of Beth McGregor's,' I added.

The lined face broke into a wide smile. 'Well, any friend of Beth's is a friend of mine. Come this way.' She moved aside to let me pass, still with her foot braced against the heavy door. It clanged shut and she led the way down a long corridor, panelled in the same dark fake wood as the waiting room, to an office at the far end. I could see the bright sunshine outside, but in here the light was dull, the windows shaded by battered Venetian blinds which were probably once cream coloured but were now turning brown.

I glanced round as Nita squeezed behind her desk. The cream walls were dominated by a large tinted photograph of a heavy-set middle-aged man wearing a dark blue uniform and a gold badge like Nita's.

'That's my husband, Jim,' commented Nita, noticing my interest. 'He used to be Sheriff till he was killed in a car wreck about twenty years ago. The townspeople voted me into the job after that – sort of a widow woman's pension.' She hooted with laughter, a surprising sound that reminded me of a flock of wild geese honking. Abruptly she stopped. 'Now you said you were interested in some suicide or other. Who would that be?'

'I'd like to see your records on Kelly Swartz.'

Nita cocked her head. 'First time I've had *that* request.'

'Beth said she'd vouch for me,' I coaxed.

Nita nodded slowly. 'Now why on earth would you be interested in that?'

'Oh,' I improvised, 'I work for a television company in the UK and we're always on the lookout for good stories.'

Nita considered for a moment then smiled. 'Oh, well. I guess it won't do no harm, especially since you're so well-connected.' She showed me into a small office along the hall

165

from her own, and went to fetch the files.

'The Swartz case,' she announced a few minutes later as she steered a small trolley loaded with dusty folders into the room. 'If you can come up with any answers from that lot we'd be real grateful! Don't be surprised if you come across a few mouse droppings. I don't suppose anyone's looked at those for years.' She closed the door and left me to it.

I sat in the dim light, far removed from the outside world. Occasionally I would hear cars or trucks drive by slowly. No one seemed to be in much of a hurry around here. The baking sun seemed to paralyse everyone.

Leafing through the folders, I homed in on the coroner's summing up. He had concluded that Kelly had indeed committed suicide, citing Harlan's testimony that he had told her only that afternoon that their relationship was over. The note that Harlan had discovered the following day was quoted as further corroboration.

I set that page aside and riffled through the remaining files until I found what I wanted. The autopsy had been performed by Dr Peter Ottinger, Senior. It gave his age as sixty-three and his address was Rapid Falls, so I guessed he must be Pete's father. Presumably there was so little need for a full-time pathologist in this part of the world that the local doctor carried out any autopsies that were required.

The body had been in a pretty bad condition. Not only had it been immersed in the quarry water, but there were a number of injuries to the head and limbs. These were consistent with blows the body would have received as the car plummeted downwards and then hit the water – since Kelly had not been wearing a seatbelt. There was no evidence that she had consumed alcohol or drugs, either legal or illegal. Death was by drowning and the doctor estimated that it occurred between nine p.m. the night of her disappearance and two a.m. the following morning. Kelly's watch had stopped at 9.37 p.m.

I turned to Harlan's account of the events that afternoon. According to him, Pete had dropped him off at Kelly's around one o'clock and he had driven her to the quarry in her car. His own car was being repaired after an accident. He broke the news to Kelly that he wanted to end their relationship. When she became upset and told him to leave, he had walked back out to the highway and hitched a lift into town. He had eaten a hamburger at the diner then joined the poker game in the back room of the Beer Garden where he had stayed all night. The next morning he arrived home to find Kelly's suicide note and phoned her mother, then the Sheriff's office.

I leaned back in my seat and gazed at the empty street outside. It was all very plausible. I could understand why there had never been any suspicion that Harlan might have been more than an innocent bystander to the tragedy. I glanced at my watch. It was getting late.

Quickly, I leafed through some of the other witness statements. As far as I could tell, they were remarkably consistent in their versions of what they had seen that evening. At least five people – including Marlene McKinley, I noted with interest – had seen Kelly drive into the parking lot of the diner at about 8.30 p.m. It was already dusk but even so, they had easily recognised Kelly's white Mustang because it was custom painted with orange and red flames spreading out from the radiator across the bonnet.

Kelly was in the driver's seat. It was definitely her. Apart from anything else, none of the other girls in town had hair like that and all the witnesses at the diner noticed her new diamanté sunglasses because they sparkled when they caught the light. They were unique.

Only Marlene had a feeling that something was wrong, that maybe Kelly was upset about something. She was driving way too fast, swerving into the parking lot, skidding round in a tight U-turn, barely stopping before she roared off. Marlene had commented out loud to everyone that she thought Harlan and Kelly had had another of their bust-ups and that she was out looking for him. That was the last time Marlene had seen her friend.

I flicked over a few more statements, then stopped. The last one in the pile had been provided by Pete Ottinger. He had been mailing a letter when he spotted Kelly driving by the post office on her way out of town. His description echoed all the others, except for one small thing. According to Pete, Kelly had been wearing her old Ray-Bans.

It was a tiny detail, but it caught my attention. It could have been simply an error on his part, or perhaps Kelly had exchanged one pair for the other. But there was something strange about this whole business of the sunglasses and it bothered me.

The door behind me opened loudly, making me jump, and Beth walked in, accompanied by the Sheriff.

'Well, there you are,' she exclaimed. 'I was beginning to think you'd been arrested.'

Nita was grinning. 'Find anything worthwhile?' she asked.

'Not really. It's all pretty much as Beth said. There is one thing, though. All the witnesses agreed that Kelly was wearing sunglasses that evening. It seems a little odd.'

The two women looked at each other thoughtfully. 'Well,' Beth said finally, 'I suppose that's possible. If she'd come into town from her home or the old quarry she'd have been driving due west and that sun can go straight into your eyes when it's lying there on the horizon just before it sets. So she may have been wearing them for that and then not noticed she still had them on. Specially if she was upset and all.' She shrugged dismissively. 'But who knows? Kids are a law unto themselves. Maybe she'd been crying and didn't want anyone to see. Maybe she thought it was cool to wear them. Kelly was really into attracting attention with that automobile of hers and everything. It's anybody's guess.'

I rose to my feet, beginning to pile the manila folders back on to the trolley. The one I'd been reading last was still open at Dr Ottinger's report. I placed my hand on the open page. 'D'you think I could have a copy of this?'

'I don't see why not,' Nita agreed easily.

'And these as well?' I asked, indicating the six witness statements lying on the desk.

'No problem. Here, leave all that. I'll have someone come and take it back to the basement. We can have these Xeroxed on the way out.'

She led us down the hall towards the exit, pausing long enough in the outer office to run off my copies. Beth and I said our farewells and walked out on to the street. Instantly I noticed that the temperature had dropped. I looked around me. A thick wadding of clouds hung low over the town. It was unbroken except for a lurid bar of greenish light on the horizon.

I felt the uneasiness of the atmosphere. There was no wind and it was eerily silent – no dogs barking, no birds twittering in the trees. I shivered involuntarily.

Beth was looking around her appraisingly. 'Storm coming,' she commented in a tight voice. 'We should probably get back to the house.'

'A tornado?' I'd read the *Wizard of Oz*.

Beth squinted at the sky again, then shook her head. 'Naw. There's been no tornado warning issued. I think it's just a storm, but a real good one,' she added with feeling.

I glanced at my watch. It was after six. I dialled the number for Joe's mobile phone. He answered at once.

'Joe, it's me. Where are you?'

There was a chuckle. 'Well, you're not going to believe this but we're at the diner just about to have some supper. I know it must seem like we never left but we haven't spent the day eating, honest.'

I turned round as he spoke and looked up Main Street. I could see the crew van parked in front of the diner and I thought I could make out Joe and the others seated in the window.

'Has everything gone OK?'

'Absolutely fine. What do you want to do about tomorrow?'

'Look, can we meet you for breakfast at your motel? I still have some things I need to do tonight.'

'No problem. See you in the morning.' He rang off and I saw him wave to me from the window of the diner. The crew had been booked into the tiny local motel, but Beth had invited me to stay with her at the farm. I turned to her now.

'Can we drive by the old quarry on the way back?' I asked impulsively.

She looked dubious. 'Well. I suppose so. Just as long as the rain doesn't hit before we get there. Better hurry.'

There was almost no other traffic as we drove out of town, heading east on the two-lane highway. Suddenly Beth swung the car off the road again on to another dirt track winding through undulating scrubland dotted with a few spindly trees, stunted by the wind and huddled close to the ground. Even the short, coarse grass that stretched as far as the eye could see didn't seem to flourish in this climate. The path was deeply rutted, with large stones sticking out of the dried mud at intervals. I winced as they scraped along the bottom of the big Lincoln, but when I glanced at Beth she seemed unconcerned.

Suddenly the road veered left into some brushwood then curved steeply down and round until we emerged into a flat clearing of sun-baked mud. There were signs that the area was used for parties. Makeshift barbecues had been constructed out of stones and there were several beer and soft drink cans lying around.

Slowly, I got out of the car. Before me was a sheet of dark, sullen water, the surface choppy from the wind that had suddenly got up. Towering over it, ominous against the surging storm clouds, was a rocky cliff. The path we had come down followed the edge as it descended to the clearing. That was where Kelly had plunged to her death.

'This used to be the only place to swim for miles around till they built the pool in town,' Beth commented, coming up beside me. 'The kids still come out here because it's private. They have parties in summer and they can do their courting and parking here undisturbed.'

When I said nothing in response, she continued. 'It was never really a quarry, although I think they may have started to dig here originally for fence posts. They used to make those out of stone in these parts because there wasn't any wood to speak of. But the limestone layer for that was very thin and only a few feet below the surface so it wouldn't have been very deep.

'It was my daddy and my uncle who really dug it out to make this a sort of reservoir for the livestock. There's an underground spring that feeds it, so there's water here most all the time, even when there's a drought. It's shallow for quite a ways out, but it suddenly goes down real steep somewhere in the middle. They reckon that just beneath the cliff it could be forty feet deep or more.'

'Was that where her car went off?' I asked.

Beth nodded. 'It must have been. They found it right below there.'

I considered for a moment. 'Could she have missed the path when it veered to the left and gone over by accident? It was dark by that time of night, wasn't it?'

Beth shook her head slowly. 'I doubt it. Kelly knew this place from the time she was a little 'un. You can't drive fast on that road, as you probably noticed, without tearing up your vehicle and grinding to a stop. And all the use that track has gotten over the years has dug it into the ground pretty deep. So even if she couldn't see where she was going, she'd have felt her automobile going up over the edge of the bank and stopped before she ever reached the cliff.' There was a pause. 'Of course, she could've been drunk or something.'

'Not according to Doc Ottinger. His report said no drink or drugs. Ah well. Let's get back. This place gives me the creeps.' I turned to go and was hit by a sudden powerful gust of wind that seemed to come from nowhere and knocked me sideways. At almost the same instant, it started to rain, a fierce, battering downpour.

'Quick! Get back to the car!' yelled Beth, struggling to keep on her feet. Clutching each other, we reached the safety of the Lincoln and managed with difficulty to pry one of the doors open against the force of the wind and squeeze inside.

'My God! I've never seen anything like this!' I gasped. We were both soaking wet and shivering. Rain drummed against the car, sluicing down the windows so that it was almost impossible to see anything outside. The big vehicle was rocking violently from side to side with each roaring gust of wind. The noise was deafening.

Suddenly there was a long rolling crash of thunder followed by lightning which cracked overhead, tearing the sky in two and illuminating the old quarry in syncopated flashes. I cowered in my seat, too frightened to move or make a sound. I glanced at Beth. She had gone white and her jaw was tight, but she was sitting upright, arms resting on the steering wheel, looking out resolutely at the storm breaking around us.

I don't know how long it went on. It seemed for ever. But gradually the wind dropped and the car settled back on to its shock absorbers. I held my breath, waiting for another whiplash of lightning, but it didn't come. The rain was still pouring down the windows, but it was quieter now. I sighed with relief and turned to look at Beth. She smiled weakly.

'I'm glad that's over.'

'Was it a tornado?' I asked.

Beth laughed. 'No, no, no.' She started up the car and turned it round. 'If that had been a tornado, we wouldn't still be here, believe me. No.' She steered the Lincoln up the track towards the top of the cliff. 'That was just an ordinary Kansas storm. We get a lot of them here.'

I leaned back in the padded leather seat and let the tension flow out of my muscles. We had almost reached the ranch before I felt calm enough to think clearly. By visiting the old quarry I had hoped to find something in the terrain that would prove conclusively that Kelly couldn't have committed suicide. I hadn't done that. But the elemental violence of the scene we had just witnessed had made a deep impression on me. Somehow it merged with the image I had of Kelly's plunge into those sullen waters. Now I felt to the depths of my being that her death had been brutal and that she was still not laid to rest.

It was beginning to get dark when we reached the ranch house. Stepping inside was a shock as the cold air conditioning struck us. 'Time for cocktails,' Beth announced firmly, heading for the kitchen. There was the sound of the fridge door opening then closing with a resounding thud. Moments later she emerged from the kitchen with tall glasses of what looked like orange juice and handed one to me. 'Let's sit outside.'

She led the way through the kitchen to the screened-in porch at the rear of the house. The air smelt damp and musty and already the temperature was rising again. Perhaps we both felt drained by the storm, but for almost half an hour the only sound was the clinking of ice in our glasses. The orange juice had a strong taste of vodka in it.

I thought about Janine in that mausoleum of a house, each

day tending and preserving the relics of her daughter's life – the cheap nail polish, the snapshots, even her aspirin. Was that how she would spend the rest of her days, dusting the girlish mementoes on the dressing table, cleaning the unused bath? Did she renew the solution for the contact lenses, refill the atomiser of perfume when the contents evaporated?

I turned to Beth. 'Something just occurred to me. Can I call Janine?'

Beth looked puzzled but she nodded assent. 'Why sure, honey. There's a wall phone just inside the kitchen door. I think you'll find her number on the piece of paper tacked up beside it.'

I dumped my glass on the wooden floor of the porch and made my way back into the house. Janine was at home as I expected and didn't seem to be particularly surprised to hear from me.

'Janine,' I said tentatively, when our initial civilities were over, 'how bad was Kelly's eyesight?'

'How bad? Why she couldn't see a thing without her contacts or her glasses on – so pretty bad, I'd say. But she had the loveliest eyes,' Janine replied.

'And her sunglasses – were they prescription lenses?'

'No. She thought the ones you got from the optician were so old-fashioned. She always had Ray-Bans or those new diamanté ones I told you about. They were just ordinary lenses.'

'Did she have another pair of contacts or did she leave that day without them?'

'No, she had just the one pair. She didn't ever wear them when she went swimming in case they got lost. That's why Harlan drove her car to the quarry. She couldn't see well enough to do it herself.'

I felt a surge of triumph go through me. 'Thanks, Janine,' I said happily. 'I'll talk to you later.' I hung up and stood for a full minute, savouring what I had discovered. Then I went back out to the porch.

Beth watched me as I sank into my chair again.

'Are you all right, honey?'

I nodded. 'You know, the thing I thought was so odd about everyone's account of seeing Kelly that night was that she was wearing sunglasses. Now, you and Nita gave several plausible explanations for that,' I continued hurriedly as I saw Beth about to speak. 'Any one of them could have been correct. But it suddenly occurred to me, sitting here, that the sunglasses weren't the key to all this.' Beth had perched on the edge of her seat and now I turned to look at her directly. 'It was the contact lenses. I noticed them soaking in solution in the cabinet of Kelly's bathroom. I remembered them particularly because they were aquamarine and I realised that Kelly must have worn them to make her eyes look more striking.'

I paused, but Beth's attention did not waver. 'That was what I wanted to ask Janine about. She told me Kelly was really short-sighted. And the day she died she wasn't wearing her contacts.'

Comprehension dawned on Beth's face. 'So that means,' she began, then stopped and shook her head as if she couldn't quite take it all in.

'That means,' I said quietly, 'that with or without sunglasses Kelly couldn't have been driving her car that night. It must have been someone else.'

Chapter Eleven

'So if it wasn't her, who do you think it was?'

Beth's voice had a thread of anguish running through it and I thought I understood why. The idea that Kelly had committed suicide had been bad enough, but now it seemed as if her mother's claim that she was murdered might be true and that opened up a great many painful issues.

'I don't know,' I said. 'But all those people who stated they saw Kelly that night must have *assumed* it was her because the woman had red hair, wore Kelly's sunglasses and was driving her car. Those three things were so distinctive.'

I swivelled my glass so that the ice circled round and a little vodka and orange spilled over my hand. 'And remember, it was dusk. The people who saw her were sitting in the diner, where the lights were probably already switched on. That would have made the parking lot seem even darker. I bet they only had a general impression of who was driving that car.'

Beth nodded slowly, deep in thought. 'I don't think they had any lights in the parking lot itself, except one just at the entrance so folks wouldn't trip over the step,' she offered. A deep sigh escaped her. 'But why? Kelly was alive at that time anyway. Why would someone be driving around in her automobile pretending to be her?' The pain was still in her voice.

We sat in silence. I looked out over the endless fields stretching to the horizon. Steam was rising from the ground in a low mist. A few clouds had gathered where earth and sky met, glowing with the rosy light of the setting sun, which had returned once the storm passed, as if to say all was forgiven.

Shortly after sunset, Beth disappeared inside the ranch house, returning five minutes later with a simple meal of what she called 'cold cuts', which turned out to be a selection of salamis and ham accompanied by coleslaw and potato salad.

When we had finished eating, we retired to our rooms for an early night, partly because I knew I would have to be up at dawn to start filming the next day, and partly because I was becoming a little drunk. The combination of heat and the chilled vodka and orange which slipped down so refreshingly seemed to have gone to my head.

Before I fell asleep, however, I phoned Mags back in Kansas City. The news about Amanda was not good. She appeared to have gone into a deep depression and was eating nothing and talking to no one. For most of the day, she simply lay on her bunk with her face turned to the wall. I asked Mags to give Martin a call to keep him informed. Then I went to bed, deeply concerned.

Nevertheless, I slept soundly and awoke just as dawn was breaking. I got out of bed and went over to the window where I looked out on a mysterious world. A heavy mist lay low over the landscape, to perhaps waist or shoulder height. It drifted across the fields in thick, languid swirls. A pearly rim on the eastern horizon showed where the sun was about to rise.

On impulse, I grabbed my jeans and pulled them on, hastily adding a T-shirt before racing through to the kitchen. There I paused to write a quick note for Beth. During the long drive out here, she had mentioned that I could borrow the Lincoln any time I needed. I left a message to say I'd taken it for now but would be back within the hour, then grabbed her car keys off the table and rushed out. Minutes later I was nervously steering the huge vehicle down the dirt track towards the highway. Once I was on the tarred road, I speeded up, heading towards the little motel on the outskirts of Rapid Falls where the others were staying, intending to knock on Joe's door to see if he was awake. As I arrived, he was loading his camera into the crew van.

'Hello. What are you doing up this early?' he asked, smiling.

'I was hoping to persuade you to film the sunrise,' I said boldly. 'It looks so beautiful.'

He grinned, swinging his camera bag on to the back seat. 'Snap. Come on. We'll get some nice pictures.' Without more ado, I climbed in beside him and we set off, driving around the countryside, looking for suitable locations. We didn't have a monitor with us, but as I watched Joe at work and took occasional glimpses through the lens, I could tell that we would have some beautifully atmospheric shots as the dawning light refracted through the mist and clouds of vapour floated mysteriously across the pastures, revealing trees and bushes in ghostly procession.

By six thirty we had done enough and headed back towards the motel where we found the others already waiting for us. Quickly I phoned Beth to say I was coming to pick her up to go for breakfast. She was standing out in the yard when I arrived back at the ranch.

'You must have been up with the birds,' was all she said, settling herself in the passenger seat as I turned the car round and drove back towards Rapid Falls.

I'd arranged to meet the others at the diner. It was the first time I'd been there and as I entered I felt as if I'd been caught in a time warp. Chrome and plastic-topped tables lined one side against the windows. Opposite them was a long counter, complete with revolving cabinet displaying slices of pie, and in front of that was a row of metal stools bolted to the floor and covered with pearly green PVC. The room was crowded with customers, mostly men in dungarees or jeans, T-shirts and baseball caps, clearly all regulars and with the air of people who had already done half a day's work.

We found a table in the corner and sat down. Beth had said almost nothing during the journey into town, but as soon as she'd ordered she leaned across the table towards me and asked, 'Have you thought any more about what we discussed last night?'

I shook my head, then rapidly explained to the others my theories about Kelly's death. Lewis had already wandered off and was playing a video game in the lobby. Evan showed only mild interest and soon ambled away to find himself a newspaper, which he read quietly until his eggs and bacon arrived. Joe, Beth and I tossed around various suggestions as to why someone had posed as Kelly, each one wilder and more improbable than the next. Mine were the least inspired of all.

'The thing is,' reasoned Beth finally, 'Kelly drowned when her automobile hit the water. Harlan wasn't there for that, so if she was killed, it couldn't have been him who did it. So the link with Sharon's murder is gone.'

'OK, let's leave that aside for the moment,' I conceded unwillingly. 'We know that two of Harlan's girlfriends have died in suspicious circumstances. If we believe Amanda – and we do, right?' Joe and Beth nodded. 'Then we also know that in both cases there was another red-haired woman involved in the murder. Either she killed Sharon and Kelly out of jealousy or whatever, or she knows who did. The connection between the two killings is still there.'

'And,' Beth broke in eagerly, 'if you can prove that, then perhaps it ties in with Marlene's murder and we could prove Malcolm's innocence too. Marlene knew Harlan, and Kelly.'

I looked down, unable to meet her eye. If the link between the first two murders was tenuous, the connection with Marlene's death was virtually nonexistent.

Joe pushed his plate away and leaned back in his seat. 'But who could have masqueraded as Kelly that night? This place is so far out of the way it had to be someone local, and if your theory is correct, they had to be living here fifteen years ago and have been in Kansas City very recently.'

Beth shook her head doubtfully. 'No one around here had hair like Kelly. Not that same bright red colour.'

'Well, what about a wig?' Joe was beginning to sound as frustrated by all these dead ends as I was.

'Joe, this is a tiny community. Less than five hundred people. We all know each other. If someone gets a new dress it's a talking point. I can't imagine that anyone could have a wig that striking without the rest of us girls knowing about it – unless, of course, they'd never worn it in public, but that wouldn't make sense, would it? Keeping a red wig in the closet just in case you might need one some day?'

'Unless it was planned,' muttered Joe softly.

Evan laid down his newspaper and stood up with a bright smile. 'Think I'll wander over to the drugstore. When d'you think you'll want to get started?'

I glanced at my watch. 'Ten minutes. Sorry, Evan, this thing is occupying more of our time and attention than it should.'

'No problem.' He wandered out and strolled off down the street accompanied by Lewis.

Beth was deep in thought. 'The only person with hair that length was Crystal but it was a different kind of red, more chestnut. She didn't have the golden highlights that Kelly did.'

'Who's Crystal?' I asked.

'Crystal was – I guess she still is – a lost soul. She grew up here, but her folks were both alcoholic. She wasn't the beauty that Kelly was, about the same build but not what you'd call graceful and her features were kinda, I don't know, kinda ordinary, I suppose. She had a big nose and a strawberry birthmark just below her neckline. The other kids always teased her about it. I used to feel so sorry for her. She was in the same high school class as Kelly and she'd hang around the fringes, never quite one of the gang. Her clothes were all worn out or hand-me-downs.' Beth shifted in her seat, as if uncomfortable with the memory.

'I remember once seeing her at the school fair and she was wearing a red cotton dress that was kinda big for her and some kid pointed at it and said, oh look, there's Mom's old housecoat, and the others all howled with laughter. Crystal just turned and left. She didn't give any sign she was upset, not in front of us anyways, but I swear she probably cried her eyes out when she got home.'

Beth's face was riven with pity. 'She got herself a job as a bus girl at the truck stop south of town. She'd hitch out there after school. Sometimes we'd see her if we stopped late at night, just a kid, thirteen, fourteen maybe, dog tired, you could see that, clearing tables, yes sir and yes ma'am to everyone. God knows, she must have hitched a ride home after she got off work. It's terrifying to think she did that so late at night.' Beth shook her head. 'I guess it was the only way she could get the money to feed herself.'

There was silence for a while, Beth lost in her memories of the past, her face grave.

'Did she know Harlan?' I ventured.

Beth nodded almost imperceptibly, still deep in thought. Her voice seemed to come from far away. 'But Pete was the one she was really close to. They were always real tight, even when they were little. He was kind of an outcast like her, in a way. Oh, his father was rich enough, being the local doctor and all, but Pete's mother died when he was three and his father didn't really have time for him. He was an only child, just like Crystal, and he was shy and lonely. So they sort of hung out together.

'When they got older, he'd pick up the tab for her when they were out with the gang. I remember once when I was looking for Marlene, I saw Pete and Crystal together at the quarry. She was crying and he had his arm round her and was talking to her real soft and gentle. I couldn't hear what he was saying but you could tell they were real close. And I suppose that after a while, they fell in love. They got married when Pete graduated, but it didn't last. It wasn't Pete's fault – he's always been a good-hearted person. That's why I'm so pleased he's sweet on Lola. She couldn't ask for a better man.'

I glanced at my watch and rose to my feet, reaching for the bill. 'So what happened to Crystal?' I prompted as I counted out the money.

'What happened? Oh . . .'

Beth gathered up her handbag. 'She'd lived on the edge, lived on her nerves, you might say, for so long that I guess she couldn't settle to keeping house and being a suburban wife. She took to disappearing for a few days at a time at first, then it got to be weeks. I know, because we were all living in Kansas City by this time – me, Pete and Harlan – and Pete would come over to see me because I was like an older sister, I guess, and he had no one else to talk to. He kept it pretty quiet, but he was so worried about her and he loved her so much.

'It was like she was on a mission to self-destruct. She got into drugs eventually and she was running with a pretty wild crowd. Nobody else knows this except me, but she got picked up by the police once for prostitution and Pete got her out of it. Talked the cops into letting her go. But then she left for good. It was so strange, after all those years of pulling herself up by the boot straps to just let everything go to hell like that.'

We had reached our vehicles. Evan was leaning against the crew van, smoking a cigarette, and Lewis was throwing small stones at a Coke can set up on a nearby wall.

'Where is she now?' I asked Beth. 'D'you think she's the one we're looking for?'

Beth shrugged. 'I have no idea. The last I heard she'd disappeared – gone underground. She and Pete got divorced two or three years ago.'

The others were clearly impatient to start work. Reluctantly I put all thought of Crystal and Amanda out of my mind and tried to concentrate on the day ahead.

We began at the family farmhouse, filming Beth as she showed us around the various rooms and described her memories of her sister's early life and character. Later, we all walked across to the old homestead and recorded some sequences there. At one point, when she was in the sitting room, telling how Marlene and her friends had used it as a place to hang out, Beth knelt down and picked up a burgundy coloured garment which was lying on top of a pile of rubbish. She stopped talking. Tears formed in her eyes and several minutes passed before she regained her composure and was able to continue. 'I suddenly remembered seeing Marlene wear that dress the summer when she was nineteen,' she explained to me in a low voice a little later.

Afterwards we went outside to take shots of the landscape and the places where Marlene and Malcolm would have wandered when they had first fallen in love. The mist had long since burnt off and a hot muggy wind blew over the grasslands, tilting the leaves on the trees so that their grey-green undersides showed. By mid-afternoon we were done and ready to head back to Kansas City.

I dozed fitfully part of the way, tired from filming outdoors in the heat. But my mind kept returning to Kelly's death. I seemed to have got nowhere. My theories were pure speculation and likely to remain so. After all these years, the chance of proving any of them were true was negligible. Many of the people involved must have moved away and lost contact with the community. Memories were dimmed or unreliable. It was hopeless. And even if it wasn't, one thing was sure. The murderer could not have been Harlan. And that was my only interest in the case.

It had been a wild card, this idea of mine that if I could prove Amanda's husband guilty of killing his girlfriend all those years ago, somehow it would help to convince the police he had done it again and that Amanda was innocent. It wasn't even logical, I told myself sourly. Supposing I had shown he was Kelly's killer. No court would convict him of Sharon's murder on the strength of that without further evidence. The only tiny, tiny chink of light in this gloomy picture was the possibility of tracing the mystery woman. But that was a long shot. And always lurking at the back of my mind was the dread of finding out Amanda was lying – not consciously perhaps, but lying nonetheless – that we were wasting our time and would never be able to prevent her from spending most of the rest of her life in jail.

Recoiling from that prospect, I turned to Beth. 'How can I find Crystal?'

Beth thought for a moment. 'Ask Pete. He'll tell you he doesn't know but if you push him, I'm sure he can help. I'll give you his phone number.'

It was after eight o'clock when Beth dropped me at the hotel. Joe and the others waved as they drove past, heading for the freight lift at the back of the building. When I picked up the keycard for my room, the receptionist handed me a couple of faxes from Martin. They contained minor queries about the production, and repeated requests to know how Amanda was faring. I shoved them into my bag, hoping that Mags had kept him informed. There were also two messages from Carl. I made a mental note to call him back as soon as I could.

I reached my room and wearily slid the keycard into the appropriate slot, holding the door open with my foot as I swung my overnight bag inside. A heavy object landed on my back, pinning me to the ground. I was just starting to drag myself to my feet when I heard Mags's voice behind me.

'Oh Bel! I'm so sorry! That's my fault.'

I sat down on the edge of the bed, rubbing my sore knees. Mags was standing just inside the door, which was held open by the overnight bag I had dropped. The entrance to my room was blocked by a large suitcase and several smaller packages which I recognised as belonging to Amanda.

'Are you all right?' Mags was frantically trying to move the suitcase to one side. 'I packed up Amanda's stuff and told the manager to move it in here because my room is piled high with presents for the children and—'

'I'm fine,' I assured her, gingerly rubbing my back. 'I wasn't expecting it, that's all.'

'How about a nice cup of tea?' Leaving the door propped open, she disappeared next door. While she was gone, I telephoned Carl, but he wasn't home and I had to content myself with leaving a message to say I'd call back later. Mags reappeared with her little electric kettle and some teabags and within minutes, we were seated on my balcony sipping away contentedly.

'I phoned Martin like you suggested,' she told me.

'What did he say?'

'He thinks it's gone too far now to keep it secret. He'll tell old whatsit first thing tomorrow. He's not sure what the verdict will be, but his instinct is that we should keep going as best we can with our documentary on Malcolm.'

'That's mine as well,' I agreed.

'He said he could send us out another researcher if we want

one. He thinks the insurance will cover the extra expense but he'll check into it.'

I shook my head. 'I think it would be more trouble than it's worth to bring someone new in at this late stage. I'm sure that between us we can cope with the rest of what there is to do.'

Mags nodded. 'Fine. How did your filming go?'

Briefly, I described what we had done and then told her about my discoveries concerning Kelly.

Mags gazed out at the evening crowds strolling on the Plaza. 'So,' she said slowly, 'if you're right about Kelly, then Amanda could be telling the truth.' She turned to look at me sharply. 'There could be another redhead who's going around bumping off Harlan's girlfriends.'

'But why didn't she kill Amanda?'

Mags rested one foot on top of the balcony railing, then crossed the other one over it. 'Perhaps she would have if Amanda had stuck around long enough. She got out, remember. Fast. I wonder if she had any inkling that she might be next?'

I was gazing absent-mindedly at Mags's neat white sandals propped up on the railing. There was a tiny streak of what looked like red nail varnish on the leather at the cutout for her toes.

'You know,' Mags said, turning to me with a worried look on her face, 'Lois thinks she could probably persuade a jury to believe Amanda's story if it wasn't for Patsy's testimony. That's what will scupper her.' There was a pause. 'D'you think there's *any* way to pick holes in her evidence?'

I shook my head resignedly. 'Patsy comes across too well. She's quite definite about what she saw.'

'But there must be something, some little flaw. There must be a detail like Kelly's contact lenses that will give her away.'

I closed my eyes, trying to picture what Patsy had seen. The redhead wearing Amanda's dress. What was it she had said? That she looked as if she had walked through a pool of blood. It was on her dress and her legs and spattered on her shoes. I could envisage nothing that would undermine that testimony.

I opened my eyes again. Slowly I focused on what was in front of me, literally under my nose – the red stain on Mags's sandal. 'There might be *one* thing,' I said.

'What?' Mags's voice was sharp.

'Patsy described quite graphically how there was blood on the woman's legs and shoes. Except,' I said, turning to meet Mags's intense gaze, 'you and I both know that Amanda was wearing her new navy pumps that night. I saw her the next morning and she was still wearing them. They were pretty battered, but they were the same shoes and they didn't have any blood on them that I could see.'

Mags considered for a moment then made a face. 'They'll argue that she had time to wipe it off.'

'You're missing the point. The thing is, how could Patsy have noticed blood on Amanda's navy shoes at night, from that distance?'

Mags looked at me with hope dawning in her face. 'Phone her up,' she urged, rising to her feet so quickly that she knocked her cup and saucer to the ground.

With one bound, I was back inside my room and had crossed to the desk in the corner and begun pulling open drawers. The phone book was in the second one down, under a large copy of the Bible.

I located Patsy's number and punched it into the keypad. 'It's after ten,' I muttered worriedly. 'She's probably already in . . . Patsy! Hello! This is Bel Carson,' I sang out, trying to sound nonchalant. The voice on the other end mumbled something, as if I had just woken Patsy up.

'Look,' I breezed on, 'I know it's a bit late but there's something I really need to ask you.' I paused for Patsy's laconic response before continuing. 'Remember that night you saw Amanda leaving her house after the murder? She had blood on her shoes, isn't that so? Can you remember what colour shoes she was wearing? Uh-huh. That's right.' I listened to her answer and then said hurriedly, 'Patsy, thanks. I really appreciate it. Talk to you later.' I hung up and sank down on to the bed.

Mags hadn't taken her eyes off my face during the entire conversation.

'What did she say?' she demanded.

I looked at her thoughtfully. 'Patsy is quite certain that she saw blood on the woman's shoes. She's equally certain those shoes were white.' I jumped up. 'I'd better tell Lois at once.'

I riffled through my organiser to find the number and dialled quickly. There was only an answering machine, however, so I had to content myself with leaving a message to call me back because I had some urgent information. I hung up and paced around the room restlessly.

'I suppose there's nothing more we can do until morning,' commented Mags wearily. 'Christ, I'm tired.'

I was still walking up and down. 'I know I won't be able to sleep. I feel I want to do something!' I punched one fist into the palm of my other hand. 'This is the first real indication we've had that Amanda could be telling the truth, that she's innocent! It means there *was* another woman masquerading as her that night, however far-fetched that may seem.' I stood stock still, gripped by a sudden conviction. 'I have to find Crystal at once. I'm going to see Pete.' I reached for my shoulder bag.

'Hang on!' Mags sounded alarmed. 'Why don't you just phone? It's late.'

'Uh-uh. Beth said he would probably deny all knowledge of her whereabouts. It's easier for people to be evasive over the phone. I stand a better chance in person.' I'd found the car keys and was heading for the door. 'He's a nice man. This is not some dangerous lunatic I'm going to see,' I added to try and pacify her. 'I'll be fine.'

'I'm coming with you,' announced Mags with determination.

'No.' I put a restraining hand on her arm. 'You're knackered. You just said so. This isn't going to be any big deal and one of us needs to be awake and on the ball tomorrow. Goodness only knows we're just scraping by with this documentary by the skin of our teeth as it is.'

She held my eye for a full ten seconds, unconvinced, then gave way. 'OK,' she said in a resigned tone of voice. 'But promise me that after that you'll come straight back and go to bed.'

'Yes, Mum,' I said as I hurried out the door.

Chapter Twelve

I drove through dark streets. As soon as I left the main thoroughfares and turned into the neighbourhood where Pete lived, traffic became almost nonexistent.

I found Pete's home with some difficulty because street lights were few and far between and the houses half hidden by trees. It turned out to be a charming two-storey brick house with dormer windows in an up-market, older neighbourhood. I parked the car on the street and walked up the dark driveway. There was a light in one of the downstairs rooms, to the right of the front door and as I approached, I could see Pete sitting in the glow of a lamp, speaking into a dictaphone. He leapt to his feet and answered the door at once when I knocked.

He seemed younger than I remembered, more boyish, dressed in a T-shirt, shorts and sandals. If he was surprised to see me, he was too courteous to show it. Stepping aside, he invited me into his home. I found myself in a tiny, square hall. Ahead of me was a steep flight of stairs leading to the upper storey and as Pete closed the front door I noticed an archway on my left with what seemed to be a dining room beyond.

'Please.' Pete nodded in the opposite direction towards a small sitting room. The off-white walls and creamy linen curtains lent it a calm, comfortable atmosphere. It was furnished very simply with a pale apricot coloured sofa, an oak desk in the corner and the armchair in which Pete had been sitting beneath an overhanging brass lamp. As I sat down on the sofa, I noticed that he had some beautiful Native American paintings on the wall, very similar to those I had admired in Lois's office.

'Can I get you a drink?' Pete asked solicitously, gathering his papers and dictaphone together and stuffing them into a manila folder.

I shook my head, sinking deeper into the sofa. 'No, thanks. I'm sorry to bother you at this time of night, but I need some help.'

'No problem.' He smiled and the blue eyes regarded me sympathetically. 'What can I do for you?'

I gave him a level look and said, 'I'm trying to get in touch with your former wife. I wondered if you could tell me where she is?'

Something flickered across his face, but it was gone before it could register. 'Why do you want to talk to her?' A note of concern had crept into his voice.

I shrugged. 'Various things, really. I understood that she and Marlene knew each other well when they were teenagers. I haven't been able to track down any other friends and it would be nice if she could say something about what Marlene was like as a girl.'

He nodded as if he understood, but there was something guarded about the expression in his eyes. 'Well, I'm afraid I can't help you much. We're divorced, you know, and I haven't seen Crystal for at least a year.'

'And you've no idea where she might be?' I pressed him.

He shook his head. 'None. The divorce was perfectly amicable, but she wanted her own life and to make a clean break.' He got to his feet and walked across to the roll-top desk in the corner of the room. Opening one of the drawers, he pulled out a torn piece of paper, inspected it then held it out to me. 'Here.

You can take this. It's the last address I had for her. She's not there any longer though, I'm afraid.'

I stood up, glancing at the lines scribbled on the paper. 'Thanks,' I said, smiling gratefully.

'You know,' he said in a quiet voice as he accompanied me out to the hall, 'I can't believe you came here at this time of night just for that.'

The softness of his tone caught me off guard and I looked up sharply with an expression of guilt. He wasn't fooled.

I made a snap decision. 'You're right. I wanted to find out what Crystal knows about Kelly's death.'

An alarmed expression came into his eyes. 'You'll be opening up a lot of old wounds. Why Kelly?'

'I don't know,' I hedged. 'Her death intrigues me for some reason. I thought Crystal might be able to answer some of my questions.'

He stared at me sceptically and for a moment I thought he was going to ask me further questions. But he shrugged dismissively. 'Perhaps she might. Who knows? Anyway, I wish you luck with finding her.'

He reached forward and opened the door, but on the threshold I paused. 'Harlan said you're a good friend of his.'

Pete's face stiffened but he answered evenly. 'That's right. Although perhaps not as much as we used to be. We were inseparable when we were boys.'

'So what came between you?'

Pete looked uncomfortable. 'Oh, you know how it is. Partly we just grew up and drifted apart. And also, I don't . . .' he hesitated, as if searching for the right word, 'I don't feel comfortable with some of his views about things.'

'Such as?' I was in journalistic mode.

Pete looked around him for inspiration. Apparently he found none because his gaze came back to me. 'Look, you won't get me to say anything bad about Harlan,' he started firmly. 'I think he's a really great guy – he has style, intelligence, charisma, he's a born leader. He stands head and shoulders above dull old accountants like me.' Pete laughed self-deprecatingly. 'But I suppose the downside of that is that he attracts a certain kind of woman, good-looking like him but also highly-strung and neurotic, I'd say. Perhaps they're the only ones who can match his level of energy and . . . flamboyance.'

I was silent, watching him closely.

'The problem is that Harlan is the sort of person who has no time for fine detail – except in his job of course. There's an . . . an impetuous streak in his nature and he gets impatient with pettiness or nagging.' Pete's expression was anguished as he continued. 'I feel partly responsible for Sharon's death. I should have done something.' He looked at me, and I noticed with a sense of shock that there were tears in his eyes. 'You see, I knew Amanda was dangerous. She was always neurotic and demanding in her relationship with Harlan. That sort of behaviour just turned him off, of course, and he'd ignore her, which only made her worse. You could just see her level of frustration escalating until you could sense something was going to blow.'

He shrugged. 'I thought the problem was solved when she finally left for Britain. When I found out she'd come back, I should have predicted what was going to happen. I felt it in my bones but I didn't want to believe it. I could have saved Sharon's life, I'm sure I could.' He seemed tortured by that thought.

'Well, if you knew it was going to happen, then surely Harlan must have too,' I pointed out gently. 'He could have saved Sharon.'

Pete shook his head. 'Sometimes,' he said softly, 'the people around Harlan get hurt, not because he's cruel or callous but because he doesn't understand ordinary people. He doesn't see their frustrations. He doesn't notice what's going on.'

'Did Harlan have other girlfriends, that you know of?' I asked.

Pete nodded reluctantly, unable to meet my eye. 'Yes. I know he did. Amanda knew it too and it made her even crazier. But don't ask me who they were. I'm not proud of this but I've allowed Harlan to have . . . assignations here in the past when I was out of town. I thought it might help to take some of the pressure off his situation with Amanda.' He shrugged. 'Perhaps I was wrong.'

I decided to take a risk. 'I've been looking through the old files on Kelly Swartz's death,' I said. Pete frowned. 'On the night she died, you reported seeing her driving by. You said she was wearing her Ray-Bans. Is that right?'

He considered carefully before replying. 'I don't recall. If that's what the records say I'm sure that's right.'

'You don't remember anyone pointing out she was wearing some fancy diamanté glasses when she drove by the diner earlier on, do you?'

Pete shook his head, clearly puzzled. 'No, I don't.'

'So you've no idea why she had changed glasses?'

'No. I'm sure the likeliest explanation is that I made a mistake.'

I nodded. 'OK. Thanks, Pete. You've been very patient.'

He stood at the door until I was safely into my car and had pulled away from the kerb.

As I drove through the deserted streets, I struggled to come to terms with what he had told me. I disliked Harlan intensely. But was I allowing that to colour my perception of his guilt, making me ignore what was under my nose? After listening to Pete, I was full of doubt once more. His description of Amanda had rung true. I had witnessed myself how emotionally unstable she could be. I had been present when she had tried physically to assault Sharon.

195

Was I struggling to prove her innocence when I should be accepting the obvious? Could it be that Patsy had simply got one tiny detail of her story wrong?

It was after midnight and I felt a wave of tiredness wash over me as I waited at the last set of traffic lights, ready to turn into the hotel parking lot when they turned to green. At that moment, a van crossed in front of me, from the direction of the hotel, swerving round a corner towards downtown. It took a second to register that the driver was Joe. Whatever Amanda had done or not done, he had to have been involved. On impulse, I gunned the accelerator as the lights changed and sped after the van.

By the time I had turned on to Main Street, it was already a couple of blocks ahead. That was probably just as well. There was hardly any traffic around, and on these wide empty streets Joe would have spotted me at once if I'd been any closer. So I followed at a distance.

After about ten minutes' driving, the tail lights up ahead suddenly disappeared. Racing to catch up, I realised he had turned right into a side street which was virtually unlit. I drove along it slowly. Shadows lurked on empty lots and derelict looking commercial buildings added to the sense of isolation. I could just make out the lights of the van several blocks away. Then they were gone.

I came to the brow of a hill and found myself steering the car down a narrow twisting road between steep banks. At the bottom it levelled out and crossed some railroad tracks. I had no idea where I was. Slowing the car to a stop, I looked around me. There was no sign of the van. Clouds obscured the moon, but from time to time a weak light would break through and allow me to get a glimpse of my surroundings.

I was in some sort of yard. There appeared to be cranes and scaffolding silhouetted against the skyline, but something about the angle at which they'd been left, the amount of debris

196

lying around and the absence of any sign of life told me this place was no longer in use. Opening the window a crack, I listened carefully, but apart from the incessant noise of the wind, there was nothing. If the van was nearby, the engine had been switched off. Disappointment washed over me. I had lost him. Any chance I had of resolving that mystery had gone – at least for the time being.

Feeling suddenly nervous, I rolled up the window completely, checked that all the doors were locked, started up the car again and drove back the way I had come. In spite of my anxiety, I reached Main Street without any problem and found my way back to the hotel. Too tired to care about anything, I collapsed into bed and fell into a deep sleep.

There were no interviews organised for the following day, so I had decided to film what was going on in the courtroom and get an idea of how the jury selection was carried out. It was something Joe could easily handle without me, since it would be a case of choosing a place to set up the camera and then leaving it there.

'Just follow as much of the action as you can and get me some cutaways,' I told him over breakfast. 'I'm sure it's the sort of thing you can do standing on your head. I've got to check up on some stuff.' I watched him closely as he responded. But Joe was as calm and easy-going as ever. It made his nocturnal activities seem all the more suspicious.

When I had first woken that morning, all my doubts of the previous night had flooded over me again. For a long time, I had lain in bed, wrestling with the same old questions. In the end I had concluded that the only way to resolve them was to follow up every lead I could. I had to find Crystal. There was nothing else to go on.

As soon as the others had left, I set out for the address Pete had given me. It turned out to be a decaying room in a street where all the buildings jostled next to each other; the yards were little more than hardened earth and there wasn't a tree anywhere in sight. I approached it with some trepidation. White paint was peeling from the walls, revealing grey wooden planks beneath, and the screens at several of the windows were torn and curling back on themselves. Grimy-looking curtains covered the windows and kept out prying eyes.

I mounted the steps to the porch. Several of the floorboards were rotten, and those I trod on creaked alarmingly, but I persevered and rang the doorbell. A skinny, elderly black woman answered the door, staring at me wordlessly in an unwelcoming manner.

'Excuse me,' I began. 'I'm looking for someone called Crystal Ottinger and I believe she lives here.'

'Nope.' She made to close the door in my face, but I had automatically inserted my foot.

'This was the address I was given.'

The woman exerted pressure to close the door, squeezing hard against my loafer. 'She left a long time ago.'

'Do you know where she went?'

The dark eyes stared at me coldly. Then she took her weight off the door. 'Upstairs. Room Three. You got five minutes then I want you off my property.' She half turned towards the interior of the house and yelled loudly, 'Laetitia! You got company!' Then she stood aside, jerking her head towards the upper floor, motioning me to enter.

Apprehensively, I mounted the stairs. The interior of the house was clean but spartan. There were no rugs or carpets, only bare wooden floorboards. As I reached the landing, I was confronted by a young sleepy-looking black woman wearing a grubby lilac satin robe, who had just emerged from a door bearing a crudely painted number three on it.

'What you want?' The voice was not exactly hostile, but it wasn't very friendly either.

'I'm looking for Crystal Ottinger,' I said. 'Tall, slim build, long red hair.'

The woman eyed me suspiciously. 'You a cop?' I shook my head. 'Then what you want with Crystal? What that girl done now?'

'I need her help,' I answered, meeting her gaze levelly.

She considered for a moment. 'OK. Come on in.' She led the way back into the room, pulling up the pink ruched blinds at the windows. 'Aagh!' She recoiled in mock horror. 'It's too damn early for this much light.'

I looked around me. We were in a small room, furnished with a large bed, a dressing table and a carved wooden screen in the corner. On the floorboards was a grubby, fluffy, white nylon rug, and the rumpled bed, from which she had obviously just emerged, had a lace-trimmed pink counterpane which had slipped on to the floor.

Laetitia sank on to the bed and pointed to a wooden side chair against the wall opposite her. 'Have a seat. Now, what is it you want to know?'

'I'm trying to find Crystal. She used to live here, right?'

Laetitia nodded, reaching for a packet of Virginia Slims and a lighter on the table beside the bed. As she extracted a cigarette, she said, 'Crystal left about a year ago. I don't know where she went. Someone – some guy – picked her up one night and they drove off and she never returned.' She lit her cigarette.

I felt suddenly cold. 'You mean she disappeared?'

Laetitia nodded, watching me with interest.

'Didn't you call the police? Did you try to find her?'

Laetitia laughed uproariously. 'Honey, you don't call the police when you work in this profession.' She raised her eyebrows meaningfully, but it was a few moments before I caught on.

'You mean she was working as a prostitute?'

'You got it.' Laetitia tapped out the ash into the cupped palm of her hand.

'Weren't you worried about her?'

'Sure I was worried about her. But what was I gonna do? I have a john who works for the police department and I kept asking him if there was any dead bodies that looked like Crystal but there never was. Or at least that's what he said.' Laetitia shrugged dismissively. 'Maybe she just moved on. Maybe she found someone to be with. She left with a man, I remember that. He had a real smart automobile – he'd picked her up a coupla times before.'

'What did he look like?' I asked.

Laetitia pouted and scanned the ceiling while she thought. 'Oh, he didn't never get out of the automobile. I could see from up here that he wore a vest and tie, real smart he was, but I never saw what he looked like.'

'Did she take anything with her?'

Laetitia slid off the bed and bent to reach under it. 'No. That was the strange bit. She just walked out and left every-thing.' Her voice was muffled as she began to drag something across the floorboards. 'This here's her stuff. That old dragon lady downstairs woulda chucked it all out, so I put everything in a box and kept it in case she came back.'

'Laetitia!' The thin reedy voice floated up from below.

'What you want?' Laetitia roared back.

'Your caller got two more minutes then I'm going to git the police!'

Laetitia snorted and said in her normal voice to me, 'Like hell. The cops know this is a whorehouse. She has guys coming and going here all times of the day and night and she's acting like she's upset about one lady!' She hauled a small tin trunk from under the bed. 'This is her stuff.' Laetitia sat back on her heels and pried the lid open.

Inside was a jumble of tawdry garments. I leaned forward

200

and began to examine them one by one. They had been bought in cheap chain stores, in a standard size eight. I lifted the last negligee out, revealing a small collection of miscellaneous items – a few popular novels, a silver hair-brush which looked out of place amongst all the cheap artefacts, some garish plastic earrings, and a few dog-eared photographs.

Gingerly, I picked these up. There was a studio portrait showing a younger looking Pete in a dark suit, sitting slightly behind an attractive woman with auburn hair. She wore an off-the-shoulder midnight-blue evening gown which revealed pale skin covered in freckles.

'Is this her?' I asked.

'Yup.' Laetitia was raking around in a small battered fridge in the corner of the room. Now she emerged with a half-empty bottle of pink wine. 'Would you like some of this?' she asked, waving it in the air.

'No thanks,' I said automatically, going back to the snap-shots. 'I've just had breakfast.' Laetitia hooted with laughter as if I'd just said something really funny.

The second picture had a caption that identified it as a high school class portrait. Peering at the tiny images, I thought I could make out Crystal and, a few places further along from her, Kelly. One of them was now dead and who knew what had happened to the other.

I saw the inscription on the back of the last photograph before I saw the snapshot itself, because it was lying face down. Someone had written on it, 'Rapid Falls Blue Grass Festival, July 1985'. Lightly pencilled in underneath were the words 'Harlan, Pete and me, together and in love, July 1985'.

I turned it over. They were wearing fancy dress of some sort. Harlan was a pirate, with a patch over one eye and a kerchief knotted over his hair and big hoop earrings. Pete was

201

a ghost, wrapped in a white sheet, while Crystal wore heavy make-up, masquerading as some sort of vamp, or perhaps a movie star. She was very slim, wearing a red satin dress with a moth-eaten feather boa round her neck.

'Do you mind if I take this?' I held up the picture.

Laetitia was uncertain. 'I don't know. She might want that back.'

'It's been a year,' I coaxed. 'I need it to help me find her.'

After eyeing me for a few moments, Laetitia nodded.

'Seems fine to me.'

'Laetitia!' The screech from downstairs was piercing.

'Just coming.' She rolled her eyes in mock despair and saw me to the door. 'I hope you find Crystal. She's a real fine girl. I'd hate to think anything bad had happened to her.'

After saying goodbye, I took a deep breath and straightened my shoulders before descending the stairs, ready to confront the landlady whom I knew would be lying in wait. She stood in the doorway of her room, arms folded, one foot tapping impatiently, and scowled ferociously as I passed. I half expected to go up in a puff of smoke, but I reached the street in one piece.

Once outside, I sat in the car for several minutes to take stock, watched lethargically by various people lounging in the street or sprawled on their front steps. Nothing I had discovered so far indicated that Crystal could have posed as Amanda's double. For one thing, the photograph confirmed that her hair was a much darker red. But to prove it one way or the other, I had to find Crystal herself and I had no idea where to start.

I knew there must be organisations that offered help to young destitute women and to prostitutes and that I ought to start by getting in touch with them. It would have been easy at home, where I knew the ropes. But here I was lost. I needed help badly. On a sudden impulse, I started up the car and headed for Beth's house, guessing that, since the jury selection was still going on, she would be at home.

She and Lola were sitting in the summerhouse when I arrived. Malcolm, I knew, was in court. There was a palpable air of tension. Lola was lying back on a teak recliner with a furious scowl on her face and Beth looked as if she was near the end of her tether. I could sense that it required a tremendous effort on her part to play the role of the good hostess. Another time I might have been more sensitive to her situation, but today I was desperate.

Beth offered me a cold drink, hot tea, breakfast, lunch, anything she could think of. I accepted the cold drink, said hello to Lola who mumbled something in return and then closed her eyes and appeared to go to sleep.

'We've had a row,' mouthed Beth, surreptitiously pointing at her daughter's prone form.

I nodded to indicate I understood and then said aloud, 'Beth, I need your help to find Crystal. I'm desperate. Pete gave me an address but she left there over a year ago. She'd been working as a prostitute.' I spread my arms wide. 'I have no idea where to start looking.'

The muscles of Beth's face went slack in a gesture of helplessness.

'Harlan knows where she is,' said a voice behind us. We turned to stare at Lola. She had propped herself up on one elbow. 'Can I have a glass of wine?' she asked her mother.

'No!' rejoined Beth sharply. 'You are far too young and it's only just after noon.'

'I am not too young!' flared Lola. 'It's you who's too old to understand what being young means.' She made to get up out of the recliner.

'How do you know that Harlan knows where Crystal is?' I asked hurriedly before she could flounce off into the house.

Lola stopped and stared at me uncomprehendingly. 'What?

Oh that.' She scowled at her mother, then turned her body so that Beth was given the cold shoulder. Flicking back a long strand of blonde hair, Lola said, 'I saw her at Pete's house a couple of mon—'

'I told you that relationship wasn't over!' Beth exploded.

Lola whipped round to face her mother. 'She was with Harlan!' she shouted. There was a moment's silence while they stared at each other with open hostility. Then Beth gave way, settling back in her chair and gazing out at the garden.

Lola turned to me with an air of injured dignity. 'I'd gone over to Pete's house quite late at night. I was in the area and I just thought I'd drop by. There weren't any lights on, and no one answered the doorbell, but I thought I could hear voices coming from the back. So I went round. They were sitting there on the porch. It was dark, but I knew it was them. Crystal had on this beautiful red dress. I'd seen it before because she left it at Pete's once and I found it. I tried it on, but it was too big. It just sort of fell off me.' Lola grinned.

'Anyway,' she went on. 'I said hello to them and Crystal jumped up and rushed into the house, like maybe she thought I hadn't recognised her or something. Harlan told me Pete wasn't home and asked if I wouldn't mind coming back another time because he was having a private meeting. So I went out to my automobile and called Pete on his mobile phone. He was at the office and he said not to worry. He told me Crystal had been in love with Harlan for years, since they were teenagers. She only married Pete to get near Harlan. He was real hurt when he realised that, but he said they're still his friends. He lets them use his place to meet up every so often, when he's working late.'

If this was true, why had Pete lied about Crystal? Was he trying to stop me finding her? My brain was spinning.

'Bel, could you help with my video?' Lola suddenly asked in a wheedling tone of voice.

I looked at her blankly, bewildered by this abrupt change of subject. She seemed to be on the brink of tears. 'I've done something wrong. I think I've erased part of it and I could really do with some help.'

My gaze strayed from Lola to Beth. The latter had a pleading look on her face. 'It would mean a lot to me,' she said quietly.

Lola's vacation project was the last thing I wanted to think about right now, but I smiled politely and said, 'Fine. I'll be happy to help if I can.'

Lola beamed at me. 'I'll be working in the basement for the rest of the afternoon. I've got my editing set up there. Come on down whenever you're ready.' She propelled herself out of the recliner and raced towards the house.

'Thanks, Bel,' Beth said with feeling. She paused, waiting till Lola had slammed the kitchen door shut behind her. Then she turned to me. 'You heard Lola say something about trying on that red dress of Crystal's just now?' I nodded, uncertain where this conversation was headed. 'Well,' she continued, 'according to Lola, Crystal left a whole bunch of stuff in a closet in the spare bedroom. Now, I was concerned about that because I've always been afraid that Pete still carried a torch for his ex-wife. But I didn't realise she was staying there from time to time and that bothers me. I don't want Lola to get hurt the way I did.'

She leaned back to gaze up into the layers of branches above our heads. 'Lola has keys to Pete's house, and I know the combination to turn off the burglar alarm because she wrote it on the front page of her diary.' She paused, then when I still said nothing, she turned to me and said softly, 'He drove out to western Kansas this morning to make sure everything's OK before we burn down the house. I wouldn't normally consider doing such a thing, but there's a lot at stake here – my daughter's future and your friend's life. I'll go with you right

now, if you like, while Lola's busy with her editing. We won't
be long and you can look at her film when we get back. Who
knows what we might find out?'

I didn't stop to think twice. Rising to my feet, I said 'Let's
go.'

There was no sign of life as we approached Pete's house.
The windows looked blank, there was no car outside, no one
mowing the lawn. Beth pulled into the drive, squeezed my arm
once, seemed to gather herself mentally, then got out of the
car and walked up to the door as if she owned the place. I
followed.

Beth inserted a key into the lock with a firm, decisive
movement, turned it and withdrew it again. She selected a
second key and did the same with that, only this time the door
sprang open. Stumbling over the threshold in her haste, Beth
reached for the cupboard opposite, yanked it open and began
punching numbers into the illuminated keypad on the wall, all
the while muttering feverishly to herself. A red light blinked
steadily at the top of the panel.

Then suddenly it switched off. Beth turned and gave me a
gleeful smile. I had the feeling that this was the first time in her
entire life she had done anything remotely illegal and that part
of her was taking a secret pleasure in her boldness. Without a
word, she turned and led the way up the staircase.

We reached a broad landing and were confronted by several
panelled doors. Beth seemed to know where she was going,
because she headed straight for the one on the far left, opening it confidently.

'Quick, in here,' she said.

I followed her into a small room. The furnishings seemed
strangely familiar and for a moment I was confused. Then I
realised that the ruched drapes at the window, the frilled skirt
round the dressing table and the white four-poster bed with its
white lace counterpane were all reminiscent of the decor in

Kelly's bedroom. This looked like the private domain of a teenage girl.

Beth was already rooting in the closet in the corner. It seemed to contain several men's suits, swathed in the sort of plastic that dry-cleaners use.

'Here.' She sounded breathless. 'Help me get this out.'

Together we hauled at a small metal trunk. It was bright red with heavy brass fittings and had an impressive looking lock. Leaning forward, I pressed and tugged at it but it wouldn't open.

'Damnation!' Beth swore under her breath. 'How in hell are we going to get into this thing?'

'Would you like me to try?' a male voice came from behind us.

I sat back on my heels and looked up into the muzzle of a small handgun. Harlan was smiling grimly.

'May I ask what you two ladies think you're doing?' he asked in a grating voice.

Beth tried to recover her composure. 'Why, Harlan!' she exclaimed. 'What are you doing here?'

'I live here,' he answered with a tight smile. 'For the time being. But never mind that. You haven't answered my question.'

Beth was still gamely trying to play down the situation. 'Do you mind if we talk about this in the living room, Harlan?' she asked, moving towards the door. He stood still, blocking her way. For a moment nothing happened. Harlan stood there, tall and powerfully built, but Beth held her ground, her small frame resolute. The tension was almost unbearable.

After a long moment, Harlan slowly stepped aside, allowing Beth to pass, and motioned me with the gun to follow her.

Beth led the way along the hall and down the stairs to the

sitting room I had seen on my last visit. She sat down on the sofa, elbows pressed to her side, hands clasped tightly together on her knees. I sank into an armchair, grateful that Beth had taken the initiative.

'How the hell did you get in here?' Harlan ground out between clenched teeth. His eyes were dark hollows and he towered over us, still pointing the gun. I saw Beth's eyes flick towards it automatically and she swallowed hard.

'Well,' she began, then gave a little scream. But it was only the telephone ringing. She subsided into her seat again, hand on heart, and looked at Harlan. He waited without moving as the answerphone picked up the call.

A few seconds later, Lola's voice rang out across the room. 'Hi, Pete, Pete, if you're there will you pick up the phone?' Beth gave a nervous laugh. Harlan stood immobile, watching her fixedly. Finally, after repeating her request for Pete to answer, Lola hung up.

There was complete silence. Beth took a deep breath and began speaking with deliberate calm. 'I came to see for myself if Crystal still stayed here sometimes. I know it's wrong, but I was worried about my daughter. You know me well enough, Harlan, to realise that I am not a thief or anything else that's bad. And there is no need for you to tell Pete, because I will tell him myself.' She rose and made a move towards the door.

Harlan's wrist moved infinitesimally and there was an audible click as the safety catch was removed. Beth froze in her tracks, a look of terror on her face. For a seemingly endless moment, she and Harlan stared at each other. Then Harlan let his wrist fall so that the barrel of the gun sank towards the floor. Beth let out a sigh of relief.

The gun went off. I let out a loud yell and leapt to my feet. Beth had gone deathly white and for a moment it seemed as if she would pass out. But she rallied quickly.

208

'There was no call for that, Harlan,' she said in a voice that was barely audible. Without a backward glance she walked towards the front door. I followed right behind her. In silence we walked across the lawn and got into her car. Beth turned the key in the ignition and pulled away from the kerb. When we reached the main road, she said so quietly I had to strain to catch the words, 'That fucker would have killed us if he thought he could have got away with it.'

Then, visibly trembling, she drove us back to her home.

'I think I should go,' I said. 'The others don't know where I am.'

Beth seemed deep in thought. Then she looked up abruptly. 'Wait here a moment.'

She was gone for several minutes. I got into my hired car, opened the window and sat gazing out at the garden, the peaceful stretch of lawn, the shady trees. I was still in shock. If I had ever had any doubts that Harlan was capable of killing, they were gone now.

Beth came out of the house, walking purposefully. In her hand she carried several sheets of legal-size paper stapled together.

'I didn't want to mention this earlier in front of Lola,' she began in a conspiratorial tone of voice. 'She's going to be mad enough when she hears what we've been up to.' She leaned across and offered me the document in her hand.

'That's a copy of Pete's divorce papers. When he and Lola started going out together last year, I just had to make sure for myself. I sent someone out to the courthouse and got this, to see for myself that the divorce was final. Lola would hit the roof if she knew.'

I unfolded the sheets of paper. The decree was couched in legal terms and seemed to take a long time to say something very simple – that the marriage was ended and that Crystal would receive no alimony but had been given a substantial lump sum instead. I scanned the pages eagerly, then laid them down with a feeling of disappointment.

'They don't mention an address for either of the parties.'

Beth reached forward impatiently and picked up the document herself. 'I know that but . . .' She flipped the pages over, then stopped on the last one and pointed at the final paragraph. 'There. D'you see? It gives the address of the lawyers who represented her. The Women's Legal Centre. It's a charity. I was on their board for a while. I seem to recall they're open every afternoon.' Beth straightened. 'They might know where to reach Crystal and you might be able to persuade them to tell you.'

I thanked her gratefully and set off towards downtown again, my hopes raised once more.

The Women's Legal Centre was located only a few blocks away from where Laetitia lived, in an equally rundown neighbourhood. I had expected some sort of office building or perhaps a store front, but in fact the centre occupied a small clapboard house in a street where men lounged idly on the kerbstones or porches and flocks of children roamed unchecked.

As I walked up the path I noted that the trim was neatly painted and there were pots of bright flowers on the porch. The front door stood wide open and when I pulled back the screen and stepped over the threshold, I found myself in a small front room, the blinds half drawn to keep out the burning sunlight. I stood there, buffeted by the fierce breeze from a large fan, as I surveyed the scene.

Several people – elderly women and weary-looking young mothers with children mostly – sat on chairs against the wall to my left. On my right was a small desk at which a young black woman sat typing furiously on a word processor. Behind her was a white plastic board decorated with bright yellow sunflowers along the top and bearing the printed words, 'Your legal friends today are' and then scrawled under-neath in ordinary handwriting were the names 'Chris and Shareen'.

'Hi! What can I do for you?' The young woman looked up with a welcoming smile. Her expression turned to one of puzzlement as she took in my appearance. Even though I was wearing jeans and a T-shirt, they had designer logos on them and the leather shoulder bag I was carrying was expensive. I obviously seemed an unlikely candidate for charity.

Nevertheless, when I asked to speak to one of the legal assistants, she added my name to the list in front of her without comment and directed me to the row of chairs oppo-site. I sat down in the corner of the waiting area, conscious of the curious looks of the other clients. One by one, their names were called and they disappeared through a door leading to the rear of the house. Finally it was my turn.

A heavy-set woman came out to greet me, introducing herself as Chris. As I followed her through to a tiny office at the back, it occurred to me with a flash of amusement that she fitted almost every misguided notion of what a feminist should look like. Although she appeared to be quite young, her hair was already an iron grey, cropped into a masculine, crewcut style. In spite of the heat she wore heavy denim jeans and a man's khaki jacket over a T-shirt. But when she had squeezed in behind an old metal desk, the brown eyes which gazed at me through thick glasses were warm and sympathetic.

I shifted uncomfortably in the canvas seat opposite her. The room was stiflingly hot, in spite of the open window. When I told her I was trying to contact one of her clients, Crystal Ottinger, a frown creased her kindly face.

'I'm afraid I didn't handle that case, although I do know we did some work for her.' She gestured helplessly. 'The thing is, we couldn't possibly give out her address.'

I nodded. I had guessed that would be the response unless this was some fly-by-night outfit. I had made enough documentaries about rape and sexual abuse to know that no reputable agency would give away confidential information about its clients. But that experience had also taught me there was usually a way round that.

I smiled at Chris. 'I understand. However, do you think you could pass on my name and ask *her* to contact *me*?' I asked. The other woman looked at me dubiously, but I was already fishing out one of my business cards. Quickly I scribbled the name of the hotel and my room number on the back, and handed it to her.

Chris examined the card carefully, turning it over to read the RTV logo and my name and title on the other side.

'Why does someone from a British television company want to talk to Crystal Ottinger?' she asked finally.

On the way there, I had wondered how I would answer that question, inevitable as it was. If I gave any clue as to the real reason I wished to speak to her, then Crystal would surely realise she had become a suspect and would go underground. Neither I nor the police would ever find her, I was sure. But I needed to give some sort of plausible explanation.

'I'm here making a documentary about Malcolm Laurie's case – I don't know if you've heard about it?' Chris nodded immediately. 'As part of that, I'm doing a background on his wife Marlene. Crystal grew up with her and they used to hang out with the same small gang. She's the only one of Marlene's girlfriends from that period who's still around. I'd really like to talk to her.'

Chris gazed at me dubiously. 'OK. I'll see what I can do. But don't hold your breath.' She stood up and stretched across from her desk to pull the door open for me to leave. Suddenly she said, 'Don't I know you from somewhere? Wasn't your picture in the newspaper or something?'

'I haven't seen anything,' I answered truthfully.

'Oh well.' Chris shrugged. 'I must be mistaken. If I get any response to your query, you'll hear from me by the end of tomorrow.' And with those words she closed the door gently but firmly behind me.

Chapter Thirteen

Mags was pacing restlessly up and down as I entered the hotel foyer. When she saw me, she grabbed hold of my arms with such intensity that I felt myself automatically recoiling.

'Bel, for goodness' sake, where have you been all day?' Mags so rarely became upset and raised her voice like this that I was instantly alarmed. 'Amanda's in trou—' She stopped and glanced around to see if anyone was listening, then pulled me over to a sofa in the corner.

'Amanda tried to commit suicide last night,' she said in a low voice. 'We didn't find out about it till we got back from filming. She took an overdose of sleeping tablets. The prison authorities have no idea how she got hold of them. She was moved to the local hospital. Joe's there now. She's under heavy guard and they won't let anyone see her, but he's sitting waiting for news.'

I stared at Mags in horror. 'Will she be all right? Doesn't she realise we're all trying to get her out?'

Mags shrugged. 'Who knows? Apparently she's been on tranquillisers for months and that stopped when she went to jail so that may have had something to do with it. Lois thinks she just reached the end of her tether and decided it was no use going on. They're not sure if there's liver damage. It could take a few days to find out.'

'Oh my God!' I laid my head back against the sofa and

closed my eyes. Was this an admission of guilt on Amanda's part? Did she believe there was no hope of release because she had committed the murder? Or were we letting her down, failing miserably to prove her innocence and find the real killer? For a moment I allowed myself to share her sense of defeat.

Mags was speaking again, in a voice vibrant with frustration. 'There's nothing we can do, I suppose, except pray she gets better.'

I stood up. 'Come on, I need a drink.'

Mags followed me towards the bar, then stopped in her tracks. 'Oh, I forgot to tell you. Beth phoned and asked us for supper tonight. She said something about you looking at Lola's film.'

I groaned. 'I completely forgot. I'd better go. I promised. You don't have to.'

'And stay here and be miserable on my own? No thanks.'

We arrived at Beth's half an hour later to find a barbecue being prepared. Four or five neighbours had been invited, and Pete was there with Lola. In spite of the hubbub, Beth noticed our sombre mood at once, and in a quiet moment asked what was wrong. I told her what had happened. She looked deeply shocked, but said nothing, her eyes full of concern. Then I told her about the brick wall I had encountered at the legal centre.

'Well, not a *complete* brick wall,' I added. 'She did say she'd try but I got the feeling there wasn't much hope. I don't know what else I can do.'

Beth shook her head sadly. 'It sounds as if it's been a bad day all round.' She indicated the group sitting under the trees. 'Come and forget all about it for tonight. Brooding doesn't help. I can tell you that from personal experience.'

She started to lead us towards the barbecue, but at that moment Lola bounced up to me and tugged my arm. 'Bel, please, please come and look at my film,' she pleaded.

I saw Beth open her mouth as if to object, but I held up a hand to silence her. 'It's OK. It'll help to take my mind off things.'

Chattering brightly, Lola led me into the house, through a door opening off the kitchen and down to the basement. It was an enormous open-plan room, floored with terracotta tiles and furnished with a pool table and sofas and chairs upholstered in red and green tartans. In one corner, curtains had been rigged up to screen off a sizeable area which Lola had turned into an editing suite.

I don't think I had realised just how indulged Lola was until I saw the equipment she had set up in there.

'Is this rented?' I asked incredulously when I saw the computerised editing system.

'No,' Lola replied nonchalantly. 'Mom really wants me to make a go of this, so she found out what the best gear was and bought it for me.'

'But it costs *thousands!*' I couldn't help exclaiming.

Lola shrugged and sat down on the chair in front of the monitor. 'I had somebody put my film, I mean videotape into this machine,' she said. 'And then they started to edit for me. Then I decided to have a go myself but I think I've goofed up already. I've erased about half of the stuff I shot!' She turned to me with an anguished look.

'You can't have,' I said reassuringly. 'The images in that machine are just digital copies of your tapes. That's not actually the material you shot. If you've wiped some of the pictures, you just have to load them in again.'

A look of pure delight mixed with relief dawned on Lola's face. 'Ohhh, I see.'

'You would never use your original material for editing anyway, not unless you were completely stupid,' I explained. 'Even in the old days when everyone used film, we had copies – work prints they're called – made of the camera film and we edited those in all sorts of ways until we were satisfied with the result. Then we cut the original to match it.'

'Oh God, I feel so stupid!' Lola covered her face with her hands. 'Mom thinks I'm going to be a great film-maker and I just keep making these dopey mistakes.'

I laughed. 'Everyone does that.' We began moving towards the door.

'Like what's the worst thing you've ever done?'

'Ooh . . .' I thought back. 'Well, I started out as an assistant editor. When we finished a film, we'd join up all the outtakes, the bits we hadn't used, and wind them on to one big reel. To save on space, the centre was a tiny plastic core and the film was held in place by the tension as we wound it. Then they were stored flat, like big pancakes. Well, one day I was in a terrible rush, I think I had a deadline, and I went into the cupboard and got out one of these reels of outtakes. Only instead of laying it flat across my arm to support it, I just put my hand in the centre. When I was halfway across the room, the core suddenly popped out and the outer edges fell to the floor. Suddenly I was surrounded by thousands of feet of film unwound in one long ringlet.'

Lola was grinning. 'So what did you do?'

'I cried. I just sat down on the floor and bawled.' I laughed at the memory. 'The thing is, good editors are very organised, methodical, careful people and I was never any of those things. I was temperamentally unsuited to being a film editor.'

'That's what I keep telling Mom. But she's got this idea in her head that I've inherited Auntie Lenie's talent and that I'll be famous.' Lola shrugged and smiled at me. 'The thing is, I just want to get married. But Mom won't let Pete and me get engaged until I finish college. What do you think?'

'What does Pete say?' I hedged.

218

Lola made a face. 'The same as Mom.'

'Well,' I said, choosing my words carefully, 'perhaps that's the best idea. I mean, what would you do if anything happened to Pete and you had children to support?'

Lola stared at me blankly. 'Nothing. I'll have lots of money from my mom.'

'Ah yes, of course,' I agreed sheepishly. 'I'm not used to the people around me being rich. Maybe you should just do whatever you want. You can always go back to school later if you get bored.'

Lola gave a whoop of glee. 'Wait till I tell Mom you said that! She thinks you walk on water so it will mean a lot that you think I should get married.'

'Well, I don't think I said that exactly,' I protested as I found myself being propelled up the stairs and out on to the patio.

Beth gave me a mildly reproachful look when her daughter informed her with great ceremony that I had endorsed the idea that she and Pete get married.

I shrugged helplessly, deciding to keep my big mouth shut and stay out of it.

'I think, Lola, we should take your mom's advice,' argued Pete in a reasonable tone of voice. 'It isn't so long to wait. Only another two years till you graduate.'

'Three,' corrected Lola. 'Remember, I'm flunking out already. I'll probably have to repeat this one.'

'Well, Lola, I'm sure you'll regret it,' said Beth. 'You know when Marlene and I went back to Grandma's house to clear it out and she found those old films of hers, d'you know what she said? D'you know what her immediate response was?'

Lola cast her mother a mutinous look but said nothing.

'She said she'd wasted so much of her life by marrying so young. She had all that talent and she had all those opportunities and she did nothing with them.' Beth reached out to place her hand over Malcolm's. His face was expressionless.

'This is no reflection on you, Malcolm. It's just that if she'd waited a couple of years, she would have felt she'd done something.' Beth lifted her other hand to wipe away a tear which had appeared unexpectedly in her eyes. 'She never even got to edit those films. No one got to see what was in her mind, what she saw, what her vision was, if that's not too grand a term. She would have had something to show the world.' Beth's voice cracked. 'She would have left something.'

There was an uncomfortable silence, broken only by one stifled sob from Beth. Pete had an agonised expression on his face and looked as if he desperately wished he knew what to say. Lola was staring sullenly at her long manicured nails.

The awkward atmosphere did not lift and the evening ended shortly afterwards. Mags and I returned to our hotel. There was still no sign of Joe, just a message saying he was still at the hospital waiting for news, but that he would see us at breakfast the next morning, ready to start filming Malcolm's trial, now that the jury selection was over. Mags went off to bed almost at once, conscious that she had to be ready to appear on camera the next day.

When I got to my room, I found another message from Carl, and remembered guiltily that I hadn't called him back again as I had said I would. Immediately, I dialled his home number, but found myself talking to his answering machine once more. Feeling disappointed, I hung up.

I knew I wouldn't sleep. I paced around my hotel room restlessly. Then I switched off the light and stood at the window, pulling aside the curtains to look out at the Plaza, lit up and already emptying of pedestrians. I thought longingly of my TR6. I felt trapped in this high-rise building, with its weighted doors which shut resoundingly behind me, its labyrinth of corridors, its artificial ventilation. I'd have given anything to have taken the TR out into the cooling night air on some back road, to have opened the throttle and let rip, tearing up the dust and gravel behind me, letting off steam. Instead, I was closeted in here, with thoughts I couldn't bear and a desperate loneliness which threatened to overwhelm me. I had so few places to go at this time of night. I knew almost no one in Kansas City.

On impulse, I picked up the keys for the hired car – a solid sedan but a vehicle that could take me away from all this nonetheless. I walked free from the hotel, revelling in the cool air, feeling a light breeze play soothingly along my arms. But the Buick wasn't the same as a sports car. There was no kick, no sense of breaking free of restraint. The streets I drove along were broad and straight and peppered with traffic lights. The only roads I knew out of town were monotonous highways. I gave up and turned back. I couldn't outrun my loneliness. I would have to find some other way to cope.

It was only a few minutes' drive to St Dominick's Hospital where Carl worked. As I parked the car in the street outside, it occurred to me that I had no idea if he would be on duty tonight. But when I gave his name to the receptionist in the E.R., under the watchful eye of a security guard, she phoned through to him at once.

After a pause, she hung up again and said briefly, 'You can go through there and he'll meet you on the other side.'

As I approached the double wooden doors, a buzzer sounded, releasing a catch so that it swung open and I walked through. I was in a hospital corridor, much like any institutional hallway anywhere. The walls were painted cream and there was overhead strip lighting and grcy marble linoleum. Trolleys were lined up along one side and I glimpsed examining rooms full of medical equipment.

'Well, this is a nice surprise!' I turned towards the speaker and for a moment I was confused. The last time I had seen Carl, he had been wearing ordinary clothes. Now he was dressed in loose blue garments, not unlike the outfit Amanda wore in jail. 'You picked a good night. We're not busy.' He leant forward and kissed my cheek. 'I can take a little time off. Can I buy you a cup of coffee?'

He led the way down a maze of corridors until we finally emerged at a sort of large alcove which had been turned into a coffee bar. 'The main cafeteria's closed at this time of night but they have a machine that does OK espresso or latte,' he offered.

I decided on some mineral water and Carl had a double espresso. He held up his coffee cup to chink it against my glass. 'Your good health.'

'Hey,' he added suddenly after a gulp of coffee. 'Are you OK? I just assumed you were here to see me. Maybe you had a heart attack or something, and I'm offering you coffee?'

'No,' I said quietly. And then, perhaps because I hardly knew him and because I wouldn't have to face him again if I didn't want to, I blurted out, 'I suddenly felt terribly alone and I wanted to talk to someone. Anyone.'

'Oh, that's wonderful,' Carl said good-humouredly. 'It's great to know you can stand in at a moment's notice for just anyone. It must be a real problem for those people who're sort of *individual*. They must get hardly any visits at all. Boy, am I the lucky one.'

'Stop,' I begged, smiling in spite of myself. I had wanted to indulge my feelings of gloom and get some sympathy, but clearly I had come to the wrong person. He was making me laugh instead. So we talked about everything – politics and art and films and television programmes, food, even football. At one point, he asked about Amanda's situation, and expressed his sympathies, but he didn't dwell on it, sensing perhaps that it would only add to my despondence.

After a pause in the conversation, I opened my mouth to announce that it was time I left and heard myself say instead, 'I couldn't face going back to the hotel room. I can't sleep. I'm worried. I've got one of my best friends staying in the room next door yet I feel completely alone. I think I'm cracking up.'

His eyes were warm and concerned. He was fumbling in the pockets of the loose blue trousers and now he held out a set of keys. 'Stay at my place. It's two blocks away.'

I reached out thoughtfully and took the keys, examined them for a moment, then handed them back. 'Thanks. You don't know how much it means to me that you did that. But I have to go back. I have no choice. I can't stop now.'

He looked at me appraisingly for a long moment, then pocketed the keys. 'OK. But promise me you'll come back if you need help.'

He showed me to the outer door. As it opened, I could feel the rush of night air. He said, 'Will I see you again?'

'I don't know,' I answered truthfully. 'I don't seem to have much control over events at the moment.'

He leaned forward and kissed me. 'Well, you know where I am. I'd like to see you sometime when you're relaxed and not worried about things.'

'Never happen,' I said wryly. 'You may well see me again but I can guarantee I won't be relaxed.'

'Then I guess I'll settle for whatever I get.'

When I reached the kerb, I looked back. He was standing silhouetted in the doorway. I walked towards the car, hearing the sound of my footsteps echoing on the pavement. Suddenly I became aware of heavier feet somewhere behind me. Instantly, I glanced back and saw a powerfully built man emerging from a side exit.

For a moment I tensed, automatically wary of any stranger on this dimly lit street. But he seemed preoccupied. Hands in the pockets of his jeans, eyes downcast, he headed away from me, crossing the road towards the multi-storey car park on the opposite side. It wasn't until he passed beneath the bright yellow light over the entrance that I saw the cropped blond hair and Miss Piggy T-shirt and realised it was Joe.

I took a step forward, drawing in my breath to call out to him. But something made me stop. I got into my car and waited. A minute later, the crew van came down the ramp, turned right and drove off in the opposite direction from where I was watching. I started the car and pulled out after him without switching on my headlights. I was determined not to give myself away this time.

This time I kept less than a block behind, confident that he wouldn't see any telltale beams in his mirror. He headed north and then east, towards the rundown part of town I'd been told to avoid. The roads grew emptier and the street lights were mostly blown out. Such shops as there were had heavy grilles pulled over doors and windows and many of the buildings looked abandoned and boarded up.

Suddenly the tail lights disappeared. I felt the car bumping over rough ground and quickly slowed to a stop. I was in the same yard as before although I had approached it from a different direction. I looked around me nervously. As far as I could tell, there was no movement anywhere, not even in the dark areas of shadow. I rolled the window down an inch and listened. In the distance, a train hooted and I could hear the muted roar of traffic, as if the highway was fairly close.

There was no engine noise, but I knew the van couldn't be far away. It had been out of sight only seconds. On impulse, I opened the door and got out. There was the rank smell of rotting vegetation and the sound of insects – perhaps crickets – buzzing, but otherwise nothing, no sign of human life. I took a step forward, out of the shadow of the car. There was a slight sound to my right and I half turned, peering into the dark. The next thing I knew, something was tight round my neck and I was being yanked almost off my feet. Instinctively I lashed out with my heel, kicking behind me, trying for my attacker's shins.

I heard a gasp of pain and the arm round my neck loosened. It was only for a second, but it gave me the chance to free my head and I bit the hand gripping me. This time there was an audible yell and a hoarse, rasping voice roared, 'You little shit!'

'Joe!' I stood stock still. He froze and then I felt the arm fall away from my neck.

'Bel.' He sounded shocked. 'What the hell are you doing here?'

I couldn't speak, merely flexing the muscles in my neck and shoulder.

'Christ!' I heard him mutter. 'I just saw this car with no lights following me all the way from the centre of town. I thought it was a mugger, so I pulled in here, turned off the lights and waited. Are you all right?'

I nodded, then croaked, 'Yes.' I swallowed. 'I'm sorry. It sounds a bit silly now, but I was following you because I wanted to know where you went at night. There are so many unresolved questions surrounding this thing with Amanda, I thought it wouldn't hurt to find the answer to one of them.' I rubbed my throat. 'I guess it did hurt.'

'I didn't mean to, honest. I wouldn't lay a finger on any woman, ever, for any reason. It was just that this is a bad neighbourhood, it's late, it's dark . . .'

'I know,' I said quietly. 'I understand. I shouldn't have been so stupid.'

'Come on.' Joe put his arm round my shoulders, leading me away from the vehicles across the rough ground.

'Where are we going?' There was a note of alarm in my voice.

'I think it's time you learned a few things.' He seemed to know the way, even though it was pitch black. I found myself stumbling across uneven terrain, then suddenly we emerged into a narrow street.

It seemed to be lined with warehouses, tall buildings without windows on the lower floors. There was no one around and there was the sort of silence that told me that either this was a commercial area which was deserted at night, or it was completely derelict and abandoned.

Joe stopped and I realised we were standing before a door set into a long expanse of blank wall. He knocked a rapid tattoo and waited. The door opened and he stepped quickly into the dimly lit interior, pulling me after him, so that I stumbled over the step.

Straightening up, I saw that we were in a small area closed off by lengths of fabric hung from the ceiling. The only light came from a red bulb. To our left was a tiny counter behind which sat a young woman in a red satin corset and fishnet tights. There was something ghoulish about the black ringed eyes and vampish get-up. She snatched up the twenty dollar bill Joe tossed in her direction.

'Go right ahead,' she instructed us in a theatrically throaty voice.

I could hear a distant boom of rock music. Joe pushed aside the drapes ahead of us and we descended a narrow flight of stairs into a cellar painted dark red, with low-hanging beams. Strobe lights revealed a syncopated picture of dancing couples, many of them flamboyantly dressed in gold or silver lamé, silk or satin. A disc jockey was visible sitting behind a desk on a raised dais in one corner.

As I stepped down into the room, I noticed that the floor was semi-transparent, glass or plastic, through which flickered pastel coloured lights. The noise assaulted my ears, but more than that, I could feel it pulsing up through the soles of my feet.

Joe caught hold of my arm and pulled me after him through the crowds round the perimeter of the dance area to the bar. It was on the far side, up some steps and separated from the rest of the room by a wooden balustrade. Gratefully, I sank on to a stool. Joe leant across the counter and yelled an order for drinks to the barman who bent forward, turning his head to catch what Joe was saying.

I looked around me, conscious of several curious stares in my direction. I was decidedly underdressed in a white cotton shirt tied loosely at the waist and a pair of khaki slacks. Although most of the men wore jeans and T-shirts, the women glowed and glittered in their exotic outfits. Pink and mauve lights flickered over the dance floor, illuminating the cloudy atmosphere and reflecting off the intense faces of those watching. A few of the dancers merely shuffled around, but several were performing for an audience, striking poses and executing intricate steps, casting occasional sideways glances at their admirers. It was clearly a pick-up joint.

Joe nudged me and handed over a glass of beer. 'What d'you think?' He grinned broadly.

I laughed. 'This is where you've been coming on your night expeditions?'

Joe nodded. He leaned his elbows on the bar, his face lit by the downlights directed on to the counter. 'I brought Amanda here a lot the first week after we'd arrived. She'd be completely wound-up. She hadn't been able to sleep without pills for months – not since she left Harlan. She was taking uppers and downers like there was no tomorrow.' He took a sip of his beer, then swivelled round, still holding the glass, and rested his elbows on the counter behind him, surveying the dancers.

'I took her here to let off steam. I was afraid that if she got too low she'd call Harlan and he'd talk her into going back.'

'Well, why the secrecy? So what if you went out dancing every night?'

Joe cast me a mischievous sideways glance. 'Notice anything different about this place?' I peered through the gloom at the crowd on the dance floor. My eyes were adjusting to the dim light. I was beginning to make out faces and features where before there had been only vague shapes.

'It's a gay bar,' I said simply with sudden comprehension. I turned back towards Joe. 'Why do you come here?'

Joe paused. 'They stay open later than the straight bars and they're more fun – less inhibited.' He paused, smiling at me. 'And I'm gay.'

'You can't be!' I blurted out. 'You flirt with everyone.'

'So?' He was indignant. 'I like flirting. It's an art form.' He grinned.

'So why keep it a secret?' I was genuinely puzzled.

Joe shrugged. 'You can never be sure how people will react. It was nothing you needed to know.' There was a note of defiance in his voice now.

I was about to say more, but at that moment a commotion broke out on the dance floor between a tall, glamorous woman in a spangly dress and long, flowing blonde hair and her partner, a Hispanic man in dark jeans and a white shirt open to the waist. I could hear them shouting even above the pounding music and I leaned forward to talk into Joe's ear.

'I always assumed you and Amanda had something going between you.'

Joe grinned even more widely. 'That's what you were supposed to think.' He drained the last of his beer and returned the glass to the bar with a thump.

There was a wail of anguish from the dance floor. The Hispanic man was triumphantly twirling his partner's flowing golden locks in the air. The woman was now revealed as a man in drag. Bursting into the tears, she turned and pushed through the crowds to the ladies' room.

Joe shook his head. 'I dunno,' he said as the disc jockey ranted into his microphone. 'All this high drama. Give me the simple life.' He held out a hand. 'Come on. Let's go and work off some of this nervous tension we're both suffering from.'

Feeling acutely self-conscious, I followed him reluctantly on to the dance floor. But as the beat began to throb through the soles of my feet again and drummed in my head, it drove out all the thoughts which had been circling obsessively for days and nights. And with a sudden feeling of release, I threw myself into the music.

Chapter Fourteen

I woke up the next morning feeling energised and less tense than I had been for days. Not even the returning consciousness of all that was going on in the lives of those around me could detract from my sense of wellbeing. I looked out at a bright day, the sun still delicate in the sky, not yet the relentless burning orb it would become later.

I had left a message to myself on the bedside table to remind me to phone Martin first thing. When I got through, he sounded anxious and I understood his concern. We were thousands of miles away, beyond both his help and his supervision, and meanwhile he had his budgets to think of.

'I'm really sorry about Amanda and of course we'll monitor what's happening with her and try to offer support,' he said apologetically, 'but I can't keep you all hanging about out there for ever. I think you should finish up by the end of next week and come home. It's really the background to the case we're interested in. You don't need to cover the whole trial – we can probably get news footage of the rest of it.'

I couldn't argue with him. There seemed to be little else we could do to help Amanda. The one possibility that remained – that Crystal would turn up and confess to being the red-haired woman at the centre of it all – seemed so far-fetched in the cold light of day that I didn't even mention it. We ended the conversation agreeing that my PA back home would book our return flights for the weekend after next.

As ever, Joe appeared fresh and rested in spite of his lack of sleep when I joined the others in reception, ready to depart for the day's work. I had decided to begin early that morning at Beth's home, recording scenes of the family preparing themselves for the ordeal ahead before going to the court.

Malcolm was, if anything, more withdrawn than ever, hollow-eyed and silent. Beth busied herself, as always, looking after everyone else, fussing over Malcolm's choice of tie and nagging Lola to wear a less revealing skirt. Pete stood quietly on the sidelines, calming his girlfriend with a restraining hand on her arm and a consoling kiss when it seemed she would explode with fury at her mother's interference.

The court was convened at nine a.m. prompt in a rectangular room, with an imposing dais built of hardwood stretching across one end. Oak panelling and elegant chandeliers added a veneer of grandeur to the surroundings. We decided to set up our camera opposite the jury, near the front where we could see the faces of most of those directly involved.

We listened to the opening arguments before the prosecution began to call witnesses to testify to the volatile nature of the relationship between Malcolm and Marlene. Joe, Evan, Lewis and I worked well together. I positioned myself slightly behind and to one side of Joe, whispering instructions and watching out for reactions from the participants that he might miss.

At noon, we ate in a small side room with Beth and the others to avoid the press milling about outside. Afterwards, we returned to our places and the legal process continued. As the voices droned on, something made me glance to my right. Harlan had slipped into the courtroom unnoticed and was sitting at the back. He had been watching me and now he smiled. It was a chilling moment.

At five, the court was recessed until the next morning and

we said goodnight to Beth and the rest of her group. It was tacitly agreed that we would leave them alone that evening to give them a chance to recover before facing the public again the next day.

'God, it's so draining sitting there concentrating on all that legal stuff hour after hour,' commented Mags as we drove back to the hotel. As soon as the equipment was unloaded and safely stowed away for the night, Evan and Lewis returned to their homes. Joe, Mags and I agreed that we would meet in the bar for a drink around seven thirty.

I planned to go for a swim and then soak in the tub. I had just pulled on my bathing suit when I noticed that the red light on the telephone was flashing. Quickly I dialled the number which allowed me to retrieve my messages. The first one was from Carl, wanting to know if I was feeling any better. He'd left his work number with a request that I call him there later. The second message was less straightforward. The woman who spoke sounded so strained and uncomfortable, that it wasn't till she said her name that I realised who it was.

'This is a message for Bel Carson on Thursday at, umm, five p.m.,' she began awkwardly. 'This is Chris Remington from the legal centre. I have some news for you about Crystal. I'll be here until six, otherwise you can call me after eight thirty in the morning.' I glanced quickly at the clock radio next to the phone. Five to six. She hadn't left the telephone number. Seething with impatience, I tore open the drawers of the desk until I found a directory. Quickly I flicked through it until I came upon the listing for the legal centre.

After four rings the answering machine picked up and I groaned with frustration. When the beep sounded to leave a message, I simply said, 'This is Bel Carson for Chris. I seem to have—'

'Hi, Bel.' Chris's voice interrupted me. 'I was just on my way out the door. How are you?' She sounded more relaxed with a live person on the other end than she had when speaking to a machine.

'Fine,' I replied quickly. 'What's the news on Crystal?'

'She'll talk to you.'

'Fantastic!' I whooped. 'How soon can I see her?'

'We-ell.' Chris sounded uncertain. 'I suppose something could be arranged for this evening, if you like.'

'Wonderful. Where?'

'Why don't I meet you in the foyer of your hotel in half an hour, if that's OK, to discuss terms.'

'Great,' I said, but she had already hung up.

For the next thirty minutes, I tried to guess what she meant when she referred to 'terms'. Perhaps it just meant that I'd have to pay her. I raked out all my traveller's cheques in preparation and counted them out. I wasn't sure how much she'd expect – I knew that there was such stiff competition in the US between different current affairs shows that they were prepared to pay out large sums of money. RTV only ever offered token payments, partly because our budgets were relatively small and partly to guard against accusations of chequebook journalism. But Crystal's testimony could be the key to proving Amanda's innocence. I made an executive decision. I would pay her everything I had – it was the company's money anyway – and sort it out later.

I had been pacing up and down in the foyer for a good five minutes before I became aware of a tiny battered car painted bright orange puttering into the parking lot and coming to a stop under the concrete canopy at the front entrance. Such a small vehicle was unusual in America and I couldn't help staring as it idled noisily outside. But my interest quickened even further when the passenger door opened and a bulky figure emerged with difficulty from the cramped interior. It was Chris.

234

I stepped forward to greet her as she came through the polished brass revolving door.

She acknowledged me with a wave of the hand, before darting a quick glance around the foyer as if checking out who else was present. Her face was pale and she was wearing the same uniform as before – dark jeans, a white T-shirt with some slogan written across it and the over-sized khaki jacket.

'Hi.' She sounded cautious.

'Why don't we talk in the bar?' I suggested, nodding in that direction.

She shook her head. 'Too crowded.' Again she looked around the foyer. 'How about there?' She indicated a small leather sofa in the corner, screened by a large fern.

'Fine.' I led the way across the room and sat down. 'Would you like something to drink?'

She shook her head. 'No. Let's get this over with.' She slumped down on to the cushions at the other end of the sofa. There was an awkward silence.

'What are the terms?' I prompted, trying to sound as friendly and unthreatening as possible.

'Right.' She coughed slightly. 'Well, firstly, if Crystal talks to you, you must agree not to reveal her whereabouts or her identity.' She gazed at me fixedly, watching for my tiniest reaction. I felt instinctively that if I got this wrong, my chances of talking to Crystal would be gone for ever.

I thought quickly. If she did have information that could help Amanda, then of course I would want her to come forward. So I was very reluctant to give such a promise. But on the other hand, if I didn't, she obviously wasn't going to agree to talk to me and I would find out nothing at all. Better, I decided, to hear what she had to say and then take it from there.

'Fine,' I said.

'You mean that?' Chris eyed me intently.

'Yes.'

Chris nodded, then coughed again before continuing. 'You know, I have seen you before. Your picture was in the paper in connection with the murder of Harlan's girlfriend and it said you were a friend of the woman who was accused.' She paused. 'Is that the real reason you want to talk to Crystal? Is it about the murder of Sharon Donovan – something to do with Harlan?'

I considered her carefully. There was something so uncom-promising about Chris, about the way she looked me directly in the eye without wavering, about the way she asked uncom-fortable questions, it was as if honesty and truth were her lifeline. She'd know at once if I lied.

'Yes,' I said.

Chris continued to regard me searchingly. 'I'm still not sure this is the right thing to do but I was persuaded by the other women at the centre,' she said at last. She took a deep breath. 'I'm Crystal.'

'No you're not!' The words were out before I could stop myself. 'I've seen pictures of Crystal. You're not her.'

Chris laughed delightedly. It transformed her rather som-bre, heavy-set face, lightening it, making her look suddenly youthful.

'You couldn't have paid me a better compliment,' she said.

I stared at her. 'You're Crystal?' I echoed inanely. 'But you don't look anything like her.'

Chris smiled. 'No. But I used to. Maybe thirty, forty pounds ago, before I stopped dying my hair and cut it short.'

'So you're not a real redhead.' I couldn't keep the disap-pointment out of my voice.

'Oh, yes. But I started to go grey in my early twenties. That's when I began colouring it.'

'And when did you stop?'

236

'Just over a year ago. I met someone else, a woman, and fell in love, and I decided to leave the old Crystal behind.' She smiled wryly. 'She was too fragile, too much what other people wanted her to be, always trying to please, to get attention.' She paused, then added in a soft, sad voice, 'Always willing to do what any man wanted her to do.' She shrugged that image aside. 'Pete paid for me to go to college. Now I'm putting myself through law school.'

'Those men you did anything for, did they include Harlan?'

Chris studied her hands for a moment, then nodded. She looked up again, meeting my gaze bravely. 'Sure. I was so in love with that jerk. But he had the hots for Kelly – she was a good girl from the right side of the tracks. She wouldn't sleep with him, so he used to come to me instead. I married Pete to be near Harlan.'

She shook her head sadly. 'I can't believe I did that but I did. I was screwing Harlan on the side all the time I was married. Then Pete found out. What made it worse was that he didn't get mad at me. But it destroyed him. I could see it in his eyes. His wife and his best friend! I hurt the nicest man I know for the sake of one of the world's worst shits.' Tears formed in Chris's eyes, but she brushed them away. 'He didn't speak to Harlan for a long time after that. But I guess old Harlan sweet-talked him into being buddies again. After all, Pete was too useful to lose.' There was a bitter edge to her voice.

'So, if you've looked like this for the past year or more, it couldn't have been you who was seen running away from Sharon's murder.'

'The redhead? No, that wasn't me. I thought that was supposed to be your friend.' Chris gave me a pointed look.

'I was hoping to prove it was someone else.'

'Even wearing a wig, I couldn't begin to look like her,' she reasoned. 'She must be a size eight or ten and I'm at least a sixteen now.' She smiled. 'This is the fat, contented, cared-for me.'

I nodded. 'No. I can see that. But Amanda swears it wasn't her that night. Lola, Pete's girlfriend, saw another red-haired woman a few months ago with Harlan. She thought it was you.'

Chris shook her head. 'I couldn't pass myself off as the old Crystal if I tried.'

So much for all my theories, I thought despondently. The only hope I had of proving Harlan's guilt seemed to have disappeared. Aloud I said, 'Harlan seems so charming. But my gut feeling is he's behind these deaths.'

Chris frowned. 'What do you mean, deaths? I thought there was just poor Sharon?'

I debated whether to tell her what I suspected. But I needed her help and I was pretty sure I wouldn't get it if I didn't level with her.

'You knew Kelly Swartz?'

'Of course,' Chris answered in a low voice.

'Well, I don't believe her death was a suicide. I think she was murdered.'

Chris looked shocked. 'Well,' she said eventually, 'I always thought there was something not right about that, but it seemed so cut and dried – the note and everything.'

I shook my head. 'I don't think so.'

'Then who killed her?'

'Harlan has an alibi. It only stands up because a red-haired woman whom everyone assumed was Kelly was seen driving her car down Main Street that night.' I looked directly at Chris. 'I accept that you weren't involved in Sharon's murder. But this was years ago. I wondered if that could have been you. I'm told you were the only woman for miles around who could pass yourself off as Kelly with any hope of success.'

238

Chris shook her head emphatically. 'Uh-uh. I had an alibi too. When I left high school, I went to work full-time as a waitress at the diner. Saturdays were our busiest night of the week.' She smiled sadly. 'I wish in a way it *was* me. Because I would love to nail that creep.'

'Can you think of anyone else it might have been?' I pleaded.

'Not that I recall. There really weren't that many people in that part of the world, full stop. And no redheads apart from Kelly and me. If anyone else had been around, people would have noticed, believe me. There wasn't a great deal of coming and going in town. Everyone knew everyone else's business.'

'Well, do you think Harlan could have been involved in murdering Kelly?'

'Oh, for sure.' She looked away. 'He beat me up a bunch of times. Smashed my face in but good. He seemed to really get off on that. He liked women to do what they were told. I can imagine a scenario where he went one step too far.'

'Did he beat Kelly?'

Chris grimaced. 'I wouldn't be surprised. Kelly was afraid of him sometimes, I know that. I never understood it because she really didn't have to put up with any shit. She had a nice home and a mom and dad who loved her. But I guess she was like the rest of us and she just couldn't stay away. There were always lots of women circling around Harlan. I don't know what it is about men like that but they seem to be irresistible to so many women, don't they?' Her mouth twisted into a bitter smile. 'But like I told you, Kelly wouldn't sleep with him. She had more guts than I did.'

'So what do you think happened that afternoon?'

A thoughtful expression came over Chris's face. She gazed out of the window, far away to some past life. 'There was a bunch of speed in town, as I recall. And Harlan loved speed. He was probably high as anything that afternoon and drinking beer out at the quarry. He would have wanted sex, I've no doubt of that. Speed and beer together always made him horny as anything. Kelly might have gone along with it so far, but then wanted to call a halt. That would've made him mad. And maybe this time he couldn't stop himself. Maybe this time he killed her.'

Chris was quiet for a moment. With one finger, she traced the outline of the studs in the leather seat cushion between us.

'In a way, Harlan and I were alike.' She looked up at me with an air of bravery, as if she were confronting something painful. 'We could both tune in to what other people were thinking and what they wanted, just like that.' She snapped her fingers. 'But I did it because I was a born victim, and I wanted to please everyone and get attention and what I thought was love. Harlan used his intuition to make people trust him, to be the sort of person they liked and felt empathy with. Then he'd get them to do exactly what he wanted. What makes him so dangerous and difficult to pin down is that there is nothing constant about him. He'll say whatever he has to at any moment to get by and he'll say it with utter sincerity.' She laughed mirthlessly. 'Ordinary people like you and me – or Kelly for that matter – don't know how to deal with that.'

'Do you think Pete could have been involved?'

'No!' Her tone was emphatic. 'Pete is the nicest person you could ever hope to meet. He was the only man I ever knew who didn't abuse me. And when I left, he paid for my education and last year he bought me a little apartment downtown. No. No one will ever get me to say a word against him. His only failing was that he never could see through Harlan. He always believed the best of him, no matter what. But he made allowances for me, too, so I suppose he's that kind of person.'

Suddenly her expression changed and she held up her hand to look at her wristwatch. 'I have to go,' she said hurriedly, getting to her feet. 'My ride will be waiting.'

We walked towards the exit. The small orange car was parked just outside. Chris waved to the driver, then turned to me, fishing in her jacket pocket to produce a small white card. She scribbled something before handing it over.

'You can contact me at the legal centre most days, but I've put my home number on the back.' She held out her hand and shook mine. 'Good luck. If you need anything else, let me know.'

She made to get into the orange car, then stopped. 'I'm sure you're right. Harlan is guilty. But God knows how you'll ever prove it.'

I watched and waved as she was driven off, then made my way back to the bar where I found Mags and Joe having a drink. I signalled to a waiter and sank into the seat Joe had pulled out for me. While I waited for the wine to arrive, I filled the others in on my meeting with Chris.

'So it's not her,' commented Mags in a flat voice when I'd finished.

'We're back to square one,' I agreed morosely. 'We're no nearer solving this than we were when we started.'

'Well, it must be someone.' Joe sounded defiant. 'Amanda isn't lying.'

I closed my eyes, trying to marshal my thoughts. 'We know she must be about five foot ten and be slim enough to pass for Amanda – at least at a distance. We know she either has red hair or wears a wig. We know she has some connection to Harlan because she shows up when his girlfriends get killed. She was in Rapid Falls fifteen years ago and she was here in Kansas City very recently.' I opened my eyes again. 'I've gone over and over Amanda's case and I can't figure it out. And as for Kelly . . .' I shrugged.

'We still don't know why this mystery woman was pretending to be her while Kelly was still alive,' Mags finished for me.

'Well, there has to be an explanation!' Joe sounded belliger-
ent. 'Three reasonably smart people must be able to work it
out.' He gazed at me beseechingly. 'Come on, Bel, you must be
able to come up with something.'

I shook my head helplessly.

'Perhaps Kelly was being held prisoner,' mused Mags.

'But why?' I objected. 'Why not shove her in the quarry
there and then if that's what they intended?' There was a
moment's silence. 'Because Harlan didn't have his alibi set up
till later,' I continued, suddenly finding myself answering my
own question. 'And if Harlan needed an alibi—' I stopped and
grabbed the other two by the arm. 'That's it!'

Mags was looking mystified, but Joe leaned forward
urgently. 'What is? You've lost me.'

I took a deep breath. 'Harlan went out of his way to set up
an alibi. Right?' I looked from Joe to Mags and saw them nod,
still mystified but doggedly following my reasoning. 'That had
to be because he was guilty. He'd done something. OK?'
Again they nodded uncertainly.

'And if he'd done something, it had to have been earlier
that day . . .' Light was dawning in Mags's eyes. 'And we
know that he had to get someone else to masquerade as
Kelly. Therefore –' I paused for emphasis – 'he must have
attacked her that afternoon and injured her so badly that he
thought she was dead or at least dying. That's when he set
up the alibi. Then someone else put Kelly into her car and
pushed her off the cliff while Harlan was playing poker.
Only she wasn't already dead and the poor kid drowned.'
We were all suddenly silent. It didn't bear thinking about.

I jumped to my feet. 'I've got a copy of the autopsy report
upstairs.'

Without a word, the other two followed me. All the way up
in the lift, we could hardly contain our impatience. When we
reached my room, I was so nervous that I dropped the keycard

and then inserted it upside down. Finally we burst through the door.

'It's on the desk.' I scrabbled through files and sheets of paper. 'Here we are.' I ran a finger down the typed lines as the others crowded behind me and read over my shoulder. 'This is what we want!' I read from the page. ' "Facial lacerations . . . broken jaw . . . severe head injury." ' I looked up at the others. 'The doctor assumed that happened when the car hit the water from such a height and she got bounced around inside.'

'But we know it was probably caused by Harlan,' said Joe.

'But, surely they can tell when injuries like that occurred so long before death?' Mags looked puzzled.

I waved the sheet of paper excitedly. 'I'm sure you can, if you're an expert. But the autopsy wasn't carried out by a pathologist. It was done by the local doctor – an elderly man whose knowledge was probably years out of date. Plus he had no reason to suspect foul play. Remember, they had the suicide note. He wasn't looking for complicated explanations.'

'Christ.' Joe sank on to the bed and rubbed his hands across his face. 'Where does that get us?'

'Yeah.' Mags sat down next to him. 'This is all conjecture. We have no evidence.'

Joe punched a fist into the palm of his other hand. 'If only it had happened last week, or even last month. We'd have had a fighting chance of finding proof. People would remember things. We could have had the autopsy redone. But fifteen years . . .' He groaned despairingly.

'There are these,' I said, holding up a sheaf of papers. 'The eye-witness reports. I've already looked at them but we can go through them again.'

'Let's see.' Mags reached out a hand.

We sat in silence for the next fifteen minutes, reviewing all the accounts given by people who claimed to have seen Kelly that evening. Joe was the first to finish, tossing the last one on to the bed in a gesture of exasperation.

'There's just one thing . . .' Mags was not an ace reporter for nothing.

'The sunglasses?' I suggested.

She nodded and waved a couple of pages in front of her. 'Why the change-over?'

I shrugged helplessly. 'I can't figure it out either.'

'What's that?' Joe looked puzzled. Quickly, I explained.

He shook his head slowly. 'Everywhere we turn with this there are questions we can't answer. We need to know exactly what happened that night and there's no chance of that now.' Joe bowed his head and ran his hands through his hair distractedly.

'Marlene's films,' I said. Joe and Mags looked at me sharply. 'I always thought they couldn't have anything to do with Kelly's murder because she died at night, when it was dark and the camera wouldn't have been able to see anything very much.'

Joe looked at me with dawning comprehension. 'But now we're talking afternoon.'

I nodded. 'The old quarry was on the McKinleys' property. She was obsessive about her project. She could quite easily have been out filming there that day. In fact –' I closed my eyes momentarily, visualising the quarry when I had last seen it, with storm clouds surging over the clifftop – 'If I were her, I'd definitely have chosen that location because it would have been much more dramatic than watching things happen slowly far away on the horizon.'

'Yeah.' Joe was becoming enthused. 'And didn't you say it was time-release stuff? She probably lay there sunbathing with the shutter cable in her hand and just pressed it every ten seconds or whatever.' He smacked his fist on to the bedside table. 'So she may have filmed Harlan's attack on Kelly without knowing it . . .'

244

'. . . and only found that out when she discovered her old student films years later,' Mags chimed in.

There was silence. 'And now they've gone up in flames.' Joe's words were almost inaudible.

'If only she'd made a safety copy,' moaned Mags.

'If only,' agreed Joe bitterly.

'But then she'd no idea they contained something so potentially danger—' Mags stopped in mid-sentence and stared at me. 'What?' she asked bewildered.

I was on my feet, pacing up and down the room. 'I bet she did! I bet she had work prints! She was a rich kid. Nothing but the best. I bet she did!'

'So where are they?' asked Mags, ever practical. Joe's eyes were fixed on me.

'I have no idea. I'm not even sure that if they existed they weren't burnt with the others.'

'Don't!' groaned Joe. 'Don't say that. For God's sake, let's work on the premise that they survived. Otherwise Amanda is as good as dead.'

'You're right,' said Mags, reaching out to pat his shoulder consolingly. She turned to me. 'So how can we find out?'

I was already picking up my shoulder bag from where I'd dropped it on the floor. 'I'm off to see Beth and Lola. If anyone can answer our questions, it has to be them.' I paused at the door. 'Are you coming?'

Joe opened his mouth as if to say yes, then closed it again and grimaced. 'I can't. I'm expecting a call from Amanda. She's on such a knife edge that if I'm not available when she needs to talk . . . In fact –' a troubled look came over his face – 'I'd better go to my room now. I didn't tell the switchboard I would be here.' He pushed past out of the room.

'I'll come.' Mags was right behind me. Without another word we headed for the lifts.

'I wouldn't know if she had other copies of her films.' Beth was gazing at us anxiously. We were in the family room at the back of the house. The curtains were still open and I could see the garden outside, looking dark and mysterious. Malcolm had gone to bed by the time we'd arrived and Beth and Lola had been sitting watching the televised news of the trial.

Beth turned to her daughter. 'Do you know anything about this?'

Lola looked blank. 'All I saw was she had four little films on plastic reels.'

'Were they in colour or black and white?' I asked urgently.

She frowned. 'Well, they were colour. Why does that matter?'

'When your aunt was making her films, people often had black and white work prints because it was cheaper.' I turned back to Beth. 'They could have been burnt already, but if Marlene didn't bother bringing them to Kansas City, where would they be? At the house?'

'Could be.' Beth sounded dubious. Suddenly she put a hand up to her mouth in a gesture of dismay. 'All that stuff is supposed to be burned sometime this week whenever the wind is right. Lola, call Pete this instant and ask him.'

But Lola was already punching numbers into the telephone keypad, tapping her foot in her anxiety. 'Oh, come on, Pete, come on!' she muttered under her breath. She closed her eyes in an expression of resignation, then looked at us despairingly. 'It's the answering machine. What d'you want me to do? Leave a message for him to call back?'

Beth jumped to her feet. 'Hell, no! We have no idea when he'll be home. Bel, I think you should head out for the old homestead anyhow. It's worth taking a chance because the weather forecast said they had high winds out there today and they wouldn't start a fire under those conditions.' She shrugged. 'If it has burnt down, at least we'll have tried. If it hasn't, well, it would be wonderful if you could find Marlene's films.'

She turned to her daughter. 'Just leave a message that we'll see Pete tomorrow as planned.' Reaching for her handbag, she added, 'Lola, where are – oh, there they are. Here, Bel.' She held out a small metal key with a red string attached. 'This is for the padlock on the door. I'll get you a flashlight.' She bustled out of the room.

I rose to leave and noticed Mags watching me with an expression of alarm on her face. 'Don't worry,' I assured her. 'If I'm not back in time for the trial tomorrow, Joe knows what I'm after. He can cope without me.'

'That's not what concerns me,' she replied, frowning. 'This sounds like a crazy scheme to me. You're chasing a murderer, for goodness' sake! He hasn't thought twice about killing before. Why don't you just notify the police and let them take care of it?'

I considered that for a moment, then shook my head. 'It would take too long to explain. I know exactly what I'm looking for and no one knows I'm going out there except the people in this room. I'll be fine.' Then as she still looked dubious, I added quietly, 'It's Amanda's only hope.'

Beth reappeared and thrust a torch into my hand. 'Here,' she said. 'You'll need this.'

Beth and Mags stood silhouetted in the lighted doorway as I jumped into my car and tore off as fast as I could.

I got as far as the Interstate before it occurred to me that I was going to feel a complete fool if this was a wild goose chase. Hundreds of miles for nothing. But it was the last chance we had of catching this killer and freeing two innocent people.

Chapter Fifteen

I drove west on I-70 without ever looking down at the speedometer. Once I had passed the state capital of Topeka and the lights of the town fell away behind me, the traffic began to thin out. Occasionally I would overtake a pickup truck or the headlights of an on-coming juggernaut would flare in my eyes. But for most of the time there was only the long, empty moonlit highway, the road markings whirling beneath the car, keeping up a rapid syncopated beat.

Obsessively, my mind returned to Marlene's films. Even though I knew the chances of finding them and somehow using them to prove Amanda innocent were remote, I could not give up now. I could not accept that the brutal killer of three young women should go free while there was the slightest chance of proving his guilt. I had to see this through to the end.

But I wondered what the films would show if I ever found them. Would they be enough to destroy Harlan's alibi? Would they reveal the identity of the mystery woman? Without her testimony it would be impossible to convict him of involvement in Kelly's murder. And she was also the link between that killing and Sharon's. The only hope of breaking the case was to find her. She had to confess.

I wrestled again with the tantalising fact that she must belong to that tightknit community. But who was she under that disguise?

Fleeting images flew at me out of the darkness – Kelly's double in diamanté sunglasses, swerving round the forecourt of the diner, the sullen waters of the old quarry closing with a rush over her car, Marlene lazing in the grass, unwittingly filming the murder of her friend, and threaded through it all the strands of red hair, like a web tangled in my thoughts. I knew that if I could only unravel them, see them from a different perspective, I would find the key to solving all three murders. But how?

I completed a journey that should have taken five hours in just over half that time by treating the sedate Buick as if it were my TR6. Driving up the dusty track to the farm, I could just make out the ranch house brooding amongst the dark cluster of trees surrounding it. And to the right, across the dry, crumbling earth, was the old homestead, silhouetted in the thin moonlight, crippled and listing to one side but still defiantly standing. As I slowed to a standstill, I noticed a big hole had been gouged out of the ground on the far side, ready to inter the charred remains.

It was eerily silent as I emerged from the car. The wind had died down as it often did at night and I paused, listening intently, looking around me slowly. The monochrome grey-brown of the ploughed field stretched into the darkness as far as the eye could see. To my left lay the deep shadows of the trees.

I fished in my jeans pocket for the key that Beth had given me. The porch sank a little under my weight as I walked across it and undid the padlock. The door gave a loud juddering creak as I pushed it open. Then I waited, but there was no sign of life from inside, no indication that anyone was there before me. Switching on the torch, I stepped over the threshold gingerly.

The sweet-sour smell of rotting wood met me as I entered and stood in the pool of moonlight that cascaded down the stairs from the hole where the roof had caved in. As I moved forward I could feel an occasional breeze against my face and hear the whispering of air moving through a honey-comb of crevices and cracks. It was as if the house were sighing.

I picked my way carefully towards the archway and through into the big living room, following the wavering beam of my torch. It looked exactly as it had during my last visit. The finger of light reflected off the black rubbish bags piled up on one side and picked out the big fireplace with its fairy ring of log seats. Somehow darkness made the house seem more cavernous. The bare wooden struts where the plaster had crumbled to dust and the beam that had fallen across one corner cast distorted shadows. They were like bones, ribs perhaps, as if I were inside a carcass.

The thought made me suddenly shiver with apprehension. Brusquely, I told myself to get a grip, then propped the torch on top of a box and began searching systematically through all the black bags. I worked quickly, pulling out old clothes, worn cowboy boots with badly cracked leather uppers and hundreds of torn pieces of paper, bills and magazines, a shoe box of ribbons, some junk jewellery.

After about an hour, I noticed that the torch beam had begun to flicker and, with a sickening lurch, I realised that the battery might be going down. Panicking, I looked around, hoping to find an old oil lamp, anything that would give light and enable me to continue my search. I crossed to the fireplace, stubbing my toe on one of the upended logs, thinking that perhaps I could start a fire in the grate. Instead, just before the torch beam flickered and finally died, I caught sight of the two candles left on the slate hearth.

I spent the next fifteen minutes fiddling with the cigarette lighter in my car to get them lit. When I finally returned to my task, they turned out to be surprisingly effective. The sight that greeted me was not encouraging, however. I had torn apart some thirty or forty bags. Now there were only three left and my chances of finding the films were looking slim. Wearily I rubbed the aching muscles of my back.

What if the work prints didn't exist? Resolutely I pushed that thought aside. But if they weren't in the black bags, where could they be? There was nothing lying around in any of the other ground-floor rooms. I turned and looked to where the cold, pearly moonlight poured down the stairwell. Could Marlene have put them on the floor above? But almost at once I dismissed that idea, recalling the rotten treads and the broken banister which swung dangerously loose. She wouldn't have been that stupid. She could have killed herself going up there.

Yet Beth had said her sister hadn't wanted to leave without some sort of ceremony. Marlene had wanted to make her mark. She'd put together a little pyre of her memories and dreams and hopes, she'd said, so they would soar to heaven from the ashes and mark the end of an era. But I had come across nothing that looked as if it had been assembled with any forethought or specific intent. Rubbish had been stuffed into the black bags at random. I looked round me helplessly. If she had decided to hide the films in some secret place, they could be anywhere – under a floorboard, behind a loose skirting board, perhaps in a gap in the crumbling plaster.

I took a deep breath and began tearing the last three plastic bags apart. Clouds of dust billowed out as I tipped them on to the floor and disconsolately began poking the contents with my foot, searching for anything that could be a container for film.

Suddenly something caught my eye. At first I thought it might be a stuffed animal of some kind, or an old fur stole.

But as my foot teased it out of the pile, I was able to see more clearly and it was nothing like that. It had long, tangled strands. Bending down, I picked it up, shaking it so that the candlelight caught glints of gold and auburn as the long tresses unravelled. It was a wig of red hair.

With mounting excitement, I began scrabbling through the other things strewn around on the floor. Almost at once, my hands touched something soft which gleamed scarlet in the candlelight. Holding it up, I saw that it was a red satin dress, fitted and sleeveless, with a flounce round the neckline. I looked at it thoughtfully. Lola had been right when she'd said the dress was too big for her. This was at least a size twelve. Marlene, Sharon, Crystal and Amanda – and Kelly, for that matter – had all been very slender, size eights. The mystery woman couldn't have been one of them.

I stared at the dress, trying to visualise the person who would have worn this. Mentally, I added the wig, but it didn't work. No image sprang to mind. I laid the satin gown aside.

That was when I caught a glimpse of some fabric with a swirling pattern buried beneath a heavy black garment. Extricating it from the pile, I saw that it was a copy of Amanda's silk dress, only larger, still in one piece and stiff with dark splashes of what I realised, with a shudder, must be dried blood.

I gazed at it, my mind reeling. Who could have put this here, knowing that within the next few days it would be burned? Could it have been Marlene? Could she have been the mystery redhead all those years ago? Was that why she was killed? But it didn't make sense. She was a witness at the diner that night. And she was dead before Sharon was murdered.

Was it someone who had a key for the padlock? Someone who had broken in? One of the people involved in preparing the house for destruction?

Exasperated, I tossed the dress aside and closed my eyes again tightly, praying for a flash of inspiration, willing the solution to appear before me. I conjured up all the visual fragments of the mystery woman's identity and tried to piece them together into a coherent picture. I saw again the faceless figure in the red dress and the flowing wig. Mentally, I added the silly diamanté sunglasses. Something about them had always, always tugged away at my subconscious. Why would Kelly's double have changed them? Did Pete simply get it wrong? And all the time at the back of my mind was the nagging thought that all I had to do to solve the puzzle was turn the pieces round.

In my mind's eye, I reversed the glasses until it was as if I was viewing the world through their darkened lenses. But from this angle, they were no different from any other pair of sunspecs. They could have been any shape or design. This was getting me nowhere. I concentrated harder. In slow motion, I twirled the wig around so that the heavy tresses drifted through the air. Gradually, they began to pick up speed, spinning faster and faster, whirling aloft, catching the light. Something stirred in my memory, an image from the past. And suddenly I could see the mystery woman in my mind's eye, her identity revealed at last. It was so simple. But it meant I hadn't a moment to lose. I had to find those films and get away as fast as I could.

There was only one person I could think of who could help me. I stumbled towards the door and out into the blue moonlit landscape, feeling the cool night air.

That must have been when he entered the house. Surely I would have caught the sound of floorboards creaking, the sigh of another human being's breath? Or would they have merged with the dying sounds of the house, the straining timbers, the wind that suddenly got up and began to prowl restlessly through the rooms as dawn approached? Could he have been part of that all along, a shadow among shadows?

I reached for my bag lying on the passenger seat and riffled through it until I found Chris's number.

Someone answered with a sleepy 'Yes?'

'Chris, this is Bel.'

'Bel who?'

'Bel Carson. I spoke to you earlier tonight.'

There was a sigh and the sound of movement, of fabric rustling, then a click.

'That's better. Now I can see. What can I do for you, Bel? It better be good because I've just seen my alarm clock.'

'Chris,' I spoke urgently, 'I'm at the old farmhouse near Rapid Falls, the one where you and Marlene and the others used to hang out. If you were going to hide anything here, where would it be?'

'The old farmhouse? Boy, you get around!' She took a deep breath. 'Well, let's see. Same place we always hid our dope, I guess.'

I was pacing up and down with impatience. 'Where exactly?'

Chris yawned. 'Well, we used to push it up into the chimney, but Marlene's father found our gear and hit the roof, as I recall. So we had to try something different. I don't know if they're still around but there used to be a coupla logs – big ones we used for sitting on. We hollowed them out and kept stuff in there.'

'Thanks.' I hung up abruptly.

There was something innocent and childlike about the ring of logs clustered round the fireplace, as if they had been set up for a children's game. I hoisted the nearest one on to its side, swivelling it so that it caught the candlelight. There was a circle cut out of the flat bottom and held in place by some pieces of rag wedged into the crack. I broke two fingernails before I realised that the scraps of fabric had been cleverly

255

rigged so that by pulling on the end which protruded, I dislodged the wooden core.

The log was empty apart from a homemade pipe welded together from pieces of brass tubing and a clear plastic bag containing what looked like marijuana seeds. My movements tense, I turned to the other seat and kicked it over. This time the makeshift stopper was wedged in place with bits of styrofoam and came out easily. As it did so, the contents fell on to the floor with a clatter.

I reached forward and lightly felt amongst the motley collection of items. There was a copy of the wedding photograph which had appeared in the newspaper, rosettes won at rodeos, a high school graduation picture, what looked like a blue satin garter, another snapshot, this time of Harlan, Kelly, Pete and Crystal all hanging out of an open-topped sports car that Marlene was driving. And then I whooped with joy as my probing hands found four small orange canisters.

Hardly daring to breathe, I picked one up, and pressed down on the plastic cover. The core popped out. Inside was a small reel of film. I felt a surge of triumph. Scooping them all up, I swung round to head for the car and cannoned straight into something warm and breathing. At first I didn't take it in – the large figure camouflaged by the play of light and shadow. Then he shifted and I could see his face clearly. It was Harlan.

His eyes were like dark caves, and he was smiling. There was a gun in his right hand.

'Thanks for finding those,' he said. 'I always wondered if there were any more.'

My mind raced through the possibilities of escape. The windows were boarded up. Harlan was between me and the door.

'Beth knows I'm here,' I said as evenly as I could. 'If

anything happens to me, they'll come looking for you.'

He shook his head, an amused expression on his face. 'Like hell, they will. All they'll find of you will be a little pile of ash and bones and perhaps an oily patch – I'm not an expert on these things. They know you came out here to snoop around and they'll assume that somehow you started a fire. Simple, really. Why would they look for more complex explanations? The gunshot wound will have disappeared and the bullet will be a blob of metal lost somewhere in the foundations.' He looked around him with a theatrical air. 'This could all be burned before you're even missed.'

I stared at him, understanding that this was not a normal human being I was dealing with, not someone who would ever suffer remorse or whose latent finer feelings could be appealed to. The eyes I looked into were as dead black and as devoid of human emotion as a shark's.

'I've figured out what happened to Kelly,' I said to distract him.

Harlan grinned and shook his head almost imperceptibly. 'I bet you haven't.'

'But I have. I can guess what took place that day at the old quarry.' The smile faded a little from Harlan's lips. 'Did she refuse to make love? Was that it? Is that what triggers the violence? You beat her with whatever came to hand. A rock. Until she was half dead.' I was talking fast, never taking my eyes off him, stalling for time in the hope that someone would see my car and investigate. But who would come? Who knew I was in danger?

I saw Harlan's eyes narrow. He was no longer amused.

'Then when you calmed down, you thought you'd killed her and you realised you were in a mess and so you did what you always did, you used someone who loved you, who adored you so much they would do anything for you, be anything. Then you set up your alibi and let your accomplice dispose of the body. But somehow Marlene guessed the truth, didn't she? And then she found her films and could prove it.'

'Marlene?' Harlan sneered. 'Marlene was a fool.'

'Did you kill her too?'

He smiled archly.

'Because of the films?'

Harlan shrugged. 'Marlene always had a thing about me, she was a real nuisance, even when we were kids. And sometimes it was fun to string her along and sometimes it wasn't. Most of the time it was OK because she was thousands of miles away. But then she came home and she was all ready to divorce the old man and marry me.' Harlan snorted derisively. 'I told her I didn't want to see her again, so she started in with the threats. She was always one for issuing ultimatums. She said she knew I'd killed Kelly. That was nothing new – whenever she got mad at me she'd start threatening me with all kinds of stuff, trying to get me to make it up with her.

'So I assumed she was just bluffing again because there was no way she could have known about what happened. But then she started talking about these films she'd made, saying that they showed me beating Kelly to death that afternoon. She said if I married her she couldn't ever be made to testify against me. I still thought she was making it up because she'd never mentioned the films before. But when I found out they really existed, I knew I'd have to do something about it.' He gave a savage laugh. 'Stupid bitch. All she did was make herself dangerous.'

As he spoke, I could sense that he was beginning to relax. If only I could keep him talking a little longer. If only someone would show up.

'When she refused to hand over the films,' he was saying, 'I just tore out the one that was in the projector and grabbed the rest and tossed them in the fire. Then she started to scream and I had to take care of her.' He gestured dismissively with one hand. 'It was her own fault. If she'd just cooperated, maybe I wouldn't have had to do it.'

There was a pause and I had the chilling sense that he was eyeing me up, as if deciding where to aim. The gun moved a fraction.

'What about Sharon?' I broke in hurriedly. 'Why did you kill her?'

He didn't even bother to deny it. He merely shook his head despairingly. 'I don't know about you women. Some of you don't even have the brains you were born with.' He made a comical face and it dawned on me that he was enjoying this, basking in my undivided attention while he boasted of his cleverness. It made sense in a way. For someone as egocentric as Harlan, it must have been torture that his skill in duping the police had had to be kept secret and unappreciated.

'Sharon was a total bitch,' he continued. 'She was so jealous and vindictive – my God, was she vindictive! If I even looked at another woman, she'd throw a fit!' He gave a snort of laughter, recalling his dead girlfriend. 'You see, Sharon decided to follow me that night I went to see Marlene. She thought I was having an affair. I was –' he grinned at me slyly – 'but not with Marlene, at least not that night. She lost track of me when we got to Beth's neighbourhood, but when she read the papers the next day she put two and two together.' Harlan gestured widely with the hand holding the gun and every nerve in my body tensed.

'She didn't say anything at the time. But the night Amanda and I got together, Sharon came home and found me still groggy from the crack on the head my dear wife had given me – and tripped over Amanda's dress. Boy! She went berserk! Started punching me. That didn't bother me much because I was just a teensy bit bigger than her. No, the thing that got poor old Sharon in trouble was she threatened to tell the police where I was the night Marlene died. She actually picked up the phone and was dialling 911. So, goodbye Sharon!' Harlan said these last words as if he were a game show host bidding farewell to an unsuccessful contestant. It added to the surreal quality of his account.

'Even if I'd talked her out of speaking to the cops that night, it would have come up again every time she got huffy with me.' He laughed softly. 'I've been really lucky, I guess. First there was Kelly's time of death being a lot later than I thought, which made my alibi rock solid. Then, of course, it was really unexpected that Malcolm's fingerprints were on the murder weapon for Marlene. I mean, what were the chances of that? Plus, no one saw me, I was wearing gloves and I didn't make any noise. And when it came to Sharon –' he spread his hands with a flourish – 'dear old Amanda was already set up to take the rap. Three perfect crimes.'

'No,' I said. 'Not perfect.' A shadow of anger passed across Harlan's face. 'With each of your murders you got something wrong. That's how I finally knew you were the killer and the identity of your accomplice.'

His chin went up combatively. 'Oh really? And what did I get wrong?'

'Well, firstly, Kelly wasn't wearing her contact lenses that day, so I knew it couldn't have been her driving.' Harlan watched me, immobile. 'And then there were her sunglasses.' A slight frown creased his forehead. 'Everyone said she was wearing her new diamanté shades that night. But Pete reported that she had on her old Ray-Bans. That was what finally gave it away, that and the clothes. All the redheads – Sharon, Kelly, Amanda and Crystal – were very slender, all size eight or ten. Those dresses fell off Lola when she tried them on because they were too big. So none of them could have been the mystery woman.

'So who did that leave?' I asked rhetorically. 'We were all scurrying around looking for the answer when it was right under our noses all the time. I didn't realise who it was myself until a few minutes ago.'

For a moment he stared at me, as if paralysed, then suddenly he moved. I heard the click of the safety catch being taken off. He grasped the gun with both hands and raised it until it was pointing at my chest. I gazed at him, mesmerised, unable to quite grasp what was happening. This would be it. Only ashes left, the bullet a piece of molten metal amongst the embers.

The barrel tilted and I sensed the pressure on the trigger. The shot when it came was strange, a sharp crack. I couldn't breathe. But as I watched, Harlan bent a little at the knees then collapsed with a thud on to the floor. I stared at him, dazed, trying to understand that I was unhurt, while blood seeped from beneath Harlan's body. A shadow fell across me.

'Are you all right?' a familiar voice asked.

Slowly, I looked up into Pete's harrowed face. I was in such a state of panic that for one wild moment I thought that he was about to kill me too. But he laid his gun aside and gazed at me with concern. My heart was pounding loudly in my ears and all my limbs were trembling. Looking into that anguished face, I knew that at last I was safe.

'Yes,' I gasped, hardly able to speak. Then, as my breathing began to return to normal, I added, 'How did you know I was here?'

'The same way Harlan must have found out. I checked my answering machine when I got home. It had been recording all the time Lola was asking her mother what she should do. I could hear Beth shouting in the background that you should drive out to the old homestead to look for the films. Harlan was gone and he'd taken his gun. So I guessed at once that he'd

probably heard the message at the time it was left and then
followed you.'

He looked down with an expression of profound sadness at
the body lying at his feet. A pool of blood was spreading
across the floor, draining between the cracks in the wooden
boards. Kneeling down, he touched the dark head gently. For
a moment he did not move. Then he rose to his feet.

'I'm glad I got here in time,' he said, his voice husky. 'You're
safe now. Let's get out of here at once.' He held out a hand to
support me as I stepped over Harlan's corpse. When we
reached the outer door he released his hold.

'I'd like a moment alone, if you don't mind. I left some
things for you in my automobile.'

I stumbled out into the coolness of a grey dawn. In the
east, a glow of pink arced up from the horizon, promising a
new day. As I felt the breeze, tension flooded from my body
so that I could hardly walk. I only just made it to Pete's car,
parked about fifty yards away. It was unlocked, but in my
weakened state the door seemed impossibly heavy and it
took several attempts before I got it open. Lying on the
passenger seat was a small pile of audio tapes next to a
dictaphone, and beside that was a folded sheet of paper. I
picked it up, turning it in the half-light to read the inscription. It was addressed to Lola. And I suddenly knew what he
was going to do.

With a sharp cry, I spun round, preparing to run back into
the house. But in that instant I was hit by a blast of heat as the
old homestead exploded into flame. Fire ravaged the dry
timbers, a living thing which surged through the house, soar-
ing to the rotting beams until finally it brought the whole
structure crashing to the ground with a vehemence and a rage
that were final.

I stood transfixed, caught in a rush of conflicting emotions.
When I tried to think about it later, I could never be sure if I

heard Pete's gun go off again, but then perhaps I wouldn't have, not over the roar of the flames. But I hope he shot himself. I hope he didn't choose a purgatory of his own devising and go fully conscious into that inferno.

Chapter Sixteen

'It was a bizarre combination of things that just clicked into place when I found those old dresses at the homestead. I realised it was Pete I'd been looking for all along – that he was Harlan's accomplice and that he was the key to proving Harlan's guilt. I just had to look at things from a different angle.'

I had been keeping my gaze fixed on the tabletop in front of me, one tiny part of my brain absorbed with tracing the whorls in the oak. But in the silence that followed my words, I found myself compelled to look up into Beth's ashen face and see her mouth set to endure yet more pain, her eyes huge and agonised.

We were sitting in a large, anonymous conference room at Overland Park Police headquarters in Kansas City. Eamon Scott, Malcolm's lawyer, was seated on one side of Beth, and Lois on the other, both watching me intently. I was conscious also of the unshifting gaze of the various police officers ranged round the table. But somehow, everything I had been saying was directed at Beth.

I tried to explain. 'There was always the thing about the dresses being too big for any of the women who were part of Harlan's group. And when I found the wig, it suddenly triggered a memory of a transvestite I'd seen wearing a similar one in a club. It dawned on me that the mystery woman could have been a man. And that gave me another take on the sunglasses. You see –' I reached out and gently touched Beth's hand lying limp on the table – 'Pete said he saw Kelly that night wearing her old Ray-Bans when everyone else said she wore her new diamanté sunglasses. We were all trying to figure out why there was a change-over.

'In the end, I decided Pete had just made a mistake. And it's true, he did. But the reason he couldn't describe the sunglasses accurately was because he was the one wearing them. Perhaps they were lying face down when he picked them up. Or perhaps he was so distraught that he didn't notice they were any different from the ones Kelly usually wore. But he couldn't see what was obvious to everyone else.'

Beth shook her head helplessly. 'Pete was such a good man. He really was. I just cannot take this in.' Her eyes were clouded with confusion.

I knew how she felt. It was only a few hours since I had sat in a daze watching the old house bend its crippled frame and fall to its knees, before sinking into the ground in a shower of sparks. And all the while I could hear vehicles approaching, the engines labouring over rough ground, tailgates clanking as they raced along the dirt tracks. Finally two pickups burst out of the cover of the trees and tore across the ploughed field, sending up plumes of dust.

As they drew closer, they slowed and then stopped when the occupants saw that it was only the old homestead which was going to be burnt anyway and that it was past saving even if they'd wanted to. Five men got out – two from each cab and one man clambering down off the flatbed. All wore jeans and boots but two were bare-chested and a third was still doing up his belt buckle as if they had dressed in a hurry. They took off baseball caps and shook their heads.

'Well, I guess it saves us the trouble,' one of them said.

They suddenly became aware of the two cars parked a short distance behind them. They peered at the vehicles, shading their eyes against the sly rays from the sun hovering just above the horizon. Then, as they spotted me sitting sideways on the passenger seat with my legs hanging out of the open door, they broke into a run, converging on Pete's car, their faces intent as if my presence had changed things.

Of course, the news that they would find the remains of two bodies amongst the embers sent everyone into a panic. But there was nothing they could do except wait until the fire died down. I took advantage of the confusion to slip the folded sheet of paper and the tapes into my bag and called Lois from the mobile phone in my car. She was awake – it was after five by now – and listened to me in stunned silence. It was only moments, however, till she was thinking logically, telling me to say as little as possible, to report to the Sheriff, and that she would sort everything out from her end.

I don't know how long I sat there before I was taken into Rapid Falls. Nita seemed to accept that I was in shock and refused to allow anyone to question me until I had been seen by the local doctor who offered me some tranquillisers which I refused. I felt light-headed enough. Then the phone calls from Kansas City started. There was a long conversation between the Sheriff and Beth and then Lois and then what I can only assume were police officers. Finally, sometime around late morning, I was told I was being taken back to Kansas City to talk to the police there.

'We got a puddlejumper lined up,' Nita announced proudly. 'Beth's gonna pay.' Half an hour later, I was duly escorted to a dusty landing strip on the outskirts of town and helped into a tiny plane with my police escort. We took off uncertainly into the clear blue sky, tilting against the wind currents, the engine buzzing like a clockwork toy.

When I had told them about the bodies, no one had seemed to know whether or not to treat me as a murder suspect, but I wasn't handcuffed for the journey back to Kansas City. I wriggled uncomfortably in the low-backed seat, gazing down at the Kansas landscape spread out before me. The farms and small communities seemed even tinier and more insignificant from this height, almost lost in swaying expanses of wheat and grass.

As I watched, a pool of water appeared below me. I realised it was the old quarry. The last time I had seen it, it was shrouded by dark clouds, caught in the grip of a violent storm. In my mind, it had always been overhung by brutality and unresolved tragedy. But now, as I looked down on this clear, sunny day, it seemed completely different. Sunlight gilded the crests of the myriad small waves which the wind had whipped up on its surface. I could see three or four young people splashing about at the edge, swimming and playing games. It was as if the pall of Kelly's violent death had finally been lifted. An immense feeling of peace flooded through me.

Lois and Beth met me when I landed and I was taken to the police station, a plain brick building, where Mags and Joe were already waiting. Wordlessly, each of them hugged me tight when I walked into the conference room.

Harlan's three murders had occurred in different jurisdictions, but it had been decided that since he lived in this area of the city and since this was where the most recent killing had occurred, we would convene here. A young officer sat at one end of the table taking notes, but for the most part the police had been content to let me tell the story in my own way, only occasionally interjecting questions.

Now Lois leaned forward. 'But why? Why would Pete get involved in murder?'

I shrugged. 'I could guess, but I don't really know.' I turned to the burly man in plain clothes who seemed to be in charge. 'I think that's probably what the tapes are about.'

He turned slightly and nodded to a colleague sitting further along the table, and a few moments later we were listening as

Pete's voice, hesitant and troubled, filled the room. The recording had been made as he journeyed through the darkness to the ranch the previous night.

'I've always known that one day, one day it would come to this. And part of me, if the truth be told, wanted it to happen. Something you never dreamed of, never asked for, happens and your life changes for ever. But now I want to set the record straight.' He sighed and there was silence for several moments.

'I've always felt like a useless fool. The only time I didn't was when Harlan paid attention to me. He was so kind to me when I was a solitary, lost kid. He was my only friend, he saved me – my father didn't care – and I was besotted with him. I should have grown out of it, it should have become simply one of those stages that a lonely teenager goes through. But, for some reason I will never understand, it continued. If I didn't love him, I would never have gotten into any of this, I don't think.

'I felt that if someone as glorious as he was thought I was worth something, then I couldn't be so bad. It was like basking in sunlight, and when it was taken away again, when he went off with Kelly and he didn't have time for me any more, everything was dark and cold again. So I decided to become the woman Harlan loved. It was the nearest I could get to what I'd had and lost. I got everything mail order. It was like a parallel universe. I walled it off from the daylight world. People will laugh at me, I know. I think I'm laughable, believe me.'

There was a long pause before he continued. 'I killed Kelly, although I didn't find that out till later.' His voice broke. 'I never would have pushed her in the quarry if I'd thought for one moment she wasn't already dead. But Harlan fell apart that day. He showed up at my place in a panic. He thought he would go to jail for sure. It was me who thought of the alibi and decided to masquerade as Kelly. I never really stopped to consider the implications of what I was doing. It was just enough that Harlan had come to *me* for help, that he needed me, that I was important to him again. All I could think of was that he couldn't go to jail. It would have been like putting some magnificent wild beast in a cage. He would have withered and died, I know he would.'

There was a pause. When Pete spoke again, his voice was almost inaudible. 'It was only later that I found out Kelly had still been alive. I never really forgave myself. But I put it behind me. I had to. If I'd confessed, Harlan would have gone to prison, and perhaps me too, although I didn't really care about that. And Kelly would still be dead. Nothing I could do would ever bring her back.

'Of course, after that, Harlan knew about my other self. He thought it kinda funny, but he put up with it because he had to. It was our secret. Then Amanda came along and I hardly ever saw him. One day I couldn't stand it any longer. I dressed up as my other self and asked him over. He laughed. He thought I was so ridiculous. And I was. I was. But I couldn't stop. And I threatened him. I reminded him I knew enough to put him in jail. He grabbed me and told me that I was the one who had committed the murder. He had an alibi. And I was trapped. Because he was right.

'He tried to keep me sweet after that, though. If he gave Amanda a gift, he gave me one too. I had a lot of clothes that were identical to hers.

'Over the years, I managed to distance myself from what had happened at the quarry. I convinced myself it was a horrible accident and would never be repeated.

'Then Marlene started threatening Harlan with the films. He didn't take her seriously at first. But when Lola phoned that night, I called Harlan in a panic and told him they really did exist. Suddenly our whole lives were at stake. I drove him over there in my automobile and he hid in the bushes till Lola and I left. I picked him up after I dropped her off again later. I thought he was just going to get the films from Marlene. I didn't find out till afterwards that he'd killed her.

'And suddenly I was back in the nightmare and it was spiralling out of control. I couldn't deny it any more. But I didn't know what to do. There seemed to be something in Harlan, some sort of impetuous streak that couldn't be controlled, no matter what I said. Yet I still couldn't betray him. I couldn't face the thought of such a magnificent creature being locked up for the rest of his life. It was unthinkable.' There was silence on the tape, broken only by what might have been stifled sobs.

'I don't know exactly what happened the night Sharon died,' he continued unsteadily. 'Harlan never really explained. All I know is he phoned me some time after dark and told me to come over and bring the hyacinth silk dress and my shoes and my wig. So I did. But I hated it. I hated having blood on me. I couldn't stand the thought that I was involved in another murder.'

Pete sounded indescribably sad and weary. 'You don't understand how hard it has been to hold all this together. It was a part of me I didn't own. But now it has to stop. Too many people know bits of this terrible story and can guess the rest. It is only a matter of time before we're found out. And I cannot bear any more bloodshed. I only hope I can get there in time to save Bel.'

At these words, every head in the room turned automatically to me and I felt myself go weak. But it was only for a second. Pete commanded our attention as his voice carried on.

'Believe me, I thought about calling the police before I left. But they would get there before me. They would arrest Harlan and lock him up. I'm pretty sure I can get there in time.' He sighed deeply. 'I cannot tell you how remorseful I feel, how much I wish I could go back to the days of my childhood and start again. But I can't. This is the only way. Harlan could never be kept in a prison. I couldn't live without him. So it has to be him and me together. I know what I have to do.' The tape went quiet.

There was silence in the room except for the sound of Beth weeping. Everyone looked drained. But we weren't finished yet. There were still the films to watch before this ordeal would be over. After a discreet pause for Beth's sobs to die down a little, the officer in charge nodded to the civilian technician and the projector whirred into action.

The blinds were drawn but even so it was not completely dark. A screen had been pulled down at one end of the room. A 16mm projector was already in position on the conference table, with a couple of books under it to direct its beam on to the screen. It whirred into action.

We shifted expectantly in our seats. I was almost afraid to watch and braced myself for scenes of unspeakable violence.

The film was old and brittle. It broke twice during the first reel. In spite of the interruptions, we sat watching ten minutes of clouds slowly massing on a flat horizon. The next film was the same. Then we watched another one showing a static shot of the Art Museum in Kansas City. By the time the last reel was being threaded up, everyone had begun to fidget. The projectionist was taking his time, adjusting the loops, making sure everything was perfect, while we tensed with impatient expectation. Finally, the last roll began to run and a murmur went round the room.

I leaned forward, wanting to see what came next but dreading it also. Marlene had positioned her camera as I had imagined, pointed up at the cliff overlooking the old quarry. Clouds streamed overhead. There was total silence in the room and no one could take their eyes off the screen and the images which fled across it. When it was finished we sat in stunned silence.

Someone switched the lights on, then opened the blinds. The heavy-set man was playing with a pencil on the table in front of him, frowning. The projector was turned off and everyone turned questioningly to the others in the room, seeking some explanation.

'Were there any more films?' the detective asked Beth gently.

She shook her head. 'No. My daughter always said there were only four of them. I guess that's it.' She had stopped crying and had composed her features into her habitual expression of endurance and quiet suffering. She said softly, 'Marlene always did like the dramatic gesture, the showdown.' For in spite of all her threats and ultimatums, Marlene had filmed nothing, nothing except the Kansas sky on a summer's day.

'He was a good man really,' Beth intoned for the umpteenth time. She looked at the small group of people eating barbecued steaks on her patio. Malcolm was there, and Amanda, newly released from jail. They both looked so different now that the threat of a life spent in prison no longer hung over them.

Malcolm showed no sign of being grief-stricken at the loss of his wife. Perhaps, I thought charitably, that was because he had already had many weeks to come to terms with her death, but it could also have been because their marriage was on the rocks and his love for her had gone anyway. Whatever the reason, everything about him bespoke a return of his old confidence – the firmness of his facial expressions, the way he stood, legs apart, straight-backed, head held high. He was no longer a man bewildered by events. He was once again a man who controlled them. Only now he was a millionaire.

Amanda simply glowed. I had feared the effect that the news of Harlan's death might have on her, given her already fragile state of mind. But the knowledge that her husband was a vicious killer who had been willing to sacrifice her to save his own skin seemed finally to have destroyed his hold over her. Doubtless, when the euphoria of being proved innocent had abated, she would still have very complicated feelings about Harlan to deal with, but for the moment she appeared to have put that behind her. It was as if she had taken on a new lustre with her release. Her hair shimmered, her eyes sparkled, her skin was luminous with health and vitality, her movements were fluid, graceful and assured. She was once again a thing of beauty. She was gazing up into Malcolm's face with a look of undisguised admiration.

'I haven't told Lola about Pete's –' Beth paused delicately, as if selecting the right word – '*feelings* for Harlan. That note he left for Lola – did I tell you – all it said was that he loved her and I really think he did.' She paused and swallowed hard. 'D'you think we can keep that part of it out of the press?'

'I doubt it,' I said apologetically. 'There'll have to be some sort of judicial ruling or inquiry or something, won't there? And if our documentary is ever shown over here, that will tell the whole story.'

Beth bit her lip, thinking hard. 'Then I'll send Lola to study art in Italy. Or maybe film-making in London.' She looked at me for support.

Before I could say anything, there was a tap on my shoulder. I turned to look into the greyish blue eyes of Carl Scott. 'Hello.' He smiled. 'Congratulations.' I could think of nothing to say, swamped as I was by feelings of guilt that I still hadn't responded to the message he'd left several days ago, asking me to call him at work. Since the deaths of Harlan and Pete, I seemed to have been swept along by events with hardly a moment to think.

Carl fidgeted with the glass in his hand. 'How much longer are you here for?'

'We leave tomorrow,' I answered regretfully. 'My boss has decided to pull us all back to recuperate and regroup. He seems completely bowled over by the news that we've solved three murders. It was a great scoop for RTV and he was thrilled about that, but he's convinced we must be suffering from shock. He may let us return, though, if there's some kind of hearing on all this.'

Carl nodded thoughtfully and was about to say something when a burst of laughter on the other side of the patio made him pause. I looked round the group. A man I did not know had just popped the cork on the first of two dozen bottles of champagne. People clapped their hands and a cheer went up as glasses were filled.

I spotted Joe seated at one of the small white tables. A young blonde woman in a slinky black dress lounged opposite him and even from this distance I could see he was putting on the charm and that she was dazzled. Mags and Lola were engaged in a heated discussion about the film industry and Lola's future. Once her first hysterical outbursts were over, Lola seemed to be strangely unaffected by the loss of her lover, which confirmed my suspicion that she was really a very shallow person, with none of her mother's depth of feeling and compassion.

Nearby, Lois and her partner were standing close together, absorbed in some intimate conversation. Various friends of the family, lawyers and legal assistants stood around, laughing and talking animatedly. The atmosphere was one of joyous celebration tempered at times by the memory of those who had died. Then the conversation would stop and everyone would be silent for a while, lost in their own thoughts. But the mood would quickly revive. It was as if, after so much pain and such prolonged anguish, everyone present was determined to be happy.

Brimming glasses of champagne had now been handed round to everyone. Lois stepped forward into a space in the middle of the throng. She coughed delicately. Some man called for silence and everyone fixed their eyes on her.

'Amanda asked me to say this on her behalf because she's too shy to do it herself,' she began. 'But I guess this is for everyone, especially Beth, Malcolm, Amanda and myself.' She raised her glass. 'I'd like to propose a toast to thank Bel for being so single-minded about solving these murders, for following every tiny lead to the end, for never giving up. Bel –' she gestured in my direction – 'thanks.'

A chorus of voices echoed her words followed by silence as everyone sipped their drinks. I was scarlet with embarrassment. But then the chatter broke out again and the party resumed.

'It's a pity you're leaving so soon,' Carl said quietly in my ear. 'Ever since we met I've been trying to get another opportunity to talk to you – sometime when you didn't have so many things on your mind. I suppose I've missed my chance.' He waited and I was conscious of the unspoken invitation. But I was filled with ambivalence and fear. Tomorrow I would fly back to Britain. I would return to my home with its safe cocoon of memories. I would try to seek refuge in the past and turn my back on the emptiness of the present.

'There's a place I wanted to take you to,' Carl continued in a soft voice. 'You can look down and see where the railhead used to be. It's where the drovers brought the cattle they had herded across the plains. And beyond that, the skyscrapers and the lights of the city that grew from that beginning. Then if you turn your back, you can look up at the stars in the Kansas sky.' He was silent.

'I can't,' I stammered. 'I can't explain. But I can't.'

He tipped the last of his wine on to the grass. 'Sorry.' He

smiled at me. 'I should stick to Band Aids.'

I looked away, hating myself. Mags had approached, smiling apologetically.

'Sorry to interrupt. We're ready to go, Bel. We've got an early start tomorrow and these journeys are tiring enough . . .'

I nodded and turned to Carl. 'It's not you. It's me. Good-bye.' I stretched up and kissed him lightly on the cheek then moved off quickly. I found my bag and jacket and began to say my farewells. It took a long time. There were more heartfelt thanks from Malcolm and words of appreciation from his legal team, promises to keep in touch from Lola and finally a tearful leave-taking with Beth. She clung to me, too overcome to speak.

'We're friends now, for ever.' I tried to console her. 'We'll see each other again for sure. I promise.'

'We'd better.' She choked out the words. 'Or I'll hire a plane and come land in your yard!' She managed a smile as she released me from her embrace.

I walked slowly towards the limousine she had hired for us for the evening. Joe was lounging against the front passenger door. He smiled warmly. 'Me too,' he said. 'You won't get rid of me either.' I aimed a playful punch at his midriff and he winced theatrically. Then I put my arms round his neck and gave him a hug.

'Take me to some of the gay bars at home, sometime.'

'Done,' he agreed happily. 'That's a date.'

Mags appeared next to us, clutching her silk wrap round her and shivering. 'Brrr. It's suddenly got chilly, hasn't it?' she remarked. The driver who had been loitering nearby stepped forward and opened the rear door and helped her into the car. Joe followed.

I turned to look for Amanda. At that moment, the crowd clustered round the front door parted a little and I suddenly

saw her, poised on the threshold, ready to leave. Malcolm
stood next to her, backlit by the chandeliers in the hall which
cast a golden glow out into the driveway. He was speaking in
low tones but his words carried on the clear night air.

'We must get together as soon as I get back, my dear. That
shouldn't be long. Perhaps you could come out to Craigour
for dinner one evening and see the farm.'

Amanda gave him one of her most dazzling smiles. My
gaze shot swiftly round the group, seeking out Beth. She was
standing to one side of the driveway, in the shadows, watching the couple silhouetted in the doorway of her home. The
light spilling from the interior illuminated her face. She had
a look of such wistfulness that it caught at my heart. I knew
that she loved Malcolm. Perhaps she always had, from the
moment he had first entered her life, enduring even after he
rejected her, the lonely plain-looking wife of another man,
and carried off her beautiful younger sister. Now it was
happening again. Did she wish she had grasped at happiness
all those years ago when she had the chance? Or did her
innate wisdom tell her it would have turned out this way in
any case? What was it she had said to me that night at the
ranch, as her ties to the past were about to be turned to
ashes? 'We create our own destiny.'

Amanda was hurrying towards the limousine. I glanced
about, suddenly afraid I was too late. Carl was walking
towards his car parked out on the roadway, his head bowed,
not looking back. I turned and said to Mags, 'You go ahead.
I'll make my own way back and I'll see you all in the morning.'

A worried frown creased her brow momentarily. Then she
smiled. 'Tell him he'd better be really nice to you or he'll have
me to deal with. Tell him it'll be like being chased by the
hounds of hell.'

'Well, that should be a conversation stopper,' I commented,
blowing them all a kiss.

Carl must have heard my footsteps because he paused when he had unlocked his door and looked round.

'Can I change my mind?' I asked breathlessly.

His face broke into a wide smile. 'Sure.' He held the door open.

I climbed in. As we drove off, I turned and looked back. The last thing I saw before some trees obscured my view was a lit tableau – Malcolm silhouetted in the doorway and Beth, standing a little apart, waving goodbye.